Chasing Kensie

Drew Taylor

Taylor Made
publishing

Interior Design by Drew Taylor

Cover Design by Melody Jeffries

Edited by Leah Taylor

Proofread by Charity Henico

To the survivors of this sin-ridden, emotionally abusive thing called Life—keep fighting. Keep dreaming. Keep your eyes trained upon the One who lifts your burdens and carries you on.

Prologue

Kensie ~ two and a half years ago

K ensie's finger hovered over the computer mouse, her mind concocting a thousand dreadful scenarios of how he may respond.

She'd been in Alaska for a month now and had been putting off sending this email from the moment she stepped into her classroom and was greeted by an unfinished game of Hang Man on the dry-erase board—written in permanent marker. But with the school year starting in two weeks, she couldn't wait any longer. This room needed an overhaul.

"Be brave, Kensie," she whispered, closing her eyes and inhaling dust particles as she attempted to steady her breathing. After a cough, she attempted reasoning with herself again. "You moved here to start a life of your own. It begins now." Kensie's life back in Willow Bay, Mississippi, wasn't bad. She lived with her mom as an only child, had a best friend named Frankie—whom she already missed dearly—and taught at a small private Christian school.

But she'd grown stagnant. She'd felt it in her aging bones.

She'd needed a change from the ever-lingering feeling that something was missing from her life, something outside of her father abandoning them from before she could remember. Something that was just hers. Something she could control and manipulate until it was made perfect, like strategically color-coordinating ornaments on a Christmas tree.

That change she sought meant building some semblance of a community around her if she was going to survive Alaska, which was four thousand-plus miles from her home. Part of that community would be the teachers and staff of Crescent Cove High School.

"Please, God, prepare them to accept me. Just...make me useful and likable." The soft prayer was a plea for partiality.

Kensie, in her rational brain, knew that sending an email to the previous inhabitant of her new classroom, kindly asking him to remove his things so she could curate her space, was not a big deal. Emotionally, however, she was wound up like a walking toy soldier. Would she be rejected? Would he ignore her? Would he be upset that she was asking him to come in one week before teachers officially had to be back?

While the tumultuous storm inside her head raged, Kensie once more reminded herself that she'd moved to build a life of her own. She no longer resided among friends, family, and former high school foes who knew her all too well. She was blissfully alone, left to her own devices to carve out the image she wanted others to see. She could be anything—a spunky, outgoing woman, a sweet and demure lady, or a witty, playful girl. Heck, she could even choose to go by her middle name, Marie, instead of the odd name her parents had bestowed upon her at birth. But if she did that, then she'd feel like her mother since that was her first name.

The world was Kensie's for the taking, and at twenty-five, she was quite ready to make something of herself, but she wouldn't get anywhere if she couldn't send a gosh darn email to a colleague.

Kensie's anxiousness, though she didn't like to admit it, was the true source of her wavering. It tightened around her neck, like Stolypin's necktie, which threatened to send her into a panic at the drop of a pin.

Before moving, she and her mother had searched the current staff members at her new high school to see if any cute, potentially available men would be wandering her hallway. Making something of herself meant hopefully overcoming her aversion to men and securing a spouse. She couldn't find one in her small, coastal hometown of Willow Bay, but honestly? It was her fault. She would fail before she could even work up the nerve to approach an attractive man. She wasn't repulsed; she was just...scared. A type of fear that clamped her tongue and forced her to keep her distance.

As Kensie had scrolled down the current employees section on the school's website, she had noted three good-looking men who looked to be a little older than her. The next step was to see if they had social media so that she could find out if they were already spoken for or not.

Though Kensie felt a smidge yucky about social media stalking men she hadn't met yet, she felt more at ease knowing what she would be walking into. She'd stalk the rest of the staff to the best of her ability later on.

Kensie liked information, and the internet could give a woman everything she needed to know. She remembered how her mother, glancing over Kensie's shoulder, had commented on how hot the football coach Nick Lancaster was with his light-brown hair that had a slight curl to its ends, rich brown eyes, and... Was that a dimple in his left cheek?

"Cuuute," Kensie had drawn out the word, scrunching her eyes through her smile. She had bit her bottom lip as she stared at his picture.

"And he's the physical education teacher." Her mother, Marie Smith, had nudged Kensie with her elbow.

"Health, too," Kensie had added, smiling at her mother. "Maybe he will cook good food and develop a workout plan for me. Lord knows I need the motivation."

"I'm going to miss you, baby."

"I'll miss you too, Mom." Kensie's heart had clenched. Was she really going to leave her mom all alone? "I don't have to go, you know. I can stay."

Marie had responded just as Kensie had assumed. "Nonsense. You go to Alaska and create something beautiful for yourself. I'll get a dog."

Kensie had rolled her eyes and mentioned humans were better than dogs, which had led to an hour-long debate over what type of dog Kensie would be.

Shaking her head, Kensie snapped back to reality and read over the email one more time.

Hi, Mr. Lancaster,

My name is Kensington Smith, and I'm the new tenth-grade English teacher. I've inherited your former room and am looking forward to setting it up within the next couple of days. You seem to have left some things, and I was wondering if you happened to know when you'd be by to pack them up? I don't want to accidentally toss something that you want and/or need.

Looking forward to hearing from you,

Kensie

She had to stop overthinking every word she'd typed. She was polite, kind, and approachable. It was good.

But Kensie kept thinking she shouldn't say her full name. Just in case.

Inhaling a deep breath, Kensie clicked the mouse and watched as the email was sent, cemented by the sound of a woosh coming from the computer speakers. Emboldened and more at ease at the prospect of a new life and identity ahead of her, she spun in her new black chair and looked out the window behind her desk. The sun was a bright button shining down onto a sea of evergreens; Kensie knew she'd never get used to the vast Alaskan sky. She was standing on the tilt of the world when she stared up at the blue background painted with slanted white clouds.

It wasn't the same as Mississippi.

The thought of her home state came with a tinge of sadness, but it was nothing Kensie couldn't push off. The peace she felt—had felt since she received the call from the principal saying she had secured the job—was all-encompassing despite her social anxiety. God wanted Kensie here in Crescent Cove on the Kenai Peninsula. For what, she didn't know yet, but she was excited to find out. Turning away from the small floor-to-ceiling window, she examined her new space for the zillionth time.

Desks were placed in front-facing rows, something Kensie would be rearranging as she liked a Socratic seminar-style layout. The back of the room had counter space that ran the entirety of the wall, which she would use for turn-in trays and other student-accessible things. The collapsible wall on the right would serve as a blank canvas for students to fill with their work. The wall on her left would be great for storyboards to go with whatever novel unit they were on.

And then there was the front of the room where her Smartboard and whiteboard were. Kensie wasn't a fan of how the two were side-by-side, but she'd make it work by using the whiteboard as the assignment board and the Smartboard as her primary workspace. Her desk was on the other side of the Smartboard and was where she currently stood, looking at the piles of papers, discarded posters, and tons of jumbled supplies she'd moved to an empty spot of the room. She hoped Nick wouldn't mind that she'd relocated his stuff, but if he wanted it left unbothered, he should have taken it when he found out he wasn't going to be using this room any longer.

A ding sound came from her computer, and she leaned over to see what it was.

Nick responded.

Wow, that was fast, she thought to herself.

She clicked on the email.

> Kensington? That's an interesting name. Do whatever you want with the stuff. I don't care.
> - Lancaster

Kensie stared at the email, reading it once, twice, a thousand times, trying to remind herself that he was simply being short and to the point. Nick wasn't being hostile toward her. She had no idea if he meant "good" interesting or "bad" interesting. He wasn't like the guys in high school who found it hilarious to taunt and tease her by calling her Buckingham Palace until she ran to the bathroom in tears. At least, she hoped he wasn't. They were both grown adults who taught high school. Without a doubt, it was uncool of him to push his mess off onto her, but she could live with it. She'd even get free supplies out of it.

But Kensie couldn't shake the feeling she'd interrupted his important day or had intruded upon his precious time. Was it the clipped tone of the email? The few sentences compared to her paragraph? Signing his last name instead of a friendly first name?

Obviously, she wouldn't respond. Instead, she would begin cleaning and continue talking herself out of her absurd ruminating thoughts. Right as she got started, another email came through.

> Oh, and Buckingham, or whatever palace name you go by... I know you're new here, but don't call me Mr. Lancaster. It's Coach or Lancaster. I'm not my father. Got it?

Kensie shrank back from the computer, her headspace zooming right back to Willow Bay when her crush consistently called her Buckingham Palace. *You're not in high school anymore, Kensie. Chill out. It's not a big deal.* But to Kensie, it was a big deal. She had worked so hard to love her name again after those years, and it was as if all that effort flew right out the window with that short, quipped email. She couldn't give this man-child authority over her emotions like this.

All her insecure and doubt-ridden feelings bubbled into anger. Nick Lancaster may be hot, but he was not going to be worth a moment of her thoughts moving forward. She'd treat him with due respect as a colleague, but she would not dream of pursuing anything more with that rude man. If Kensie knew how to do one thing, it was how to slam the door and forget someone existed.

But that night, while sleeping soundly, she smiled as a tall, handsome man who looked a lot like Nick's picture on the school website cuddled with her on her brand-new cocoa-brown couch while they watched her comfort movie, *Jane Eyre.*

Chapter One

Kensie

"How do you drink that dirt water?" A female student curled her lips in disgust as Kensie took a long, deliciously bitter sip of her iced Americano she'd gotten during her lunch break.

"I like my espresso diluted by water alone." Kensie scribbled an annotation on the board with her free hand, unphased by her students' active aversions to her choice of coffee. "But back to the text! Who can tell me what the mockingjay is symbolizing?"

Blank, hopeless stares met her gaze as she looked out on the sea of tenth-grade students.

"Come on, guys. You know this. We've talked about it for three days." Nothing. Crickets. Kensie sighed deeply and closed her eyes momentarily, reminding herself these babies needed her to have grace upon grace with them, just as Jesus did with her.

Kensie always looked for the good in people.

The man who shoved his shopping cart into the side of the railing while she got her coffee earlier? He was probably upset over how much his groceries cost. She would be too. Alaska was expensive, as she'd quickly learned after moving here two and a half years ago.

The middle-aged woman who flipped Kensie off as she passed her on the highway in the no-passing zone? She was most likely in a hurry and needed to be somewhere quicker than Kensie was willing to go. Five over the speed limit was pushing the boundaries, thank you very much. Especially on these ice-coated December roads.

The teen boy who stomped his feet as he stormed out of Kensie's classroom moments ago because he refused to turn in his cell phone after getting caught with it under his desk?

She was certain he was telling her the truth that he was texting his mother.

Ha, as if, she snorted to herself. Thinking of the situation threw her off-kilter as she faced the new Promethean board she'd received at the beginning of this school year. One could not laugh at a student's misbehavior in front of an entire sophomore English class.

Kensie may look for the good in people, but she was no pushover. At least when it came to teenagers.

She couldn't be if she wanted to survive the jungle of high school for three more weeks before her blessed Christmas break. She glanced at her reflection in the mirror by her desk. Her dried-out auburn hair was a frizzy mess—and not the cute kind with little curl ringlets—as it sat on top of her head as a nest for the bees. She rocked dark circles under her stormy-blue eyes, though it seemed that was most likely her supposedly waterproof, berry-brown mascara failing her.

Looks like I'll have to try a new brand.

It was tough to find that shade, which perfectly complemented her cream, freckled skin.

"Well, what questions do we have, then? How can I better clarify the symbolism of the mockingjay?" she asked the class as she turned to face them, setting her shoulders back and acting like she did not, in fact, look like the poster child for a tired teacher running on copious amounts of coffee and persistent prayers to get her through the day.

Her students continued to stare at her as if she'd grown a tail and sprouted wings. Internally, Kensie was screaming. Outwardly, she pasted on a pleasant smile and clasped her hands together. She knew they enjoyed the book and would enjoy the movie at the end of the unit, but why didn't they want to dig deeper?

Would they ever want to know more about the art of storytelling? Were the metaphors, symbolism, and philosophical ideas presented in *The Hunger Games* by Suzanne Collins forever lost on the next generation of teens? Would they understand the connections to *The Tragedy of Julius Caesar* when they read it next semester? Would they be able to tie it back into their first unit on Greek mythology?

"I have a question, Miss Smith." A small girl with dark-brown hair, golden-brown skin, and the roundest glasses Kensie had ever seen raised her hand. *Finally, someone cares!*

"And I hope to have an answer."

"How much longer do we have in class?" Her bored tone and lazy gaze stirred a swirl of aggravation within Kensie. She bit her tongue to keep from blurting out something like, "Learn to read an analog clock, dummy."

But of course, that would not be appropriate and would result in an unwanted parent-teacher conference. If the child's parents cared enough, that is.

As Kensie looked out across the blank faces of her seventh-hour class—the last of the day—she felt a morsel of remorse over thinking of them as dummies. Many of the teens lacked the proper upbringing to see the importance of literature. Comprehension skills weren't taught or supported at home for the majority of her kids. So, as always, she leaned into the core values of reading and writing as she dismissed them for the day.

"Remember that in this class, we learn to think critically and analytically, formulate our own opinions, back up our opinions with sound facts, and articulate our arguments and reasoning. Why?"

The majority of the class responded while a few woke up from their daily snooze. "Because thinking deeply leads to perceiving deeply, which leads to healthy and dynamic relationships."

Kensie gave her head a firm nod just in time for the bell to ring, signaling the end of another exhausting but fulfilling day.

"Enjoy the rest of your dirt water, Miss Smith!"

Kensie waved goodbye and took another sip, laughing to herself. They were interested in anything and everything *except* learning. At least they enjoyed her teaching methods enough to take an interest in her subject at times.

See? Always look for the good!

Smoothing down her light-brown and beige plaid, pleated skirt, she moved to the dry-erase board and began changing the plans. She had riveting discussion prompts prepared after they concluded the book tomorrow. Kensie was not unaware that most of the teens would either crack jokes about the stilted flow of the story, as they had been for the past three weeks, which Kensie couldn't complain about, or they would only piggyback off of someone else's answer just to get their participation points for the day.

But still, she hoped that someone would say *something* and that *something* would lead to a serious conversation and debate about the theme of individuality, representation of the Roman Empire era, or even a character analysis of Katniss and her plethora of layers.

"Hope is a dangerous thing," she whispered, laughing to herself and rubbing her tired eyes as she wrote on the board with the other hand. She'd never read a Stephen King novel as horror and suspense were not her preferred genres, but that certain quote had stuck with her for some reason after she'd heard it.

Perhaps because she thought it ridiculous.

Hope was life-giving. It sparked joy and crafted a vision.

Life without hope caused angry men to misplace their shopping carts with abrupt force and led to middle-aged women flipping people off as they passed them on the highway.

"Tell me, Windsor."

The voice stopped Kensie mid-marker stroke as red flared at the edges of her vision like a warning signal. She didn't have to turn around to know he was smirking, leaning against her doorway with crossed arms, wearing a classic dress shirt that would pull around the buttons holding on for their lives. Not that she'd ever paid *that* close attention—it was simply hard to miss.

"Tell you what, Mr. Lancaster?" She replaced the cap on the marker and turned to face her workplace nemesis. Sure enough, he was in the predetermined position, but the smirk he was wearing ran deeper than her vivid imagination could conjure.

He hummed, looking around her classroom like a bird of prey before landing his deep brown eyes, many shades darker than his chestnut hair, on her. "What exactly are you hoping for that is such a dangerous thing?"

Before she could respond, he dropped his arms and strode into her room as if it were his own, only stopping when he was a yardstick away from her, not caring that she took a small step backward. Kensie's pulse jumped, loud enough she was certain he could hear it.

His voice dropped. Lower, rougher, toying. "Are you holding out hope to date me? If so, I'll take you out of here right now. Dinner. Movie. Maybe I'll even kiss you.

No more dangerous thoughts on your end. It can be a one-and-done situation, yeah?"

The insufferable man dared to wink.

Kensie burned with fury, and she wasn't sure she'd be able to control her tongue if she opened her mouth.

She released her breath and closed her eyes, but when she opened them, he had stepped even closer. If she reached out her arm, she'd touch him if she didn't bend at the elbow.

Fear echoed in the quick beat of her heart, and her voice trembled. "Please leave, Mr. Lancaster. I don't have time for your petulance today."

"Do you have a date?" Nick maneuvered to her side, leaning against the board, feigning a pout. Kensie exhaled at the distance created. "Man, it sucks to be me right now."

"I'm pretty sure it always sucks to be you, Mr. Lancaster. Now, would you—"

"For the thousandth time, call me Nick. I call you by palace names. You can call me Saint Nick if it pleases you. Anything but Mr. Lancaster. I'm not my father." He cocked his head to the side, a lock of obnoxiously shiny hair falling into his face, though Kensie didn't miss the way his teasing voice darkened when he spoke of his father, Senator James Lancaster.

She recalled the email where he said to address him as Coach or Lancaster, but there was no way she'd drop the "mister" in front of his name. Not when it bothered him this much. An eye for an eye and all that.

"I've asked you not to, but you refuse to honor my wishes." Kensie folded her arms across her chest, arching an eyebrow. "I will continue to refer to you as Mr. Lancaster because the only type of relationship we have is a professional one."

"It's too easy," he mused. He opened his mouth, but Kensie wasn't inclined to hear whatever else he had to say, so she interrupted.

"Is there something I can help you with, Mr. Lancaster?"

He grinned a sardonic, white smile. "Just wanted to drop in and see how my favorite pretentious English teacher was holding up." He feigned a whisper. "Don't tell my sister."

Unable to control herself, Kensie rolled her eyes. She loved Nick's sister—Braelee–who taught in the room next to hers. Braelee quickly became Kensie's best friend a month into teaching at Crescent Cove.

Nick continued his explanation of his current uninvited attendance in her classroom. "The students can be absolute beasts this time of year. And, well..." He glanced up at the board. "Teaching *The Hunger Games* is probably not helping with their...animalistic instincts. Tell me. Are they enjoying the story? Are they eating knowledge out of the palm of your hand? Or are they bored out of their minds, counting down the minutes until they can have some fun in my P.E. classes?"

"Plato said physical training must be balanced with cultivating the mind. Literacy is important." Kensie's tone was quipped. She'd had it with this self-important, cocky, tone-deaf man. Why wouldn't he just leave her alone already?

"I never said literacy wasn't essential." Nick grinned, popping off that ridiculous dimple of his, and Kensie knew she'd made a mistake in the heat of her anger. "Come on, now, Windsor. You teach rhetoric. You know that's a straw man tactic. Don't use logical fallacies on me, especially quoting Plato while doing it."

"*You're* a logical fallacy," Kensie muttered under her breath.

"Stop talking dirty to me, Windsor," he leaned forward and whispered coyly, "we're in a classroom."

"You sound like such a—" Kensie bit her tongue for the second time today. Only this time it was to stop herself from laying into a coworker, which would be equally as bad as laying into a student. Maybe she wasn't cut out for teaching after all?

Nick's stupid grin was miles wide. "Like a what? A caveman? Alpha wolf? I can work with that type of name-calling."

"Like an alpha-hole!" she relented, frustration getting the best of her as her scowl deepened. "And don't even say it's name-calling, because it's true. It's logically factual that you, Nicolas James Lancaster, are an alpha-hole."

"What even is that?" He raised one sharp eyebrow in question.

Kensie smirked and tilted her chin up. "You'd know if you picked up a book once in a while."

"Oh, Buckingham. I read. I just don't read your little fictional stories. I read real books. Nonfiction. Truth."

The building anger toppled over like lava spewing from Mt. Redoubt. "Listen here, Mr. Lancaster. Nick. Saint Nick. *Alpha-hole.*" She stood in front of him, pointing her finger and poking him in his solid chest. "Stop calling me palace names! My name is Kensie, but to you, it is Miss Smith. Your sister is my best friend, but you and I do not have a relationship that transcends professionalism, got it? Fictional books are real and meaningful. Now get out of my classroom and don't come back. I do not like you, and I don't need you checking in on me." By the end of her speech, Kensie's chest was heaving and pressed against Nick's, her raging blue eyes glaring into his sparkling seas of brown.

They were lighter than she once thought; flecks of gold danced in his taken expression. It was then she realized she was *touching* Nick Lancaster. Her body shook involuntarily as she dropped her arm and took giant steps backward to create a wide girth between the two of them. In the clarity of space, fear wove its way around her throat as she recalled her horrific words. What had she done? Would she get written up for this?

Nick, either satisfied he'd riled her up enough or deciding to heed her warning, threw his hands up and detached himself from her freshly prepared whiteboard. "Message received." He walked backward, never looking away from her as he clenched his jaw between his words. "But for the record, Buckingham, if you want me to play nice with you, then treat me how you treat everyone else instead of like I'm gum beneath your shoe."

He turned around and stormed out of her classroom. With him leaving, she was able to breathe, and her frustration outweighed her fear of potential repercussions. She had ample things to report to District if he wanted to play that game.

But she was the one with the last laugh. Her board may need to be redone, but it was worth it to see a red marker line down the back of his white dress shirt. He was the only P. E. and health teacher she'd ever known who dressed nicely for work every day. And now his outfit was ruined.

Served him right.

Kensie looked for the good in people, but she was convinced there was not a crumb to be found in the depths of Nick Lancaster's wretched soul.

Chapter Two

Nick

That maddening woman would make a phenomenal center in a football game, Nick was sure of it. The force with which she snapped the ball of innocent banter back to Nick caused his hands to tingle.

The problem was that he couldn't pinpoint if that fatuous feeling was from hardening frustration or folly of the heart. Some days, he thought he might want to take her on a date, and other days, he'd give his left kidney to never speak to her again. Unfortunately, the days of date-taking often outweighed days like today, when he hoped he never came across the Princess of Crescent Cove again.

Nick walked down the congested hallway, fist-bumping students while remembering the countless times he had gone toe-to-toe with the pompous people-pleaser. He hated how she always went above and beyond for everyone; her kindness was a disease, and her disease ran away screaming from him as if he were the cure.

He was certain Kensie had a dartboard at home with his face on it and hundreds of bullseye marks. She smiled at the world and reserved her scowl for him. She said yes to anything anyone asked her to do, unless the request came from him. She was lenient and doled out second, third, and even tenth chances with everyone. Everyone except for him.

Nick had always enjoyed being an exception, but he found that it was weighing on his shoulders like a loaded barbell during a squat set. From day one, she had treated him, as he'd just mentioned to her, like gum on the bottom of her shoe.

As he stepped outside the side door and into the biting December air, his thoughts turned to the way Kensie called him an alpha-hole. That was a toe over the boundary line. Sure, Nick liked to poke fun and flirt harmlessly. He enjoyed being able to verbally spar with someone of Kensie's intelligence and wit. It reminded him of his time in debate and in law school. And, yeah, he could be a bit obnoxious at times, but that was part of his charm. Everyone else loved him and jested with him. Why couldn't Kensie get over whatever prejudice she held against him and get in on the good times? Laughter sure made the long winter days and nights warmer and brighter.

Nick settled firmly on the feeling of frustration as he finished making his way down the sidewalk and into the school gym, where his office was located.

"Hey, Coach. About time. You've kept me waiting." Vickie, the senior English teacher and head cheer coach, stepped away from behind the dumbbell rack.

Nick shook her outstretched hand. "Sorry for the hold up. I was across the school in the English wing."

"Visiting your sister?"

Nick motioned Vickie to follow him into his office. "Nah."

The two coaches sat down—Nick in his chair and Vickie in the one on the other side of Nick's desk.

"Ah, so getting spat on by Kensie?"

Nick laughed, though he didn't care for the way she said Kensie's name as if it were a name beneath her own. "Verbally, yes. But what's new?"

The chair creaked as Vickie leaned back and played with her wedding band. "She's so nice to everyone else."

Don't I know it, Nick thought as he nodded in agreement.

Vickie continued after a pause. "But I guess she shows you her true colors. You should see her in our department meetings. Always volunteering to do stuff for us." Vickie laughed. "I think she'd bark and roll over if I asked her to. She's so nice that she's actually a—" *curse.*

"Whoa, Vickie. Don't call her that." Nick sat up straight and stared at the woman. "And don't talk about her in those terms."

She held up her hands in defense. "My bad. But, seriously. Come on." Vickie leaned closer to Nick and made a hand motion as if Nick was supposed to understand what she meant.

"What?"

"She's only nice and helps everyone because she wants to be everyone's favorite. Surely you know that, right? You, of all people, know how she really is. It's so obvious. She just wants all the attention on her and for people to praise her. It's gross."

Nick rocketed to his feet, slamming his hands down on the desk so hard his pencils rattled in the tin can. "Enough! You don't get to talk about her that way. Kensie hates *me*, yeah, but she's one of the kindest and most genuine souls I know. And I'd advise you not to mistake her kindness for weakness. Take it from me. Don't *ever* let me hear you say those things again, or I *will* take your name to Principal Dan for creating an unsafe work environment among colleagues."

Anger burned in Nick's veins as he glared at the woman, who'd visibly shrunken into herself. He closed his eyes momentarily and regained his composure, forcing his taut muscles to relax. When he opened his eyes again, he met Vickie's and spoke slowly. "She's your coworker. A fellow teacher. We don't gossip about each other like teenagers."

"Yeah, sorry." Vickie stood. "I'll send you an email with the times I need gym use for my squad." And with that, she left.

Nick wondered why they couldn't have just used email in the first place instead of scheduling this meeting.

He also wondered why he was so quick to come to Kensie's defense when the woman did nothing but, like Vickie said, spit on him. Moments earlier, his eye was twitching over her calling him an alpha-hole, and here he was now, defending her against someone name-calling her.

It reminded him of the first day of school, the first year she started at Crescent Cove High School.

Hungover and masking it with cologne and breath mints, Nick had walked into the library for their back-to-school meeting with rain clouds hovering over his mussed hair. He had smiled and waved at everyone, the majority of whom were bright-eyed and cheery, ready to take on another year, but the greetings were plastic and the smile was a facade. On the inside, Nick had been ripped to ruins by the woman from Mississippi that he'd loved.

The introductions had started, and when the name Kensington Smith was announced, Nick had groggily turned his head to get a look at the new English teacher. She was a stunner with a soft complexion and auburn curls that reached the small of her back. Her smile had been nervous and new. Nick's mood had reached a moment of new heights from the obsidian summer he wallowed in. Maybe, just maybe, this year wouldn't completely suck.

"Hi, y'all. I'm Kensington Smith, but please just call me Kensie. I'm teaching tenth-grade English, and I'm from Willow Bay, Mississippi." Her southern accent was thick, and it reminded him of when he'd first met the woman who broke him. Nick had sunk into his chair, disinterested. He wouldn't consider dating another girl from Mississippi.

Nick's phone rang, lifting him from the memory.

"What's up?" Nick answered.

One of his lifelong friends spoke. "Can you pick up some cases of napkins and bring them to the bar? I'm about out and can't leave to grab some."

"Yeah, man. Be there soon." Nick hung up, sighed deeply, and pinched the bridge of his nose. He was thankful for the distraction.

If he thought God cared for his conflicting emotions toward the feisty redhead, maybe Nick would ask for clarity, but he knew the Big Man wasn't listening to him. God had tuned Nick out for some time now.

One too many unanswered prayers showed the line of communication was clearly one-way.

Chapter Three

Kensie

"If you keep letting him get under your skin, he's going to keep trying to dig deeper. He's like a mite." Braelee Lancaster—Nick's sister, Kensie's best friend and wall buddy (they shared a retractable wall between their English classrooms)—shuffled papers on her desk before switching off her computer for the evening. The two ladies were heading out for drinks, and after Nick's little show, Kensie needed an Old Fashioned so that she could start to process his asinine behavior.

Or ignore it into oblivion.

She knew the man was ridiculously smart, even though he taught physical education classes, health, and coached football, all while acting like a certified meathead. Before teaching, he was in law school at Harvard. For someone with so much brain, he sure did lose it sometimes. The moments where he did use his skills and challenged her in debate, however, ended up fueling her dreams at night. When she lost their little skirmishes, after her embarrassment faded, she'd play it over and over, the same way she'd play a new song she loved. Then she'd dream about it, and in her dreams, the debate never ended with him storming out of her classroom.

Why did spitting fire back at him feel unbelievably empowering?

Kensie shuddered at the thought of kissing Nick in her dreams tonight. "Let's get going."

They grabbed their bags and walked into the hall. With the bright overhead lights and white walls, it had the feel of an asylum. That was why Kensie kept her room lit with incandescent lights, pastel colors with touches of sparkle. The male students never complained; she surmised they secretly enjoyed the softness and homeyness of the classroom. Too many classrooms in modern society overstimulate the teenage brain—and the teacher brain as well—so Kensie strived to create a calm environment at all costs.

It cost her a pretty penny, but she was making more money here in Alaska than ever before. She could afford to make her classroom a home.

"Kensie!" Janet, an older math teacher, waved from down the hall before Kensie and Braelee could walk out the door.

Kensie waved and smiled. "Hi, Janet. What's up?"

She jogged toward them, stopping in front of Kensie, a bit breathless. "I'm glad I caught you before you leave. Would you mind covering tutoring for me tomorrow? I hate to ask, but I need to leave for a doctor's appointment at noon."

"Sure, no problem," Kensie responded as if on autopilot. She didn't want to, as she had covered for Janet at least once a week since the school year started, but she couldn't stand to hurt her feelings, nor did she want to risk making Janet not like her by saying no.

"Thank you so much, Kensie. I owe you one." Janet said that every time, but she had yet to give Kensie anything. Oh, well. At least Kensie was being helpful. Useful.

Braelee and Kensie said their goodbyes to Janet and left the school.

When the friends arrived at the local dive bar, The Siren's Call, they plopped into their usual spots in the dimly lit, dusty building. Kensie looked around the familiar place. Fishing net hung on the ceiling with seaweed twined throughout. A small stage for musicians was erected in the corner, and a warped billiard table sat in the middle of the tables. That was precisely why Braelee and Kensie chose to sit at the actual bar. There's nothing quite like getting butted by a billiard stick.

The bartender, Big Bear—yes, that's what they called the six-five brute of a man who had the softest heart; his real name was Panuk—had already begun preparing their drinks. They were returning customers of the place, even if they didn't choose to drink on any given day. The fries topped with cheese curds and brown gravy were to die for, especially in the cold, dark months of the Alaskan winter.

"An order of poutine today?" Big Bear asked.

Braelee smiled sweetly, batting her eyes at the single man who had to be in his early thirties. Probably thirty-one like Nick.

Ugh, stop thinking about him, Kensie chided herself.

"Yes, please," Braelee responded. When he winked at her, she turned to Kensie, covering her mouth to stifle her giggles.

"Just ask him out already." Kensie nudged her friend, and Braelee wobbled on the stool, reaching out and grabbing Kensie's arm to steady herself. The women laughed together, releasing the pent-up emotions of the day.

"I don't do the pursuing," Braelee whispered, flipping her wavy chestnut-brown hair, which was the same shade as Nick's, just as Big Bear set down her Jameson, ginger, and lime mix on the counter.

The tawny, bulky man with a classic military haircut left Kensie's drink below the counter.

"Braelee Lancaster, will you accompany me to dinner Friday night?" Big Bear tucked one arm underneath him as he leaned against the bar. His dark eyes were smoldering under the hanging lamp, and if Kensie were Braelee, she'd have melted into a puddle on the floor. She bit her lip to hide her grin, turning away to give the two a little privacy.

Kensie was not about to walk away, however. She yearned to hear every moment of this exchange that had been a long time coming. Reaching over the counter subtly, she grabbed her drink and took a sip, tuning in to Braelee's words.

"Depends on where you're taking me, handsome."

He chuckled, a rich and deep sound. "I'll take you anywhere you want to go, but I know you're a teacher and probably don't want to make a decision right now, so let's say The Hydeaway at seven."

"And what if I have to cancel for some unbeknownst reason?" Kensie could hear Braelee twirling her hair. Okay, not really, but it was obvious given the tone of voice her friend was using.

Swoon. Kensie longed for someone to take decision-making off her plate outside of contract hours. She barely ate a real meal in the evenings simply because she didn't have the mental capacity to decide *what* to eat.

"We should exchange numbers." Big Bear's voice was low and sultry, and Kensie knew Braelee would be up all night long reveling in this moment.

Braelee must have shifted positions because she knocked against Kensie's back, sending a splash of Old Fashioned against her light-blue collared shirt.

Kensie gave in to the unintended peer pressure and left the new lovebirds alone to place their souls into each other's handheld devices. She scooted around old wooden chairs, hip-checking a few of them as she navigated the tight quarters and headed for the world's tiniest bathroom.

Noting the trident carved into the swing door, she pushed it open and slipped inside, not bothering to lock it behind her. No one else was in the bar at four in the evening on a Monday.

Kensie took in her frazzled appearance in the dirty mirror. More auburn waves had fallen out of her bun. She sighed deeply within her soul, wishing for the millionth time that she had straight, silky hair. Maybe a man would be more apt to notice her as a woman. Her messy curls held her appearance captive as young and naive—childish. Smudges beneath her eyes brought out her inner raccoon, and finally, her ruined blouse topped off her eccentric English teacher vibe. It wasn't a look she was going for, but it always seemed to find her nonetheless.

She placed both hands on either side of the fishbowl-looking sink and let out a puff of air. Kensie was truly happy for her friend. But if things worked out between Braelee and Big Bear, where did that leave her? Braelee was her only single friend in her age range. All of the other friendships she'd managed to stumble into here were composed of married women with kids or older women who were in their fifties. Kensie loved the friendships she'd made over the past two and a half years living in Alaska, but she cherished Braelee because they were in similar walks of life. That was rare to find in a small town at Kensie's age.

Pegging her mirror-self with a stern look, she said, "Kensington Marie Smith. You will not throw a pity party because your best friend is in the middle of securing her future husband. God has someone out there for you, and you will continue to walk in joy knowing He holds your next steps. You will love your name. You will love your curls. You will not succumb to selfish sadness."

Right as she wiped the black from her eyes and adjusted her bun, giving herself a firm nod and pleasant smile in the mirror, she turned and—

"Ah!" she yelped as the old wooden plank on hinges swung and hit her in the face. It didn't hurt her as much as it startled her. She was known to be hardheaded, and not just in the metaphorical sense of the word. Rubbing her forehead, she glanced up to see the culprit.

She wished she hadn't.

What was he doing in her space? Since she'd been coming to this place with his sister, he had never appeared. She assumed Braelee had scolded him to stay away. Why was he here now? In this capacity?

"Oh, sh—" Nick cut the swear off before continuing. "Shoot, Kensie. I'm so sorry. Are you okay? Wait." He held out three fingers in front of her face. "How many fingers am I holding up? Is anything blurry? Do you feel nauseated?"

"Only because you're in front of me," Kensie mumbled under her breath, swatting his hand out of her face.

Nick let out a relieved breath, shoving his hands into the pockets of his khakis. "Glad to see you're clearly okay."

Kensie lifted her head and met his eyes, hoping to convey "move!" without having to say it. She was not in the mood for a verbal tussle with Nick.

No such luck was in her corner.

That's when it hit her that she was in this tight, cramped space with a man, and anxiety gripped her movements.

Nick lifted his hand, and before she could stop him, he swept aside her hair, examining her forehead. The touch of his fingers probing her hairline sent shivers running down her spine, cooling her blood.

"Ouch!" she shouted as he poked a tender spot.

"It's going to bruise. I'm so sorry, Kensie." His breath was warm and inviting, and she realized that was the second time he said her name.

Her real nickname.

Not some random English palace version of it.

For only a second, the world closed around them, and Kensie wondered what it would be like to be looked at like this by him all the time.

The moment faded. He was too close for comfort, so she pressed her back as far against the splintered wooden wall as she possibly could.

She swallowed a lump in her throat as she gazed into his sincere, warming brown eyes. She knew how to deal with the typical rude and flirty Nick. She knew how to avoid him when necessary. But she had no clue how to deal with a version of Nick who said her name in a caring, regret-ful-for-his-actions tone, while looking at her as if she was something worthy of precious protection. Especially when he was this close and the hairs on her arm were standing on end.

"It's okay. I have makeup." Kensie didn't know what else to say. She couldn't justify being mean to him because he wasn't currently being a nuisance to her. But she also didn't want to stick around for more conversation in this bathroom meant for a single hobbit, not two fully-grown adults. "If you'll excuse me."

As she slid around him, knocking him out from in front of the door she needed to pull, something strange took place in the molecules of her body. Her blood reacted as if someone had lit a match beneath her ribs. As her back brushed against his chest, heat warmed her veins. As his hips moved against her, turning with her, it reminded her of a sensual waltz. One she was not prepared to dance to, though, for the first time in her life, she thought she might want to.

Once clear to open the sorry excuse for a door, she bolted, leaving Nick in her rippling wake.

"Braelee. He's here." Her friend looked at her with a dazed expression and smile that Kensie was positive she couldn't erase from her face.

"Hm?" Braelee hummed, and then she came to her senses. "Oh, Nick. Yes, he came in not too long ago. Said he had to give Big Bear something. He asked for the restroom and then—" It dawned on her. "Oh, Kensie. Did you not lock the door again? How many times do I have to tell you to lock the door behind you?"

Kensie swept her arm around the bar. "No one is here, and I was just fixing my hair. I thought I was safe." She took a sip of her drink. "What is he doing here?"

"I told you—"

"No. How does he know Big Bear?"

Braelee grinned. "They're good friends."

"Then why haven't we seen him here before?"

"I told him not to come on Fridays when we were going to be here because you needed to have that time to vent freely about him. Today is Monday." Braelee shrugged, turning her full attention to the approaching bartender. Kensie's face grew hot, and she felt a stab of betrayal. While she was thankful Braelee had told Nick not to come all this time, she wasn't a fan that she had said it was because Kensie wanted to talk about him. To *vent*.

"Nick's my best friend." Big Bear smiled meltingly at Braelee. "Which is why I haven't made a move on his beautiful sister." Then sheepishly, which was an odd look on such a massive man, he said, "I told him a week ago I wanted to ask you out, Brae. He gave me his permission."

"Not that you needed my permission, but it was still nice of you to ask." A familiar voice approached from behind Kensie, causing her to stiffen. She went ahead and downed the rest of her Old Fashioned for good measure.

Nick took the empty stool next to Kensie, and she didn't miss how Braelee and Big Bear turned their backs toward them and proceeded to carry on hushed conversation. Regardless, Kensie angled herself away from Nick and stared beyond Braelee's shoulder, taking in the old wooden planks making up the walls of the small dive bar.

"Do I drive you to drink, Windsor? It's not good to drink when you're mad." Nick's voice had one setting: sarcastic. At least, that's what she once thought. The way he spoke to her in the bathroom after almost knocking her out made her reconsider. Should she attempt to play nice since he genuinely seemed sorry?

"I'm not ever 'driven to drink.' After a long week of work in single-digit temperatures, I enjoy a drink on a Friday evening." There. Honest, polite, and straightforward.

Nick smirked. "It's Monday, and I can think of better ways to keep you warm."

Nope.

She was wrong.

So wrong.

Should have stuck to her original assessment: There was nothing good about Nick Lancaster.

"I'm leaving. Y'all have fun." Kensie covered her mouth as she grabbed her purse. She hadn't meant for her southern accent to slip out, but that happened on occasion when she was mad, excited, or had just spoken with her mom or best friend Frankie from back home.

Grabbing her phone from her purse as she walked out, she called Tarin, a fifty-two-year-old woman she went to church with and considered a close friend. She knew she could vent to Tarin and that she'd give her words of wisdom. "Can I come over?"

Tarin's gentle voice was a cooling balm to her hot frustration. "Of course. Text me when you're on your way."

"I'm leaving The Siren's Call now."

Kensie whisked a pot of Mexican hot chocolate ferociously as a white-haired, thin woman pulled enchiladas from the

oven before chiding Kensie. "You have to love him like
Jesus. There's no other way around it. You work together,
and you're best friends with his sister. You've melded
circles, so there's no avoiding him. Love Nick like Jesus and
pray."

Snow fell in slow motion outside the broad windows
lining the kitchen and living room as Kensie contemplated
her response. "I know. I know that I'm supposed to do that,
but it's so hard when he's so unlikable."

"I'm sure people find you unlikable at times." Tarin
arched a brow as she set down the oven mitt. "We all have
things about us that make others cringe or turn their nose
up to us."

Kensie scrunched her nose and dropped the whisk,
groaning into her hands. "Why are you always so wise and
right? Why can't you give me permission to hate him?"
Tarin huffed a laugh and ignored Kensie's nonsensical
questioning. Instead, she fixed them plates while Kensie
poured the drink into two mugs. They sat down on the
couch in the sunroom, which was littered with a variety
of plants wishing the sun were out, and watched the snow
sprinkle down as they ate in companionable silence.

Tarin was the first to speak after finishing her enchiladas. "Do you remember the book study we did last
winter?"

"The puritan one? What was his name... T-something?"

"Thomas Brooks," Tarin finished as Kensie took a sip of
warm and peppery hot chocolate.

"Yes, that was a great and challenging read."

"Remember the first device of Satan he mentioned, which was to present the bait and hide the hook?"

Kensie nodded, unsure of where she was headed with this.

Tarin sipped her drink and continued. "Nick is your bait. The rage you feel for him, it's a rush of dopamine to your system, hooking you into this cycle of push and pull, tit for tat. You get pleasure from arguing with him."

Kensie shifted on the leather couch, tucking her feet underneath her. "I don't understand. I genuinely don't like him and wish he'd leave me alone."

Biting her lip and leveling Kensie with a hard stare, Tarin shook her head. "That's not true, and you need to realize that. You and Nick, for lack of a better term, rage-bait each other, and you both enjoy it a little too much. That's a sin, Kensie."

Kensie swept her eyes over the plants before landing on the little Yorkshire Terrier, who was lazily lying on his dog bed. She called for him, and Vixen, in all his black-fur glory, jumped into Kensie's lap after she set her drink down on the side table. She petted him while thinking over Tarin's words.

"I don't know, Tarin." She couldn't fathom the idea that she somehow secretly enjoyed getting put down by Nick. "I know hating him is a sin, and I do need to work better to not succumb to his attempts at rage-baiting me, but I don't see how you think I enjoy this." Kensie thought a little more as she stroked a soft, contented Vixen. "Well, I guess I enjoy it when we have actual debates. But that's not the norm when it comes to our arguments. Enjoying debate isn't a sin, though."

Tarin nodded her head, tucking a strand of straight white hair behind her ear. "Okay, I hear you. Give it some thought, okay? I'm praying for you, I love you, and I'm always here to listen."

Kensie smiled and took her friend's hand, squeezing it as Vixen jumped up and sat between them. The ladies laughed before moving the conversation into what they were currently gathering from the Bible studies. The entire time, however, Kensie was thinking of what Tarin had said. Love Nick like Jesus. Kensie didn't know if Nick was surrendered to the Lord, but she knew he never came to church and people were always asking Braelee about him while they were there. Guilt pricked her heart. She didn't need to be a stumbling block to him coming to church. Maybe she should invite him one day. Or at the very least ask him why he didn't come with Braelee.

Could she set aside her annoyance at him long enough to let the love of Christ shine through her?

Chapter Four

Nick

Fire flickered in Nick's vision as he lost himself in thought.

Why had Kensie grown cold and fearful when he touched her earlier? He only wanted to check and make sure she wasn't swelling on her head. He may pick fights with her whenever he could, but he would never even come close to hurting her purposefully.

He wasn't his father, who liked to throw things like a child when he was angry.

"Nick?"

Nick turned his head to Big Bear as they sat on log benches around a fire in Nick's backyard. He managed to keep this area plowed mainly so he could have these nights with his two closest friends—Big Bear and Alexei Selanoff. Nick took a sip of green tea before answering Big Bear. "Hm?"

"You spaced out. Alexei was asking you about coaching a little league football team come July." Nick cut his eyes from his tall, brawny friend to his shorter, paler friend. Together, all three of them were a mix of colors and heights and various thicknesses of hair.

Nick had the best hair. His friends would admit it and say it was the sole cause of his lady woes. *If he didn't have nice hair, girls wouldn't care for him and would leave him alone,* they would say.

"I don't know if I'll have time, Lex. We're gunning for our fifth straight state championship victory next year." Nick slipped his coat off. Three layers and a fire had thoroughly chased away the early December chill. "Why don't you coach the team?"

Alexei narrowed his eyes. "That is what I was asking you about. I need pointers."

"He was too busy daydreaming about Braelee's friend Kensie." Big Bear's toothy, wide smile shone brightly even in the dark of the evening.

"Are they a thing now or something?" Alexei asked. "I thought they hated each other."

Big Bear guffawed while the smoke from the fire shifted to Nick's direction. It was an unwanted spotlight on him.

"Not a chance," Nick stated, standing to stretch his legs and step out of the smoke spotlight. "She's standoffish, stuck-up, and sour. Nice to the world but the devil to me." Nick thought about the last part of Alexei's statement and added, "But I don't hate her. She's just not my favorite cup of tea." He held up the lukewarm mug of green tea he was drinking for effect. Nick didn't drink alcohol like his friends, but as long as they consumed responsibly, he was fine with them drinking at his house.

Nick *was* thinking about Kensie earlier, but he only landed there because Big Bear was recounting how he finally asked out Nick's sister earlier this evening to Alexei, and Nick didn't want to listen too closely. Braelee and Big Bear had been a long time coming, and Nick was thrilled at the prospect of Big Bear becoming his brother-in-law one day. Nick wasn't worried that his parents wouldn't approve; they only hounded him, not his sister. She was overlooked in a lot of ways by their parents, which is why Nick made sure to pay close attention to her.

And that meant paying attention to Kensington Smith.

"I think their constant bickering is a sign," Big Bear spoke up. "Love and war and all that mess. You know, I still recall you and that Noah Prewitt guy taking up space in my bar, droning on and on over how the woman you liked hated you and the woman he loved forgot him."

"I never said I liked Kensie. All I did was attempt to relate with a man in distress."

Big Bear shook his head. "You didn't have to say you liked her. It was implied, because it's true. She's the only woman who won't bow to your charm."

Alexei raised his drink. "Hear, hear!" The two delusional men clinked their glasses together, laughing.

Nick would be lying if he said he had never thought about Kensie in that way, because he did. Too often to care for. Kensie was smart, capable, and obviously hot. But she was crazy. Uptight. A know-it-all. Slightly unhinged when it came to him.

Nick couldn't manage that hot mess express, but he did enjoy flirting with it. Teasing it. Arguing with it.

"On that note, I think the two of you should head home. You've obviously lost your minds in the bourbon." Nick stood and stretched.

"This was our first and only glass," Alexei said blankly. Nick's best friend since childhood was always like that—blank emotions and logical to a fault. Big Bear, on the other hand, was not scared to get in touch with his feelings.

Nick found himself somewhere in between. He knew how to name his emotions or whatever crap society now demanded of men. He was not as tall as Big Bear but was taller than Alexei. He was tanner than Alexei but not as dark as Big Bear. Though all three had brown eyes, Nick's were the middle, muddy color, whereas Big Bear's were almost black, and Alexei's had a strange golden hue to them.

I have the best hair, though, Nick reminded himself, sipping his tea.

But continuing with the comparison game, he *was* falling into last place in one category: life.

It was his own doing. Nick dropped out of law school during his third year because he finally found the courage to tell his parents he didn't want to follow in his dad's footsteps. He wanted a low-key life, wanted to give back to the community that raised him while his parents politicked the state and bent it to their will.

Nick chose to be a high school teacher and a football coach. He chose to stay in Crescent Cove, Alaska. He *didn't* choose for Jesena, his ex-girlfriend, to cheat on him and then leave him, so there's that.

But he did choose the way he responded, which was to stop dating seriously while he attempted to heal from the unexpected pain. He had loved her. Considered proposing to her.

Nick shook off those unwanted thoughts and smiled at his friends. "I have to go to work in the morning anyway. It's time I get ready for bed."

"All right, man. Let's finish our drinks first." Big Bear pointed to the log bench Alexei had built for Nick and his weekly Monday night bonfires.

He sat back down and changed the subject back to Alexei coaching little league, anxious to turn his thoughts away from the fact that he'd crawl into bed by himself tonight.

Sleeping alone was getting old.

Nick had taken several women on dates since Jesena, but he never slept with anyone. He hadn't waited until marriage and had unfortunately slept with women prior to his ex, but he and Jesena had waited until they were serious. He knew it wasn't Biblical, but he sincerely thought he'd marry her. And he was only a man made of flesh and bone who could resist for only so long when she constantly put herself out there for him to take. She had always initiated.

Feelings for his ex were nonexistent, though. The thought of her didn't do anything to or for him, something he was just now realizing as he vaguely recalled the past. What did that mean?

Kensie popped into his head again, and he had a strange vision of holding her while she laughed. That thought stirred something, though he didn't think it was because of Kensie. It was the idea she represented.

Was he ready to start dating seriously again? Not Kensie, but...someone?

He wasn't sure, but he would save those thoughts for another time.

"I can help you develop some plays," Nick replied to something Alexei said, though Nick was only half-listening. But as his friend started talking football runs, Nick focused and pushed away thoughts of his parents, dating, his ex, and Kensie, who always seemed to linger in his brain like a dormant viral infection.

Big Bear kicked snow his way.

"What was that for?" Nick dusted snow off his pants.

"You keep zoning out. I was asking if you were going to try and come to church with Braelee and me this Sunday."

"Church?" The word was bitter on his tongue, but he laughed nervously. "I thought you'd given up asking me to go."

"You could always come with me to the Russian Orthodox church," Alexei chimed in. Nick was more tempted to go with Alexei than with Big Bear. Big Bear attended the church he grew up in, Crescent Cove Presbyterian.

Members had stopped reaching out to him after a year of absence, but Big Bear and Braelee had kept on. Though, over the past few months, neither had asked. Nick was getting comfortable.

"Thanks, guys," Nick said, throwing back the last of his tea. "But I'm good. I'll go again when I'm ready."

Why wasn't he ready? Nick originally stopped going after he and Jesena broke up because she went there, too. But she hadn't been back in the area for over two years. And even if, he knew he was over her. Nick knew Kensie went there, and it could be fun to see her in that environment. Would she fight him the same way she did at school?

But everything inside him scattered like roaches under a light at the thought of stepping foot back into church. He changed the subject to planning a skiing trip to Frost Resort in Snowdrop, Alaska, one day.

When he was dousing the fire after his friends went home, he received a call from Lori, the school's head secretary who was like a second mother to Nick. "Hey, Lori. What's up?"

She breathed a sigh of relief. "Oh, good. I'm glad you're not asleep. We have an emergency with the student council advisor, which impacts the Leadership class and upcoming dance, and I really need you to say yes to what I'm about to ask you..."

Chapter Five

Kensie

Kensie did not sleep a wink, as evidenced by her heavy makeup, the twenty-four-ounce cup from her favorite coffee cabin in her hand filled to the brim with iced Americano, and her braided, unwashed hair.

She'd spent all night tossing and turning after Tarin told her to "love Nick like Jesus" and planted the seed that her actions may have been sinful. Conviction had swept over her. Nick was a hard person to love, to be kind to, but that didn't mean he wasn't a human being deserving of it. Kensie honestly didn't know if she could, but she'd spent a fair amount of time thinking it over at three in the morning while kicking one leg in and out from under the blanket when she got too hot or too cold.

"Kensie. Your right eye is twitching." Braelee, who looked positively radiant this morning in her red sweater-dress and gray boots, held the door to Kensie's classroom open. They exited the blinding white lights of the hallway and entered the dark room. "Are you absolutely certain you should consume the beverage in your hand?"

"I am most certain, my sweet friend." Kensie had made it to her desk before Braelee plugged in the lights. The warm glow welcomed her to another day, and she was hopeful class discussions would be better than yesterday.

Braelee sat atop the desk nearest to Kensie's, dangling crossed legs off the edge. "How is planning going for the Winter Solstice dance? Do you need any more chaperones?"

During her first year at work, Kensie had taken on the role of activities advisor, a position she split with the student council advisor, Marlene. Together, they made up the Leadership Directors at Crescent Cove High School. While she was running around like a chicken with its head cut off during event times, she enjoyed the responsibility and getting to know people around the community she'd lived in the past two years. Having something to occupy her time and thoughts so she didn't sit at home in the throes of loneliness all the time was nice too.

Well, only *sometimes*.

"Currently, no. But teachers tend to come up with a last-minute excuse as to why they can't help." Kensie sighed, thinking of the homecoming dance earlier in the year when she was short three chaperones. She went home throwing up and with a fever just from over-exhausting herself.

"What theme are you doing this year?"

"Aurora Nights. We'll have posters up soon. The kids thought it'd be pretty, and we are all kind of hoping the aurora actually makes an appearance. How cool would that be?"

Braelee's eyes lit up as she clapped her hands together. "I will start praying for that miracle now."

The two women chatted for a bit longer before Braelee stepped out, allowing Kensie to settle in for the morning. Thankfully, she had her prep during the first period of the day, so she took her time taking off her snow boots, smoothing the wrinkles out of her plaid bell-bottom pants where they'd bunched up in her boots, putting on her black ballet shoes, unpacking her pink backpack, sipping her coffee, and combing through emails. She enjoyed easy, slow mornings. Even before coming into work, she spent time in her Bible and in prayer, sipping that first cup of coffee in nothing but an oversized T-shirt and fluffy socks. No rush, no pressure. Just an ample amount of hours to center herself so that she could be a witness to the kids instead of someone they resented.

After responding to parent emails—fretting for an un-holy amount of time, reviewing every word to make sure she came across as kind—and viewing her notes for to-day's reading, she made sure she had her class partici-pation grades logged from the previous day. Kensie stood and stretched while looking out at the dark morning sky from her window. When her shirt rose above her belly button, she didn't bother to adjust it because no one was in the room or peering in from outside.

But that's when she caught sight of someone standing in front of the window in the history wing. Her section of the school was shaped like the letter "L," so the English classes could easily see the windows of the history wing.

With her hands still reaching above her head in a deep stretch, Kensie watched as Nick wrapped Marlene Patalok's hand between his own, giving it a firm shake before pulling her into a friendly hug. Then he turned his head, and Kensie swore he was looking right at her from across the way. Her lights were dim, but in the midnight-at-eight-in-the-morning Alaskan atmosphere, she knew he could see her. The same way she saw him clearly through the wall of windows.

Nick briefly signed the words, "Creeping much, partner?" before patting Marlene on the back. But before Kensie could react, Nick turned toward her once more, and she watched as his head dropped down her body. He lifted his expression while signing, "Nice butterfly tattoo." That one caught Marlene's attention, and she followed his gaze right to Kensie before nodding her head as if the random signing finally made sense.

Kensie came to *her* senses at that moment, yanking her sweater down and, for good measure, grabbing the white string that would ensure her privacy while Nick pranced around the history wing. The blinds fell, cutting off her sight and snapping her back to reality. What was he doing in Marlene's room when she had a class? Kensie knew Nick had first-period prep like she did because he made it a habit to be the biggest nuisance he could be at least once a week, popping in just to say "hey" and lingering for a good twenty minutes to flirt with, insult, and argue against Kensie before she booted him out.

Playing with the end of her long braid, Kensie had bigger questions to ponder like when did he learn American Sign Language? She only knew ASL because her grandmother was deaf, and her mother had taught her.

Dread filled her as she wondered what insults he would conjure up since he saw her butterfly tattoo, which she had gotten with her mom when she turned eighteen, on her lower ribcage. And what in all things holy did Nick mean by calling her his partner? Kensie wouldn't collaborate with that man if her job depended upon it. Thankfully their subjects never seemed to intermingle.

He made no secret of the fact he found her attractive, but Kensie was certain it was all a ruse. A game. She was simply a prize he could win, play with for a season, then discard when he was bored of her, just like her father had done to her and her mom. Nick knew what Kensie thought of him, and she knew he thought her a know-it-all, uptight, and snobbish woman.

She'd overheard him once saying those exact words to his sister, though she'd never told Braelee about it. The words had stung—still stung—and it made her all the more armored up against his falsified flirting.

He was her best friend's older brother who got a kick out of irritating his sister by constantly toying with and harassing her best friend.

That's all. Kensie would not succumb to his childish game. She would not let her heart get strung out like a yo-yo in the hands of a man-toddler. Besides, Kensie was certain that if she suddenly started flirting back with Nick, he'd run. He'd run so far and so fast that Usain Bolt would never catch up with him.

Hm. Maybe that's not an awful idea?

No, Kensie thought. She would not stoop down to his level, which just so happened to be the level of the high school boys she taught every day. Nick coached football, and well, she had a sinking suspicion that he coached it because he had never truly left high school himself.

Love him like Jesus. Tarin's voice in her head made her gut churn. She wasn't Jesus. How could she love like Him? It was too hard when it came to Nick, the one person she didn't care if he liked her or not.

The bell rang, and she shook away all thoughts of Nick Lancaster. She had six class periods to tackle today, and she would do everything in her power to get her students to start analyzing *The Hunger Games* from a literary perspective instead of just viewing it as an enjoyable and interesting story.

"Any luck today with your lessons? Mine have all fallen flat. These kids are just ready for the Christmas parade tonight." Braelee took a bite of her sandwich after asking her question to Kensie, who was standing at Braelee's microwave waiting for her leftover vegetable soup to finish heating. She had left Tarin's house with three days' worth of soup that Mr. Paul, Tarin's husband and her coworker, had whipped up a couple days ago.

"Same. I had better interaction today, but it's still not what I was hoping for. Maybe I should move this unit around next year."

Braelee's dark eyes lit up just as the microwave dinged. "So you're staying for another year?"

"I think so. Unless something drastic happens to take me back to Mississippi."

"Yay," Braelee squealed. "I don't know what I'd do without you here. You've become my absolute best friend."

Kensie went to sit down in front of her friend's desk. "And you are mine."

"Aw, isn't this sweet," a familiar, arrogant voice said.

Kensie didn't even bother to turn around and address Nick.

"Go annoy someone else, Nicky," Braelee said in a stern voice, using the nickname she had given him when they were kids. Though Braelee didn't talk about her and Nick's childhood stories with Kensie anymore, when the two women first met, Braelee had downloaded many stories into Kensie's brain. But then Braelee found out Kensie didn't care for her brother and stopped bringing him up as much in their conversations.

"Nah, I like my palace view." Nick's tone was deep and velvety, and Kensie could hear the taunting smirk.

Why did Nick Lancaster make it his full-time job to hunt Kensie down and annihilate her? A thought from earlier popped into her head, and she found herself acting before she could stop herself.

Rocketing to her feet, she smoothed her cropped sweater down and squared her shoulders, walking with intention until she was chest-to-chest with Nick. Well, her face was staring into his chest. She swallowed down the fear in her throat over the nearness. The thin blue shirt he wore might as well have not been there because the tightness showed off his pectoral muscles well. Feeling a blush creep across her cheeks at the image of a shirtless Nick, which she had unfortunately seen due to sneaking over to his house with his sister to use his sauna when they thought he was away on a hunting trip—spoiler alert, he came home early and joined them in the sauna—Kensie snapped her eyes up to his face. She leaned into the blush, knowing it made her softer and more attractive.

"The view of me, Coach?" Kensie batted her eyelashes and tilted her head. This was how they flirted in the movies, right? She'd never tried it in real life. Sweat prickled her skin under her sweater. She was miles out of her comfort zone, but there was no backing down now. What came next? She needed to draw his attention to her lips.

Using the tip of her tongue, she licked her top lip and batted her lashes some more.

"My favorite view," Nick said, his eyes dropping down to her mouth. Instead of his face flushing, his eyes widening, or something else that would indicate she was successful, Nick rolled his lips into his mouth to keep from laughing.

She could tell by the crinkles forming in the corners of his eyes and that annoying dimple popping out to say hello.

Fury burned in her stomach, and he must have seen it on her face because the laugh he was suppressing broke free. It sounded hair-brained and frantic, which was how she felt, and Kensie knocked into his large shoulder as she pushed around him, leaving her soup on the student desk at the front of Braelee's room as she walked into the crowded hallway full of students. She kept her head down as she marched to the office, needing to confide in someone who wasn't related to the awful Nick Lancaster.

Her skin still buzzed where his eyes had rested on her. Not because she wanted him, but because humiliation was its own kind of fire. She kept her gaze fixed ahead, refusing to look back, even though she could *feel* him watching her go from the doorway of his sister's class-room.

With every step, she attempted to breathe through her burning rage. She kept a smile on her face and nodded to students who were eating lunch by their lockers as she made the long trek.

"Kensie, are you okay?" an older teacher, Mr. Paul, placed a hand on her shoulder, and Kensie froze at the contact before slowly turning around. His hand felt like a rock though his touch was featherlight.

Through a forced smile, she replied, "I'm good, Mr. Paul. Thanks for checking on me. Just need to get to the office."

The white-haired man gave her a genuine smile and patted her back. Kensie wanted to crawl out of her skin and hide away. She knew Mr. Paul was a nice, loving man. He was Tarin's husband. She had seen him just last night before she left their house and was fine near him. She went to church with him. He'd taught biology here for many years. The kids loved him. Why did fear overrun her even at his gentle touch?

Before she could contemplate it further, he gave her another smile and let her go.

Finally, she arrived at the faculty-only entry, and when she crossed the threshold, her smile fell flat.

One more turn and she was in front of the administration secretary's office. After taking one look at Kensie's face, Lori motioned for Kensie to come into her office.

"He's awful, Lori. Fire him. Please." Kensie plopped into a chair while Lori chuckled, tucking a strand of pale-blonde hair behind her ear.

"What did Nick do to you this time?"

Kensie's face flamed. Did she really want to admit that she tried to flirt with Nick, and he laughed at her? The awkward hilariousness of the situation settled upon her like a pressing weight, and Kensie crumbled, burying her face into her hands. No use in lying. "Nick laughed when I flirted with him."

Lori's snort echoed through the small office. "That was a little muffled. Can you say it one more time so that I'm sure I heard you right?"

Kensie shot Lori a glare, but Lori continued laughing.

"You'll fire him, right?"

"For laughing at your flirting attempts? No, Kensie. I won't fire Nick for that. But I will give him a good, motherly scolding if you want."

"Just forget it," Kensie mumbled under her breath, defeated as she deflated into the chair. She glanced at the woman who was one of her closest confidants when it came to work matters and watched as her face transitioned from playful to uncertain. A sinking feeling pooled in Kensie's stomach. A warning. Kensie could pick up on it as it saturated the air. "What is it?"

"I do have something to tell you, and I don't think you're going to like it. But I swear it's the only way we could make scheduling work for the remainder of the year." With every word Lori spoke, Kensie's nerves heightened. Was she going to be let go? Were her classes changing mid-year? Were they pulling her from activity advisor duties? She desperately didn't want to lose that...

Home got a little too lonely sometimes, and now with Braelee starting to date Big Bear, it might somehow get lonelier.

"Marlene has a family emergency, and she is going to be leaving for Minnesota tomorrow for the remainder of the school year. We have a long-term substitute to cover her classes, but we needed someone who already knew the ropes when it came to student council advising and had schedule availability." Lori paused, and she almost looked as if she was fighting a grin. "The only certified staff member who met those qualifications and was willing to step up was Nick. Did you know he is certified to teach history and government?"

Ice froze the hot blood in Kensie's veins; her body chilled colder than the Alaskan winter outside of these warm school walls. The walls that were caging her in, closing her off to air. She couldn't think through the cloud of doom in her head. "I'm sorry. Say what now?"

"Yeah, Nick majored in history, and so he—"

"Not that," Kensie bit out. She knew of Nick's unused intelligence. Lori's tired face softened.

"Nick is going to help you with the dance and will take over the student council portion of Leadership, Kensie. Play nice with him. He's a good man."

Kensie left Lori's office, her journey down the crowded halls a haze. *Nick*. His name was a detonating bomb. She had to work hand-in-hand with *Nick*. She made it back to her room before the end of the lunch period and plopped into her spinning chair with earthquaking force.

"Why, why, why?" she cried out to God, glaring at the mold-stained mineral fiber ceiling tiles. Gathering her wits as the bell rang, she sent a quick text to her mom, her friend Frankie back in Willow Bay, and her closest friend outside of Braelee here in Alaska, Tarin.

SOS. Pray for me. I'm being forced to dance with the devil now. He's officially helping me with the school dance.

Her mom responded immediately.

> Don't be dramatic, baby. Just give me a
> call whenever he ticks you off like you
> always do. It'll be okay.

Frankie replied soon after.

> Maybe you'll kiss and make up with him.
> That's what I'm cheering for.

Kensie responded with the eye-rolling emoji.

Right as the students were sitting down and class was set to begin, Tarin texted back.

> Love him like Jesus. Maybe this is what's
> supposed to happen.

Chapter Six

Nick

The red suit was insulated well enough. Nick was sweating even though the temperatures had dropped to the negatives after the sun set at three-something in the afternoon. It was now six, and the Christmas parade was about to roll.

It would end at Crescent Cove Park, and if this year was like anything in the past, the entire population of the three nearest towns would come out.

Nick was volunteering his time a lot lately. Agreeing to take on the student council class, assist in Leadership duties, and now, he found himself dressed like Santa Claus. Mr. Paul, a fellow teacher who usually took on this task, broke his leg this afternoon, slipping on ice when leaving work, and Nick kindly volunteered to take his place after driving him to the doctor, where he met up with his wife, Tarin. Nick wasn't necessarily close with them, but they went to the church he used to attend. They were one of the remaining members of the church who even bothered to reach out to Nick on occasion, and he respected them both. They were good people, so it made sense to help him out tonight.

After his father called unexpectedly, Nick begrudgingly told him that he would be Santa tonight. To Nick's surprise, the senator was glad Nick was doing it, not because Nick was helping out a friend, but because it looked like he was being "an involved community member," as if that wasn't what he did daily. His father was only happy that Nick would be in photos that would circulate the state, since this was one of the biggest Christmas events on the Peninsula.

Speaking of photo opportunities, Nick's photo area was set up under the park pavilion. He sat on an oversized black chair that was about as comfortable as perching on a sharp rock after a long day of salmon fishing in the summer. Beside him, his "elves" stood at attention, waiting for the parade goers to start forming the typical long line to snap pictures with Santa. There were candy cane poles erected around him, and brightly lit stars and fake icicles hung from the inner ceiling of the pavilion.

The real icicles had been cut down for safety reasons.

Children's laughter, soft Christmas music, and the smell of hot chocolate and funnel cakes wafted through the air. Nick hoped he would get a break to go purchase a funnel cake at some point. If not, he might send one of his elves on a mission.

Santa had to eat.

"Don't you look like a snack."

Nick froze in place, his fingers mid-scratch on his cheek because of the fake beard that was irritating his skin. How did she recognize him? "Jes, hey. Good to see you." *Not.*

The tall woman with long, light-brown hair stood in front of him, her hands on her hips and deep red lips stuck in a snakish smile. "It's been a while. I thought you would have called me by now. Your father mentioned you were playing Santa tonight."

Her voice was like nails on a chalkboard, but Nick forced a smile, though he wasn't sure if she could see it through the white monstrosity on his face. "I've been busy. You know how teaching is." It was a lame excuse, but if he was honest, he didn't owe anything to Jesena Hayes. Was it two years ago she'd ripped his heart from his chest and stepped on it with her black stiletto heels? Who wore stilettos in Alaska anyway? *Only a southern belle from Mississippi who refused to change her dressing habits after moving here,* Nick thought to himself. And there it was. Another reason he would never get involved with Kensie. She was from Mississippi, too. Thirty minutes from the town Jes was from, if he was correct in his geography. He knew the women were not the same. He knew that intrinsically, even if he liked having his excuses to be noncommittal to Kensie.

Commitment? Kensie? What in the world was Nick thinking right now as he faced down his ex?

Jes, in all of her usual boldness and brassiness, sat herself on his lap, crossing her long legs as she leaned against his left shoulder. She'd sat there plenty of times in the past, in less innocent situations, and it'd turn him on every single time.

But now it made his stomach roll.

"Jes. What are you doing?"

"I miss you, Nicolas." Her voice lost all traces of playfulness, and when her light-blue eyes met his, she looked on the precipice of tears.

Nick shifted underneath her, uncomfortable with this conversation. He hadn't seen or talked to her in ages. Just last night, he was thinking about how he felt nothing. But he wasn't sure that was true now that she was in front of him. "How did you know it was me in this suit? There are other Santas here tonight walking around."

Her perfectly sculpted brows lifted, and she smirked. "Please. I'd know you anywhere. Wearing anything." She leaned in, ran her finger down the front of the jacket until she found a button, and whispered, "Or nothing."

"Jesena," he growled her name, though, to his frustration, Nick couldn't figure out if it was a remnant of desire for her or if he was annoyed.

She cackled a fake laugh, and Nick firmly settled on annoyance.

"You broke up with me, remember?" Nick's voice was colder than the snow surrounding the pavilion. He hated the man he had been then. He had finally found the courage to stand up to his parents about his career choice, but only a couple of years after that, he found himself giving Jes an ultimatum: him or the man she was cheating on him with. His stomach soured that he even gave her the choice.

"I do." She sighed. "And I made a mistake."

Nick couldn't help himself. How dare she come here, sit on his lap, and say these things to him after what she did? "What? Was Senator Garrett not good enough in bed for you? Was he not romantic enough for you? Not sweet enough on you? Not available enough for you? Not ready to propose to you? Like I was?"

Jes stilled, her tanned face paling as her lips parted. Guilt crept into the edges of Nick's brain from the frost-bite-inducing tone he'd used. But he swatted the feeling away. She cheated. She did what she did. He kept it quiet for the senator's sake. But he didn't have to pretend to be okay with the idea of the situation, even if he had moved on from it.

"I–" Jes began, but Nick cut her off.

"Please get off me. Children will be showing up anytime now, and they do not need to see a grown woman sitting on my lap."

Jes stood, remaining in front of him. Nick heard the Crescent Cove High marching band's rendition of Jingle Bells, signaling the parade nearing the park. He silently willed them to pick up the pace.

"I'm sorry, Nicolas. I realized after Garrett left me that I never wanted him. It was always you. I told Chase, and he said I should try to make amends."

After Garrett left her. Figures.

"It's too late. You are what you did, Jesena. You're a cheater. I can't forgive cheating. Chase should know that, and if he doesn't, please tell him for me."

Chase Hayes was Jes's younger brother, and he stayed with Nick quite a bit when he came to visit. They had quickly bonded over politics because Chase had a thriving career in political analysis and commentary. He was one of the most sought-after voices in the conservative movement at the young age of twenty-nine. He was a published author, and Nick tended to agree with his well-articulated viewpoints. Nick liked Chase and remained his friend, but he'd have to question the guy if he continued to push his sister on him.

Jes finally nodded once and walked away, but Nick had an eerie feeling that she wasn't finished with her reconciliation attempts.

Would he end up falling for it?

They had dated for almost two years before he figured out she was seeing Garrett, a young Alaska state senator who was good friends with his father—and at one point, Nick—behind his back. That summer was a tough one, but he made it through. Threw himself into his job, his family, and his friends. It'd been two and a half years since Jes, and he had fully healed.

But that didn't mean the sting that came with the knowledge he wasn't enough for her wasn't still present at times.

It kept him from being honest with the women he found himself interested in. He kept them at arm's length, letting his flirty exterior and nonchalant personality rule the land. He didn't think his heart could take another romantic blow.

Nick had loved Jesena. A cut like that takes a while to stitch up, and the phantom pains that echoed in his chest may never fully go away. Only more time would tell, he guessed.

"Are you good, son?" Wayne asked. He was the photographer tonight and also a dear friend of Nick's family. Nick's grandfather had been a raging alcoholic, and it had put him in an early grave, which was one of the reasons Nick prefered not to drink. His grandmother followed behind him because she didn't know how to function without serving her husband and bowing to his every drunken command. Wayne and his wife, Delilah, stepped up and treated Nick and his sister as their own. Naturally, Nick's parents didn't have the time to care that this older couple from their Presbyterian church started taking care of their children. They were too busy running back and forth from Crescent Cove to Juneau. Nick's father was an Alaskan state senator, and his mom was the proud wife of said senator, never leaving his side if she could help it.

Nick supposed it was good his mom stuck by his father's side, but it left him to raise Braelee alone at times. A burden a teenager shouldn't have to bear.

"All's good," he said to Wayne, then Nick deepened his voice, trying to give his best Santa impression. "That woman is just a ho-ho-ho."

Wayne pegged Nick with a stern, fatherly expression, but Nick didn't miss the gleam in Wayne's dark eyes as Wayne suppressed his laughter. He ran one hand over the black beanie covering his bald head before checking on "Santa's helpers."

Moments later, the parade arrived, and families began swarming the hot chocolate stand, which was next to a large sign that read: PICTURES WITH SANTA.

The chaos began.

Some children lit up, bursting at their little seams to talk to Santa. Other kids eyed Nick warily but complied with their parents' wishes. Then there were the kids who had zero desire to see the weird, stuffed-fat man in a red suit. Their screams would pierce Nick's ears as Wayne rushed to snap a picture and hand the children back to their parents.

An hour later, Nick still had a sizable line. However, it now consisted of high school students who had somehow heard their teacher and coach was dressed as Santa. Nick sighed internally as another group of girls posed for a picture around him. He did *not* allow them to sit on his lap as children had. Nick could only imagine the social media posts that would be going around—how the students would turn him into a meme and post printed pictures around the school building—but he took picture after picture with a positive attitude. He always put his best foot forward for his students, and that wouldn't change just because he wasn't within the walls of Crescent Cove High School.

Finally, as the line shrank, Nick was able to take a small break. He chugged water, took the stupid hat and beard off, and allowed the chilly night air to kiss his face as he closed his eyes.

"Oh, this is golden," a familiar voice called. He opened one eye to see his sister, Braelee, snapping pictures of him. Nick groaned, but it was all in good fun. He trusted his sister not to post something atrocious of him, and even if she did, he had plenty of blackmail to retaliate with. If he and Braelee went into a social media leak war, their parents would have their hides.

Braelee looked a lot like Nick. She had that same wavy, light-brown hair, dark-brown eyes, and lean build. However, she was a good two heads shorter than he was, and her softer facial features looked like their mother whereas Nick had his father's sharp features.

"Hello, Lee-lee. Did you come to deliver a funnel cake to me? If not, I demand that offering before you speak with me."

"You're not a god, Nicky."

"Aren't I? I'm Santa." Nick jested, but he knew he wasn't a god. It was all in good humor. He served the one true God—Yahweh. Nick didn't serve Him well at times, and he was certain God didn't care for him, but that was neither here nor there right now. He knew better than to blaspheme.

"Goodness. You look exhausted," she said, stepping closer and placing the back of her hand on his forehead. "Are you overheating?"

"I'm sweltering, but that's okay. It shouldn't be as bad for the remaining hour of the event."

Braelee eyed him warily. "Are you sure?"

"Yeah. I'm good. But I really could use a funnel cake."

His little sister laughed, but she nodded her head and said she'd be back shortly. Nick suited back up and stepped around the black partition to greet more children and students.

After another ten minutes or so, the smell of funnel cake became stronger, calling to him like a siren. He tried to follow the scent, shifting his eyes without moving his head as he had a child in his lap. This particular boy said he wanted a new puppy for Christmas, and of course, Nick replied with a hearty laugh and told the kid that he would see if he had any puppies back at the North Pole who were ready for a new home. Nick refused to tell any kid that they had to be good to receive a Christmas present. He thought the idea was antiquated and an awful fear tactic parents used to make their kids do what they thought their kids ought to do.

When the kid hopped off his lap, turning around to hug Nick before he darted into his father's waiting arms, Nick spotted the funnel cake.

But his sister wasn't the one holding it.

Instead, a beautiful woman with long, wavy honey-red hair and a curvy figure that was annoyingly tempting in those black leggings and tight olive green sweaterdress hidden partially by her unzipped coat stood feet away from him, holding a funnel cake in her gloved hands.

Did Braelee send Kensie to deliver the funnel cake?

The better question: Did Kensie know Nick was the one in the suit?

Nick wasn't a gambler, but he would bet his entire gun collection that Kensie had no clue she was delivering a funnel cake to him. She probably thought he was Paul.

"Hi, Santa. I was kindly asked to deliver this to you." Kensie's voice was like sunlight and summer days—at least when it wasn't pointed at him. He was certain she took on the qualities of a moonlight monster when he was around.

Kensie took two more steps, a wide smile showing off her perfect white teeth as she approached.

This could be fun...

Nick still had that funny, erratic feeling haunting him from earlier in the day when Kensie flirted with him. He wasn't ignorant; he knew she was trying to dish it back to him, and she'd succeeded, though he wouldn't admit it. He had lost his mind when she had used the tip of her tongue to trace her lips. Thoughts of picking her up, setting her down on a desk, and kissing her senseless had invaded his mind like an army marching strong to conquer the land. And those charged images were still going to war in his head.

Mentally swatting the thoughts away, he focused on the here and now. Nick lowered his voice to a deeper baritone than he had with the kids. "Why, thank you so much, sweetheart."

Kensie continued to smile, her ocean-deep eyes vibrant under the lights of the pavilion. She held out the funnel cake toward him. Seemed she didn't mind being called sweetheart as long as the word wasn't coming out of his mouth.

Nick continued. "What do I owe you?"

"Oh, nothing." Her tone was as sweet as Nick imagined that funnel cake would taste, dissolving in his mouth. "My friend bought it, actually. But she had to slip away and asked me to bring it over."

"Aw, come on, now. There must be something you want for Christmas." Nick arched his brow, but between the beard and the hat and the fake white-haired wig on his head, he doubted she'd be able to tell it was him. However, he did wonder how she'd been around all night and had not caught wind that Coach Lancaster was dressed as Santa Claus tonight. But that was Kensie for you. Always lost in her fictional worlds inside her head instead of standing firmly in the real one. Nick simultaneously admired and disesteemed her for it.

Life wasn't a fairy tale. It didn't always come with a happily-ever-after.

Their rocky, tumultuous, disdain-filled relationship was proof enough of that sentiment.

But man, oh man, he sure had fun teasing her. The moments like these were bright, happy blips in Nick's days.

Kensie leaned forward and whispered as if letting him in on a secret. "There is something I want for Christmas, but I know that you can't make it come true for me, Mr. Paul." She winked, and Nick wished she were winking at him instead of the person she thought he was. Her playful behavior was addicting.

"Santa has his ways of making Christmas miracles happen." Nick grinned, losing himself in her darkened eyes a moment too long before taking the funnel cake from her and setting it on the bench beside him. Clearing his throat, he motioned her forward. "Come closer, Kensie."

Suspicion flashed across her face, but she took a tiny step to come closer as he asked. However, her snow boot caught on a wire that was supposed to be taped down, and she fell forward, right into Nick's arms. Her chest was pressed against his, causing his heart rate to pick up double-time. Her breath smelled of hot chocolate as it wafted across his face, and he found he didn't hate it. Kensie bore into his soul, causing his nervous system to glitch, and he watched the moment those irises darkened as she recognized him.

"You," she spat the word, her lips twisting into a snarl. Then she grimaced as she mixed his sister's name with a tiny little curse word. Nick grinned, his eyes growing lazy. He didn't realize she had it in her to use naughty language.

It was kind of hot.

No, it was *always* hot to watch her come unglued.

Was that the real reason Nick constantly pushed? He cursed silently and thought to himself, *I'll have to work through that later.*

Nick's voice had unintentionally lowered to a throaty whisper as he spoke. "Hi, Windsor. Thanks for the funnel cake. I'm starved." After saying one of her many palace nicknames in that tone, images he shouldn't have of his little sister's best friend popped up without permission into his brain. Images of that butterfly tattoo resting on her lower ribcage that he wanted to see again. He cleared his throat and snapped to attention. *What is happening to me?*

"You're welcome," Kensie said as if she wished she didn't have to be polite, but couldn't help herself.

See? That was her problem. For all her bark, the woman had no bite. She'd only verbally sparred with him when he pushed her too far. But her "too far" limit was miles away. He wanted her to snap back at him with a saucy comment, not say niceties after he'd toyed with her and pretended to be Mr. Paul.

Time after time, he watched as she took on all the tasks that others should have done for themselves simply because she had a hard time saying no. And for all her kindness toward others, they didn't respect her or her un-spoken boundaries. She didn't stand up for herself well, and Nick had a difficult time respecting people without a steel backbone.

Kensie's hands were pressed against his chest, their noses inches away from one another, and he didn't need to see through the lens of the camera to know she was sprawled across him. Flames coursed through his body at the realization, and he needed to get out of the heat trap that was the Santa suit.

No doubt pictures of *this* would circulate...

It was the last thing he needed. He'd get a verbal lashing from his father.

Kensie must have opened her eyes to the situation as she scrambled off of him, her hands shoving against his chest a smidge too hard, sending the big, black chair rocking backward. As he began to fall, he reached out his hands toward her. Kensie's eyes grew wide, and she grabbed hold of his hands, but it was too late. Instead of stopping him from going down, she went with him. Nick snaked his arms around her and held her close to his body as they careened toward the floor. Kensie landed firmly on top of Nick as his back hit the concrete of the pavilion with a thud. A sharp stinging sensation spread across his neck, and then he felt something sticky and wet. When he opened his eyes, he saw Kensie's face, contorted in pain, blood bubbling from her lip.

"Kensie," Nick exclaimed, his hands moving from her back to her face. "Somebody get napkins and water."

He searched her face for any more signs of injury, but it seemed to be only her bottom lip.

"I'm fine," she muttered, though the sound was distorted as she spoke around the wound.

Nick lifted her away from his body as he maneuvered from underneath her. One of the helpers put the chair back in place, and then Nick set Kensie upon it, not concerned that his hat had fallen off. He yanked the fake beard down past his chin so that he could talk clearly.

"Nick, your neck..." Kensie touched a tender spot on his neck, and when she drew her fingers back, they had blood on the tips. "I bit you."

"That's not how I imagined you would ever say those words to me." At the utterly shocked tone of her voice and the worry in her eyes, Nick had to laugh.

Crow's feet formed as she narrowed her eyes. "You should never imagine me saying those words to you, Mr. Lancaster."

"Ah, here we go again with formalities. Come on, Savoy. I'm an injured man here. And you just bit my neck like you're a starving vampire. The least you can do is use my first name."

"What do you even know about vampires? They're fictional, remember?" Though her words were pointed, her tone had lightened. If he wasn't mistaken, she was teasing him. Attempting to, at least.

Before he could reply, Wayne arrived with napkins and water for both of them. "You two look like Christmas gone horror right now."

Kensie and Nick caught each other's gaze and burst out laughing. Wayne disappeared, and they removed their gloves, setting to work cleaning themselves off. Moments later, both were blood-free, though their injuries remained intact.

"I'm not going to need a rabies shot, right?" Nick taunted. Kensie scrunched her nose at him, ticking the corner of her mouth upward.

"No, but I probably need a—" She stopped her words, clamping her hands over her mouth.

"A what?" Nick pressed.

"Nothing," Kensie squeaked. "I wasn't saying anything at all."

Nick narrowed his eyes and crossed his arms.

"Tell me, Richmond."

The nickname must have done her in. She smarted off, "An STD check."

The playful banter and humorous energy subsided. Nick knew it shouldn't impact him, but his chest tightened, and a low throb of anger pulsed within. He'd wanted her to banter back, but *that*...? "You really think that low of me, huh?"

Kensie said nothing, but she also refused to make eye contact with him.

He didn't know why, but Nick had an unholy urge to prove her wrong. He didn't like that she thought lowly of him. He may have slept with a few women in his past. With Jes, but he had been in a committed relationship with her. But since her, he'd been celibate because he hadn't committed to any woman and had grown up a little since high school and college.

Nick was a flirt and tease, but he wasn't a player. He wasn't a roguish rake of a man. It hurt that she saw him that way.

He wasn't his ex.

"Kensie," Nick said her name with authority, and when she still refused to meet his eyes, he lifted his hand to her chin and guided it toward him with his thumb. He was choosing to address her kindly instead of with more venom. "I can't wait to prove you wrong about me, partner."

She swallowed, and his gaze dropped to her lips. Blood no longer poured from her lip, but there was no doubt a nasty bruise and bump, and that would stick around for a while. Just like he'd have what would look like a hickey on his neck. He'd have to get Braelee to cover it up for him before the start of the school day each morning until it was gone.

"Partner?"

Nick pasted on a smile, still trying to overcome his anger toward her statement. "I am your co-leadership director, aren't I?"

Kensie scowled and stepped away from Nick's grasp. She placed her hands on her hips. "Right. Just stay out of my way, okay?"

Nick clenched his teeth together. Why was this woman so friendly to everyone but him? The one person who would appreciate her kindness instead of abusing it? He was getting tired of it, quite frankly. He could appreciate her teasing banter back to him, but a comment like an STD check? The sheer malice in her eyes as she commanded him to stay out of her way? That was uncalled for.

Nick had tried to be friendly, welcoming, and nice to her from the outset when she moved to the area, despite her being from Mississippi. He was drawn to her, something he couldn't deny. But from day one, Kensie treated Nick as if he were the bane of her existence. A stain in need of removal.

He remembered introducing himself to her after that first staff meeting, and the burning hate in her eyes as he had said his name had taken him by surprise. But he hadn't cared in that moment, because he was still battling a headache from the alcohol he'd briefly turned to after Jesena.

Even now, Nick couldn't recall anything he'd done to deserve *that* level of hatred from her, and he was done. He always stood up to her brazenness toward him; he couldn't help it. It was a side effect of being a coward one too many times in his life when it came to his parents.

For the most part, Kensie and Nick's banter was flirty and harmless. But the disdain radiating off her right now struck him deeply. The daggers in her eyes weren't remotely playful. Now she was demanding that he stay away from her when they were meant to be working together?

Everyone had a limit.

Including him.

He ground his teeth as he responded. "Not going to happen, Buckingham."

"Come grab a late dinner with me, Nick." Wayne had finished packing his photography equipment, and Nick had bundled the suit away into a bag that he'd bring to Paul at some point.

Nick checked the time on his smartwatch. "It's nine o'clock."

Wayne raised a bushy brow. "That's why I said a late dinner. Delilah has potato soup on the stove."

A foggy breath slid from between Nick's lips. He knew the conversation they would have, and he also knew there was no getting out of it. "Yeah, let's go."

Nick followed Wayne to his house, which was a small, three-bedroom cabin not much bigger than Nick's. As he walked into the warm interior, kicked off his shoes, and caught sight of the bear-patterned quilt thrown across the couch, he felt right at home. He and Braelee had spent countless nights here, especially after his father started pursuing politics.

Sure enough, Delilah, who had already gone to bed, had a hot pot of soup waiting for the men. Nick inhaled, catching the smell of buttery, creamy, and salty soup. "It smells divine," Nick commented as he grabbed two bowls from the cherry-oak cabinets.

"You know well enough, Delilah doesn't make anything bad."

"That I do."

After scooping out their soup, they sat at the small table meant for four and dug in. Nick was thankful; he was hungrier than he thought he was.

"Care to tell me what's going on between you and Kensie?"

There it was. The real reason Wayne invited him over.

Nick shrugged. "Nothing, really. We work together. We tend to annoy each other a little too much. What happened tonight was a pure accident."

The soup was scalding as he shoved it into his mouth, but he swallowed it down and took a sip of water.

"To be honest, I've never seen Kensie act that aggressively or on defense. At church and gatherings, she's sweet as Delilah's rhubarb pie."

Scoffing, Nick responded, "Yeah, she is. To everyone but me. For some unknown reason, she's had it out for me since she moved here."

Wayne gave Nick a quizzical look. "What do you mean?"

"Seriously. It's like she laid eyes on me and determined she would escort me to hell every day, all the while running herself ragged to do for other people, like supervise their tutoring days or clean the teacher workroom or run copies."

Wayne laughed under his breath. "That sounds like her. Even at church, she makes it a habit to help stack the songbooks and make sure no bulletins remain lying around, even though the young boys do that."

"If I asked her to do something, she'd laugh in my face and walk the other way."

"Has that happened?" Wayne took a slurp of soup, never taking his eyes off Nick as he awaited an answer.

Nick averted his eyes. "Well, no. I don't ask her to do anything for me. Why would I? I wish she'd say no to other people. She's stressing herself out and eating up all her time by letting people take advantage of her."

"You seem to care."

Uncomfortable because he didn't quite know how to answer, he spooned more soup into his mouth while shrugging again.

Wayne didn't let up. "She's pretty. And smart. I think she'd be an excellent match for you. She'd sure keep you on your toes."

Nick only nodded his head as he turned over his words.

Wayne wasn't finished, though. "And don't take this the wrong way, son, but I think she'd grow you up a bit."

"What do you mean? I'm a fully-grown man right now."

"Physically, yes. But what about emotionally? Spiritually?"

Nick coughed on a potato piece, and he swallowed it down with water. "Are you saying I'm childish?"

Wayne's sympathetic gaze cut Nick deeply.

"All men are a little childish until they meet a woman worth growing up for. But let me tell you, Nick. If Kensie is someone you even have an inkling of attraction or feelings for, you need to evaluate yourself before pursuing her."

Nick fought back against his rising anger. He trusted Wayne and knew that the man in front of him would never say something to Nick to hurt him. But Nick couldn't deny he was hurt, and as he lay in bed later that night, he knew the hurt was because...

Wayne was right.

About his attraction to Kensie.

About his boyish attitude toward her.

About how he needed to make a change.

Nick just didn't know where to start. Or how.

How could he ever be enough for a woman like Kensie?

Was it worth even trying?

Chapter Seven

Kensie

"**M**iss Smith has that Santa-rizz," one of her students said, rubbing his hands together and moving his head of full black curls like a snake.

"You have to tell us how you ended up with Coach Lancaster!" a girl shouted.

The rest of the class erupted in agreement, and Kensie's face was redder than a stop sign, eliciting more remarks about her supposed new relationship with the school's young, available, and objectively good-looking male teacher and coach. She wasn't red from blushing, no, she was hot with anger.

She was going to hunt down whoever blasted that stupid video all over social media. When she got back to her apartment last night, she had been bombarded with text messages from her colleagues, congratulating her on her new relationship. Several people said they had seen it coming.

But they were all wrong. *So wrong.*

"I will tell you this once," Kensie began, tucking her hair behind her ears. Her class fell silent, all of them leaning forward in their desks to hear her story. Of course, this would be the story they were interested in, but she was not about to make this rumor mill spin faster. "It was an accident. Mr. Lancaster and I are not in a relationship, nor will we ever be. Now, let's get back to the actual story we need to be examining."

The class groaned in unison, but they opened their copies of *The Hunger Games* as she requested. Kensie had to repeat the same mantra for the rest of the school day, so by the end of the seventh hour, she had debated quitting around a thousand times. Nick Lancaster wasn't worth her loss of income. However, she did need to talk to him about the upcoming Winter Solstice dance. Plus, she wanted to make sure he had been correcting his students as she had hers.

She speed-walked down the hallway, past the office, and took a left. After going down another hallway like she was playing Tetris in the building, she arrived at the navy-blue door that would lead to the frigid outdoors.

"Hey, Kensie!" a feminine voice called right as she was about to open the door. Kensie turned to find Vickie, the senior English teacher and cheer coach.

Kensie stiffened, but she waved and smiled. "Hi, Vickie. How's your day been?" Kensie didn't understand why she reacted poorly to Vickie, but every time they had to have a meeting or passed each other, like right now, Kensie never felt quite comfortable.

"You know how it is." Vickie shoved her hands into her pockets. "Another day trying to be the best teacher ever."

Kensie laughed awkwardly but nodded along. "I'm sure you're doing amazing as always. Are the kids enjoying the poetry unit?"

Vickie leaned against the door beside her. "Oh, yes. I thought you'd said this group hated poetry, but they're absolutely loving the way I teach it."

"That's amazing! I'm glad someone could get through to them." Kensie meant it. As a lover of words, if any person could persuade students to enjoy words too, it was a win all around. But something about Vickie's calculating look and defensive tone didn't sit right with Kensie.

"Yeah, I guess it just took a special touch."

Kensie didn't know what to say to that, so she simply agreed and excused herself. But as she shoved the door open, she swore she heard Vickie whisper something to the effect of "You're not the only one the students love."

But she was just hearing things, right? No one would actually believe she thought that about herself?

As the wind nipped her face, she tugged her jacket close around her and took careful steps through the piled snow until she made it to the school weight room, which was where Nick's office resided.

Though the small gym was warmer than outside, the cool air still infiltrated the room. Kensie imagined what this place must smell like in the summer and wanted to gag. At least the cool air kept the stench of sweat at bay. Kensie looked around the room, taking note of the various weight racks, barbells, kettlebells, wooden boxes, and ropes. There was a bunch of equipment in the room she didn't recognize, and for a brief moment, she wondered if she should take up going to the gym. She was too...soft. Maybe if she were more defined, then Nick wouldn't have laughed in her face as she attempted to flirt with him.

Kensie shook the thought off—because it was a pointless thing to ruminate on—and made her way to Nick's office. It felt like entering a cave of doom. Kensie didn't know if she was ready to face his teasing or his vitriol. She took a steadying breath and rapped her knuckles on Nick's open door to announce her arrival before stepping into his office.

Love him like Jesus. Kensie hadn't been doing a great job of that.

"Well, well, well," Nick said as he sat in a black chair, a pen to his lips as he lightly spun using his feet to create movement. He looked the part of a beautiful antagonist in a story: light-brown curls, striking cocoa eyes, full lips, and a wondrously symmetrical face. All he needed was a cat in his hands to give off full Godfather vibes.

Nick's office was small but cluttered. Neatly cluttered, which she hadn't expected. Honestly, what had she expected?

You really think that low of me, huh? Nick's words from last night echoed in her brain. A teensy-tiny part of her wondered if the version of Nick she had crafted in her head was the real him, but when he stood to his feet, took a step toward her, and leaned down to whisper in her ear, she eradicated that small question.

"It's good to see you, *girlfriend*." Nick's voice was low and dripping. The way he said that word lit Kensie up like the Christmas lights hung in the commons area of the school, and she didn't know what to do with that. Naturally, she resorted to defense, creating a chasm of space between them.

"Not if we were the last two people on Earth, Mr. Lancaster. I came to clear the air, and I request that you do the same."

"What have you been telling your students all day?" He lifted a thick eyebrow and folded his arms across his chest.

Kensie admired the way his black dress shirt stretched across his shoulders for one millisecond before she cut her eyes to his. His lips twitched as if he'd caught that momentary lapse in sanity. Kensie couldn't help it. As much as she despised the man, he was easy on the eyes. It made her resent him more. She fiddled with the sleeves of her parka. "I told them the truth. That the video and photos they saw were real, but the entire incident was a clumsy accident."

Nick huffed, an exaggerated frown painting his face. "Hm. I've told them we were a couple. Weird. I wonder who they will believe..."

"You did not," Kensie exasperated.

Nick chuckled, his arms falling to his sides. "Relax. I told them the same thing you did."

Kensie eyed him warily, but she acquiesced. There were more important matters to move on to. "We should talk about the upcoming dance. I can fill you in on Marlene's role and review all the plans with you."

"No need, Starjna."

Kensie blinked once, confused. "That's a palace in Korsa, not England."

"You know about that vague, obscure place?"

"A woman from Mississippi married the prince about four years ago. It was all over the news, and every Mississippi girl adopted the fantasy that she'd be next. I'm surprised you know about the small island country."

Nick tapped his temple with a pen. "You'd be surprised to know a lot of things about me, *Kensie.*"

The sound of her name in his baritone voice echoed in her brain as she stared dumbly at the smoldering man. He was a live-action Flynn Ryder, and she felt it right to her inner being. Molten hot.

Rotten, she reminded herself. *He is rotten to his core.*

Love him like Jesus.

How? Kensie asked herself silently. *Because it's not going to happen by developing further attraction for him.*

"Did you fantasize about marrying a prince? Having an actual palace instead of only the name of one?" he asked, one brow arched.

Kensie breathed in through her nose and out through her mouth. She'd moved to Alaska thinking she might find a man, but being here alone had taught her that she didn't need a man. Furthermore, she didn't want one.

Not anymore. Not since she proved to herself that she was capable of taking care of herself four thousand-plus miles away from her home. Not since she'd settled into her routines and had aged two years. "No. I've never wanted a prince."

"What do you want, Princess of Crescent Cove?"

Clearing her throat, she ripped her attention away from him and ignored the question and rogue nickname. She might have preferred the palace names to *that*. "We need to discuss the plans."

"Relax. A prince might be perfect to manage your up-tightness." He laughed, waving a dismissive hand. Her face fell for only a moment, but she trained it back to neutral. If he told her to relax one more time...

He must have noticed her shift. When he spoke again, his voice had a softer edge to it. "Marlene left me every-thing I need to run the class. I'll stay out of your way for the most part, as you so kindly requested of me last night. You can continue to handle the activities."

Kensie narrowed her eyes, examining his features for any hint of deception. She found none, and that pang of guilt over the way she spoke to him last night appeared again. "Okay." Her phone buzzed in her jacket pocket, so she fished it out and groaned when she read the message from one of her students, Haley, who was the student body president. Staring at the list of additional decora-tions Haley was asking her to purchase from Home Depot and Walmart, Kensie cried a little inside.

Walmart wasn't her favorite place because of all the people, and according to the list, she'd need a truck to haul the pallets the kids wanted her to pick up from Home Depot. Kensie knew several people who would most likely jump to help her, but she hated having to ask for help, especially when it came to her job.

But Sandra the Subaru was not going to get the task done.

"What's wrong?" Nick's voice brought her out of her head.

Kensie pressed the side button on her phone to black out the screen and shoved the device back into her coat pocket. "It's nothing. Just need to pick up more dance decorations."

Nick raised an eyebrow. "You make that face when you have to do your job?"

"What face?" Kensie snapped. Nick laughed once and then bit the corner of his bottom lip, pinching his eyebrows together and narrowing his eyes.

Kensie folded her arms over her chest, cocking one hip out. "You mean a look of concentration? Pretty sure that means I take my job seriously."

"Maybe I didn't portray it fully," Nick retorted. "You looked horrified."

"It's a long list."

"Is this the part where you ask me to help you, Little Miss Do-It-Yourself?"

Kensie sneered. "Not a chance. I can handle my *job*, thank you very much."

"By all means, then." Nick gestured to the door. "Try not to need me, yeah?"

"I'd rather need a grizzly bear." Kensie didn't look his way as she stalked out of his office. Prickly jerk. She never should have come here. Conversations with Nick always ended in burning flames.

Kensie lingered outside the school entranceway as she basked in the frigid air, letting it cool her hot face. When she felt sufficiently cool, she made her way to Lori's office, telling herself not to vent and to focus on securing a truck.

As Kensie approached the door, Lori smiled, welcoming her into the cozy office space. "I was just thinking about you."

"I heard you calling," Kensie jested without heart, taking a seat.

"How are you and your new *boyfriend?*" Lori looked up through white-blonde eyelashes as she typed away on her computer. "I thought the two of you were mortal enemies, but it seems love conquered war."

Kensie's eyes widened at the seriousness on Lori's face, but after three seconds of dumbfounded silence, Lori broke into a grin and laughed.

"Very funny. I actually just got back from talking to him about that."

"Oh? And how'd that go?"

"As well as one would assume talking to Nick Lancaster about a situation like *that* would go."

"So, you guys are still choosing warring over loving?" Lori asked, staring intently at her computer screen. She paused and glanced at Kensie, a sly smile on her face. "Or, as I've heard it said before, warring is loving."

Kensie snapped. "There has never, nor will there ever be, any sort of 'loving' happening between me and that conceited, prickly, self-righteous, philandering, arrogant, awful—"

"A-hem." A throat cleared from the doorway, and both of the women turned their attention to the owner of the low, throaty sound. "Want to add another adjective to that long list you've got?"

Kill. Me. Now, Kensie thought to herself. Sure, she had said similar things straight to his face, but she'd never been caught saying it to other people outside of his sister. Something akin to the nauseating feeling of guilt swarmed inside her gut, but she reasoned it was her stomach crying out to her from the amount of caffeine she'd consumed today. There was no need to feel remorse over venting to her closest work friend, right?

"Go ahead. Finish the thought, Buckingham."

Kensie cringed at the use of the particular nickname he used when he was irritated with her. When he flirted, he used Windsor. When he was jesting, he'd use Hampton Court. Occasionally, he'd throw in something random, though Windsor seemed to be his favorite tool in his toolbox because he was always flirting.

Buckingham... That one was reserved for when he was mad. When she went too far in her righteous crusade against him.

The very name she loathed.

Kensie took a quick breath and readied herself. He wouldn't do or say anything too harsh since Lori was in the room, right? She was like a mother figure to them both. Standing to be more level with him, she stared into his flaming eyes, ignoring the earthy, masculine scent being pulled off of him from Lori's open window on the other side of the office.

Crossing her arms and leaning against the doorframe opposite Nick to match his pose, she didn't cower from his intense scowling. "Fine. You want me to finish so badly? You're a jerk, Mr. Lancaster."

Nick cut his eyes from her and glanced at Lori before popping them back to her. The only sound in the office was Lori's fingers typing away on the computer, pretending to ignore what was going down on her turf.

Clearing his throat and dropping his arms to his sides, Nick nodded his head a few times, puffed out a sarcastic, disbelieving laugh, and bit his bottom lip.

Kensie went cold.

She'd never gotten under his skin this bad. At least not while in his presence. Though last night she'd come close. And maybe he wasn't over that just yet.

Love him like Jesus.

Conviction nudged her.

Right as she opened her mouth to apologize, he spoke in a rough, raised voice, and she stared open-mouthed at him as he let it all out. "That's rich coming from you. You walk around here like you're Little Miss Perfect. Never making mistakes. Always the first to volunteer and take on new responsibilities that you have no business doing. Sucking up to anyone and everyone. It's no wonder your colleagues talk about you behind your back and think you're faking your niceness to always be the center of attention. Live in the real world, Kensie. Take a good long look at yourself. You're stuck up and prissy and can do no wrong. You put that nose any further in the air, and you'll snap your neck."

Stunned, she couldn't move, cut her eyes away from him, or even swallow the raging pain down. His words seeped into her skin and blended into her blood. They nestled into her nerves and melted into her muscles before burrowing into her bones.

Little Miss Perfect.

Sucking up.

Talk about me.

Stuck up.

Prissy.

Kensie felt the water pushing at the backs of her eyes, but she held it in. She wouldn't let him see her fracture into fractals. She wouldn't let him see the skeletons from graves long buried rise and ridicule her until she was a lump of angry tears soaking into the ground.

"I know the real world all too well, Nick." She snarled his name, though her voice wavered. Kensie didn't spare a mortified look at Lori as she shoved past Nick and bolted out of the room.

"Kensie, wait!" Lori's concerned exclamation rang out down the office hallway. Kensie, however, didn't wait. She kept going, speed-walking until she reached her classroom. With her door firmly shut behind her, she crumpled onto the old, beige carpeted floor.

A key turned in her door, but Kensie didn't have the energy to lift herself from the ground. Had she been crying for two seconds or two eternities? She didn't know. All she knew was that her chest ached, her nose was stopped, and she couldn't get the voices from her college peers out of her head:

Stuck up.

Know-it-all.

Does too much.

High maintenance.

Manipulative kindness.

That last one cut the deepest.

She wasn't her father. She only built the walls and tried to be the best *because* of her father. Hoping he'd be proud of her and would come back to her and Mom.

It never worked, though she still *hoped*. She believed in hope. What would be the point of living if one didn't harbor hope? As Emily Dickinson penned: "Hope is the thing with feathers."

"Kensie?" Lori's voice carried concern and compassion, which only caused Kensie to lose her wits once more. Did she deserve Lori's care? After those horrid things she had said about Nick? Of course, he said what he said about her.

He was *right*.

Who was Kensie to claim to be a good and kind person when she thought such resentful thoughts toward her colleague? No amount of helpfulness could wipe away the bitterness she felt toward Nick.

Suddenly, arms wrapped around Kensie. Warm and strong and motherly. When Kensie lifted her downcast eyes, she threw herself into Lori's grasp, clinging to her as if she might wither away without the welcoming touch.

"I'm a horrible person, aren't I?" Kensie asked between hiccuped sobs. Lori rubbed circles on her back, shushing her.

"No, Kensie. We all get angry and say things we shouldn't. It doesn't make you a horrible person."

Kensie didn't know if she believed Lori, but she didn't *not* believe her either.

"And that also means Nick isn't a horrible person."

Kensie stiffened, but she knew Lori had a point. Pulling herself together, she released her friend and slumped against the retractable wall in her room. Thank goodness Braelee had gone home for the day. Kensie would have to tell her what happened, but at least she had time to collect her thoughts first.

Lori leaned against the wall with Kensie, both ladies stretching their legs out in front of them. Kensie had to ask. She took a deep breath and braced herself for whatever Lori would tell her.

"What did Nick mean about my colleagues talking about me behind my back?"

"It's silly. And it's all over how involved and liked you are by parents and students alike. They're just jealous of you, Kensie. Really. It's ridiculous that grown women are acting this way, and trust me, the principal and I have talked with them."

Kensie's gut churned, and she immediately thought of her weird encounter with Vickie earlier. She wanted to ask what exactly was being said and by whom, but refrained. She was better off not knowing, and she'd trust her instincts. She would just keep her head down, stay close to Braelee and Lori, and continue to be the best teacher and leadership advisor she could be. Though her anxiety might have her giving every teacher she passed in the halls second glances of unspoken suspicions. Was it better if she knew? She groaned. "Why does teaching high school sometimes feel like being a high schooler again? It's stupid." Kensie sniffled and tried to laugh, but it was a broken sound. The irony of the way she treated Nick sometimes wasn't lost on her.

God, help me to do better, she silently pleaded.

Lori replied, "Adults struggle, too. You know that. We don't get the communication thing right all the time, nor do we keep our emotions in check like we should."

"And being around teenagers all day doesn't help." Kensie finally released a real laugh. Small, but there nonetheless. She was ready to pack up and move on from this conversation, though. Tapping her fingers against her legs to calm herself, she asked, "Can I borrow your truck to go get pallets from Home Depot tonight?"

"Jim has the truck tonight, and he's in Anchorage. But I have someone in mind. Let me call him and have him meet you here. Will after dinner work?"

Kensie nodded, stood, and hugged her Alaskan mom. "Thank you, Lori. You're the best."

Chapter Eight

Nick

Show her you're a man, not a child. Wayne's voice echoed in his thoughts. How could he be anything more than he was when she treated him that way?

He breathed out a disbelieving laugh as he clenched the steering wheel of his truck. Nick's head was running back the words he said to Kensie earlier today more times than he ran back tape for his players the day after a football game.

She had deserved it, right? After saying those awful things about him? Sure, she had said similar things to his face more than a dozen times, but to disrespect him like that in front of people he had known for most of his life? And all at once like that?

That wasn't okay, and he couldn't let it go.

He enjoyed the tit-for-tat game he and Kensie had going on. But when she said those words to Lori, there was no trace of light frustration or annoyance. She sincerely thought those things about him, and when that sank in as he stared at Lori, something inside Nick snapped. Kensie had known him all of two and a half years. Who was she to hate him so much? What had he done that was so awful?

Kensie truly did not like him. It wasn't a game to her like it was for him, no matter how Nick tried to reason away that there was no possible reason for her to dislike him so much.

No, she had a reason. He'd been nothing but a man-child to her since they met, even if it was in response to her initial reaction to him. He could have chosen to rise above it and show her exactly who he was. Or, who he could be.

How did he balance being who he was naturally—flirty, laid-back, and jesty—with still acting like a man? Just because he was thirty-one didn't mean he had to give up having fun. So what was the balance?

Wayne was right. Nick was far from acting like a man. And he needed to change that. He couldn't use his sad past with Jesena or his strained relationship with his father as a reason for not being better.

Nick would not become his father...

If he ever got with Kensie, he'd never treat her the way his father had treated his mother in those early years of their marriage, which left Nick scarred emotionally and afraid to sleep with the lights off.

Nick hit the steering wheel at the thought of "getting with" Kensie. He needed to get the woman out of his head for now until he figured himself out, and he knew just the person to run to. Apparently, his body was on autopilot because he was already headed in Alexei's direction,

though there were only so many directions on a main road
one could travel on the Kenai Peninsula.

He turned onto an unpaved, icy road, taking his time
down the long and winding way. Every time he hit a rut,
he said a silent prayer that his lifted suspensions would
survive it. Finally, he arrived at a two-story log house with
large windowpanes covered by red curtains, nestled between evergreen trees buried in fresh snow packed from
the past two months of fall.

Alexei's wife, Margo, had a thing about people being
able to see inside her windows, though she lived out in
the middle of nowhere. She was a bit superstitious when
it came to evil legends like skinwalkers and wendigos.

As Nick got out of his truck and put on his coat, he
took in the Christmas lights hanging around the edges of
the house. It was a nice, warm glow against the cloudy
night sky. Maybe he should put a tree up at his place or
something?

The pathway to the front porch was paved, and as he
walked to the door, he could hear children's laughter and
Alexei's surprisingly accurate Grinch voice floating from
underneath the seals of the cozy home. A smile crossed
his face, but it was quickly followed by a frown.

An old pang of loneliness struck him.

Nick wasn't *lonely*. He had his sister, many friends, and
he knew the moment he knocked on this door that he
would be joyfully welcomed into the Selanoff home. He
was a loved teacher, coach, brother, friend, and son. Yes,

for all his parents did to persuade him to follow in his father's footsteps, he knew he was loved by them.

But standing on that doorstep with his fist raised in the air, Nick realized he wanted this.

Nights full of light, laughter, and love with the woman who held his heart and the kids she'd given him.

But there was no woman.

There were no kids.

When he left Alexei's house tonight, he'd go back to his small cabin, spend an hour or two winding down, and curl up in his bed. Alone.

And something about that wasn't sitting right.

"Nick? What are you doing here?" A tall, blonde-haired woman wearing black oversized sweatpants with a matching sweater grabbed him by the arms and tugged him into the house. "It's freezing outside. Get in here."

"Nick, hey man. What brings you out here this evening? Want to join us for dinner?"

Dinner at five p.m. was a foreign concept to Nick, but it must be because of the children. "Sure," he said, clapping his short friend's back. Alexei and Margo were as in love as could be, but they were a funny sight to look at. Margo had a good three inches on Alexei, but that didn't deter their whirlwind romance.

After he kicked his snow boots off and shrugged out of his outdoor coat, he greeted the three- and five-year-old boys by allowing them to tackle him to the ground. "What are you feeding these boys, Margo?" Nick asked, pretending that Carson, the five-year-old who bore a striking resemblance to Alexei, was too strong for Nick to fend off.

Carson was born mute but not deaf, but Nick liked to communicate with Carson the way he could talk back, so Nick signed, "I surrender." Nick had started learning it the moment Alexei told him Carson would probably never speak due to some neurological condition the doctors couldn't explain.

"Never surrender," Carson signed back with a wicked grin for a five-year-old.

Laughter rang from the kitchen as Alexei replied, "It's all in their father's genes." The three-year-old, Canaan, who resembled Margo's father, roared and then jumped on Nick's thigh.

The sound of laughter was replaced with pained groans—Alexei's in the kitchen and Nick's on the floor—before Alexei amended his statement. "Nope. It's all Margo. She's got the beauty and the brawn within this relationship."

Margo pranced into the living room to gather the boys, Alexei following behind her. "That's better, *Moya Lyubov.*" Margo's Russian wasn't great—neither was Nick's—but she nailed the phrase "my love" because of how often she used it with Alexei.

Nick also had his favorite Russian term of endearment to use with Alexei. "Yes, *Moya Solnyshkuh.* Better listen to that wonderful wife of yours."

Margo snickered, directing the boys to the kitchen. Alexei flashed Nick a rude gesture—his usual way of handling Nick calling him his little sunshine. The two men bumped shoulders as if they were going to start a real wrestling match on the floor, but Nick's phone went off in his back pocket.

"I'll be right back," Nick told Alexei, and he excused himself to take Lori's phone call on Alexei's chocolate-brown couch.

"Hey, Lori. Is everything okay?"

"I need you to do a favor for me. I forgot to ask earlier, I'm sorry." Lori's voice sounded urgent.

Nick perked up. "Sure. What's up?"

"We need to pick up the pallets for the dance from Home Depot before they close tonight, but my husband has my truck, and he's in Anchorage overnight. We could really use your truck."

Nick narrowed his eyes at the grizzly bear hide mounted on the wall. In fact, he'd rather wake up a bear from hibernation and wrestle it right now. *Should have never picked up the phone,* he thought.

"When you say 'we'..."

A heavy sigh filled his ear. "The school. The students. Leadership. Kensie. You know this, keep up."

He was silent for a beat. Two beats.

A sly smile crept across his face. "So, Little Miss Doesn't Need My Help *does* need my help."

"Nick," Lori growled his name in warning. "This is for the kids. They need the pallets to start working on the photo booth for the dance. The dance is in two weeks."

"I hear you. I'll do it. Let me have dinner first, and then I'll head over to Home Depot."

"Thank you, Nick. Kensie has the pro card. Meet her at the school at seven."

"Wait, wh—"

"'Kay, bye!"

Three beeps signaled the end of Nick's patience.

He tossed his phone on the couch, happy to never see it again, and shuffled across the heated wooden floors into the dining area. Smells of buttery rolls, garlic salmon, and fresh vegetables snaked into his senses, and though his stomach was clenching from the thought of having to spend time alone with Kensie after today's fiasco in Lori's office, Nick was never one to turn down food.

"Who shoved a sour ball into your mouth and forced you to chew?" Alexei was putting Canaan into his high chair, and Canaan began to demand sour candy, pulling at his father's beard.

Nick mocked a laugh, pulling out a chair at the rectangular, hand-built wooden table. Alexei was a carpenter and did a dang good job. Nick would trust anything built by his best friend.

"I got called in for duty," Nick said as he picked up a fork.

"This late?" Margo asked, taking her seat.

"Yep. Someone lied earlier when she said she didn't need my help."

While Nick shoved a bite of fish into his mouth, he watched Margo and Alexei exchange glances. They seemed to have a conversation without words, and Nick wondered if he would ever find a woman who would know him that deeply.

Chapter Nine

Kensie

Lori was, in fact, the worst.

Kensie sat sullenly in the passenger seat of a lifted snow-white Ram. She learned Nick called his truck Rocco—with two c's—after she had climbed in and her coffee accidentally sloshed over her cup, spilling over onto the black leather seat.

"Careful, Kew. Don't ruin Rocco."

Kensie had stared at him with a blank expression. "Rocco?"

"My truck. Rocco."

"I get that."

"Then why'd you ask?" Nick had retorted as he revved the engine to life.

"I thought only girls named their vehicles."

"You're a treat, Kensie."

Kensie had scoffed, crossing her arms. "And you're spoiled dinner."

Nick had laughed derisively. "You didn't have to accept my ride."

"Why'd you even offer to bring the woman you loathe?"

"Because Lori asked me. Consider this act of kindness a service to her."

From that moment, they rode in silence, and Kensie regretted giving Nick the benefit of the doubt and accepting a ride in his truck tonight to pick up the pallets. She had agreed because she was trying to do better, but it seemed her "better" would take some time to develop. The way she felt toward Nick wouldn't magically shift via one conversation with Lori and a whispered plea to God for change.

They arrived at Home Depot, the orange sign shining like a beacon of safety. Kensie would still be with Nick, but at least she would have a moment of reprieve from the tooth-aching tension inside the truck.

Once he shut the vehicle off, she opened the door and slinked out—there was no other way to remove herself from the monstrosity. If Kensie didn't want to fall on her bum, she had to slink out slowly like a sloth. Once safely planted on the icy parking lot, the light breeze nipping at her cheeks and burning her eyes, she started making her way into the store, not bothering to check up on Nick.

He could make his own way into the store if he wanted to help, but she only needed his truck.

Did that mean she was using him?

Oh, who cared?

But again, a small voice tugged at her soul, reminding her that Nick, even with all of his arrogance and alpha-holeness, was still a human being and deserved basic acknowledgment and respect. Just like she did with her coworkers.

Kensie stopped once she got to the entrance of the store and looked back. Nick was sitting in the truck, watching her, as if he were waiting for her permission to get out.

And he must have taken her pause as all the permission he needed.

Within moments, he was out of the truck and stomping his way toward her.

It wasn't aggression. Stomping was the only way to walk in Alaska during the winter. Sliding feet meant eating ice. Don't ask Kensie how she knew. She still felt the phantom pain pulsing in the back of her skull.

"Realized you couldn't brave the dude's store without me?" Nick stepped up beside her, and Kensie ignored the scent wafting off of him—woodsy, wintry, and a little wild.

Maybe a hint of butter? Was he pulled away from dinner for this errand of hers?

She ignored the heck out of that combination.

"I go to this store all the time without a man." The automatic door opened, and Kensie inhaled.

Home Depot always smelled like fresh-cut wood.

"Hi," an older woman greeted them from afar. "What can I do to help the lovely couple today?"

"We are not a—" Kensie began, but Nick interrupted her.

"We're here to pick up an order of pallets for CCHS."

The woman walked closer, and her name tag read: Glenda. Glenda shifted her attention to Kensie, who kept bouncing her attention from the older woman to the pompous man beside her.

"Ah, you must be Kensington Smith," Glenda said. Kensie nodded politely, then Glenda turned her soft smile onto Nick. "And you must be the famous Coach Lancaster."

Nick positively beamed.

Glenda continued. "I would know that handsome face of yours anywhere. My husband goes on and on about your success with the football team. Always reading about you in the newspaper."

Kensie watched Nick shrug like his success was no big deal, but he couldn't hide the twinkling lights illuminating his dark eyes. Kensie wished Glenda would stop feeding that inflated ego of his.

"Where are the pallets, ma'am?" Kensie asked before Nick could respond to the lady. Glenda's smile dropped a fraction, but she led the way to the pallets. Nick and another worker loaded the pallets into the truck while Kensie took care of the payment with Glenda. Within ten minutes, Kensie and Nick were back in his truck, pulling out onto the one highway that connected Crescent Cove to the rest of Alaska.

They were riding in silence when Nick's phone rang, and when he answered it, his father's voice, judging by the contact name flashing on Nick's screen at the front of the truck, filled the quiet. "Nicolas James Lancaster. What in the—curse—happened last night? There is a picture of you in a Santa suit with a woman in a tight dress sprawled on top of you."

Nick scrambled to take his phone off speaker as his father continued ranting, but Kensie heard Senator Lancaster call her a nasty name. She tried to reason with herself that his father did not know her, nor did he know it was her in the photo, but with how emotional she had been lately—and recalling the conversation she had with Lori about her coworkers earlier—Kensie couldn't stop tears from pooling in her eyes and rolling down her cheeks.

She watched the snow-covered terrain pass her by as they drove, listening to Nick try and pacify his father while "It Is Well With My Soul" looped in the background of her brain. Her heart constricted, and if she could have crawled under a boulder right now, she would have jumped at the opportunity.

It was going to be a long night in prayer, wrestling with God over these agonizing feelings she wished she could stop experiencing. Senator Lancaster didn't sound like a man to be crossed, but at least Nick had a dad who cared enough to call.

"No, Dad. Like I said, it was an accident, and if you call Kensie a social climbing bimbo one more time, I'm hanging up. We are not together, but you do not have permission to speak about her that way."

Kensie froze, her fingers that had been tapping against her thigh coming to a halt.

Nick was defending her? To his father?

She wiped at her face and snuck a sideways glance over at him. Nick had one hand clutching the steering wheel, his knuckles a ghastly white color, while he squeezed his phone closely to his ear with his other hand. His lips were pressed into a line, his brows pinched together.

Nick spoke curtly to his father for another minute before hanging up, setting his phone down on the folded-down middle seat, and releasing a long breath. Kensie couldn't look away from him.

When he noticed she was staring, he gave a sheepish smile. "Sorry about that. My father can be a bit much."

"I, uh—" Kensie said, but she didn't know what she was planning to say. She was reeling over the fact that Nick had defended her. After saying she was stuck up and prissy and everything else earlier, he *defended* her. To his high and mighty father, no less.

"He knows better," Nick continued. "He's upset people got pictures of our little incident yesterday, and he's having them take them off the internet."

"But it was an accident," Kensie finally said, her words rushed and anxious.

"I know. He knows that, too. Trust me, this is over his image. It has nothing to do with us." Nick's tone suggested he and his father weren't very close. Kensie tried to remember what Braelee had said about her parents in the past, but all she remembered were the facts: James Lancaster was an Alaskan state senator. His wife, Stacey, was the embodiment of a politician's wife. Braelee had never mentioned anything else, now that Kensie thought about it. Was it for the same reasons that Braelee tried not to bring up Nick in conversations? She knew Kensie's dad wasn't in the picture, so maybe Braelee didn't bring up her parents out of fear of triggering something in Kensie?

Kensie cleared her throat and wiped at a stray tear. She was grateful to Braelee, but she never wanted her best friend to feel like she had to tiptoe around topics. She'd have to make more of an effort to show Braelee she could confide in her about her parents. She would practice with Nick. "Has he always been this way with you and Braelee? More concerned about his career?"

Nick grimaced, the streetlight illuminating his frame. "Pretty much. Don't get me wrong, my parents love us in their own way, but Dad takes his job seriously. As he should, I guess. Participating in senatorship is a role that demands a lot of time, effort, and energy."

Kensie thought over his words as they continued to drive in silence. Was that why Nick acted carefree and unattached? Because he grew up with a father who demanded a lot out of him in his youth?

The school came into view, and Kensie refocused. It didn't matter if Nick had a rough childhood. A lot of people had bad childhoods. It didn't mean it could be an excuse to be a jerk. Kensie was Exhibit A.

But you are a jerk to Nick, Kensie's conscience reminded her. But she was a jerk to him for completely different reasons. Because he was a jerk to her first.

Love him like Jesus.

"Let's get these unloaded," Kensie said as they rolled to a stop.

Nick agreed, and the two of them brought the pallets inside one by one. It took double the time it had taken the two guys at Home Depot. By the time they finished, Kensie was ready to bolt. She hadn't stopped thinking over what Nick had said about his father, and Kensie felt like she was softening toward Nick.

She didn't like it. Understanding someone made it more difficult to loathe them.

But isn't that what you want? What you've prayed for?

"Well, thank you for your help. Sorry you had to come to my rescue so late." Kensie laughed, but she couldn't hide the nervous energy radiating off her. She couldn't stop fidgeting with her gloves as she walked beside him toward her car. She couldn't stop bouncing on her toes once they reached her car, and he reached in front of her and opened her door for her.

"I'm not a bad guy, Kensie, despite what you believe. Please don't hesitate to call if you need me."

Kensie nodded and slid into her car, dying to get away from whatever it was that was taking place in her heart. It was new. Scary. Waters were rising, and she was not prepared to tread them.

She cranked her car, and while she waited for the engine to heat up, a knock on her window pulled her attention from mindlessly scrolling through social media and thinking about how she needed to call her best friend back in Mississippi and tell her everything that had happened over the past couple of days.

"Yes?" she asked after pressing the button to roll down her window.

"I forgot to say I'm sorry. What I said about you earlier today—I, well. I meant it, but I didn't mean it like you think I meant it. Yes, you're those things, prissy and pretentious, but it's not all a bad thing, okay? I'm sorry I said it like it was. Your kindness and niceness are your strengths, and you should know that."

Kensie could do nothing but stare, her lips parted and confusion writing itself across her face. Nick nodded a few times, closed his eyes, and backed away. The movement snapped Kensie out of her stupor.

"I'm sorry, too, Nick."

She said his name. To his face. In a polite way. In a caring way. In an *understanding* way.

Kensie couldn't explain why she was sorry like Nick had done for her. She rolled up her window and drove off without looking back. Anxiety and tangled thoughts and emotions were choking her, and she had to figure out a way to understand this new territory she found herself walking in. Her head was spinning out of control.

Nick apologized? Was his apology even real? He said he meant what he said, but not the way he said it...

What was going on?

Nick. Braelee. Their parents. Her coworkers. The darkness of winter. The cold.

Too much, too much, too much.

Kensie stumbled into her apartment, unsure how she'd made it home in the raging storm that was her mind. She slipped out of her snow boots, shrugged off her coat, and allowed herself a moment to completely unravel as she cried out to God for clarity, comfort, and direction.

"Just help me, please. I don't know what to do or what to say or what to think. It feels like the life I built for myself is crumbling down brick by brick. The people I thought liked me are throwing verbal stones from afar. And I don't care if it's jealousy. *Why?* Why must someone be jealous because I take my job seriously and do it well? Why do I care so much? Why does it sting? Why am I like this? Why do I want everyone to like me?"

Kensie took deep breaths and released a truth. "Everyone except Nick, that is. And why am I still holding a bitter grudge against a stupid email from two and a half years ago? Why can't I just ignore the flirting? Why do I retaliate? Why do I not care if he likes me or not? Lord, I—" Kensie hiccupped as she lay face down on her Japanese mattress pad, her satin pillowcase soaked with tears. "I have so many 'why' questions. And the answers are going to gut me. They'll hold a mirror to my beliefs and force me to acknowledge the sinfulness within me. Lord, walk with me through this. Hold my hand as you rewire my anxious, people-pleasing brain. As you root out the bitterness I have toward Nick."

Kensie's phone rang, and when she saw that it was her mother, she dried her tears and shoved down the discombobulated feelings atop her.

"Hi, Mom. You're up late. Is everything okay?"

"Oh, I'm fine. I was up and saw you'd just got home and figured I'd call to check in on you." Marie Smith's voice was a warm balm to Kensie's cracking soul. "Have you been crying, Kensington Marie?"

Stupid mother's intuition, Kensie thought to herself, though she had to bite her tongue not to ask her mother not to call her Kensington. *I love my name,* she repeated to herself, forcing herself to believe it. "Yes."

A beat of nothing, and then, "What's going on?"

Kensie, unable to hold it in, spilled her heart to her mom. If she could be herself with any human on this planet, it was the woman who had bravely and fiercely raised Kensie. All by herself. "And he calls me Buckingham," Kensie blubbered. "It makes me hate my name again, Mom. I'm sorry. I'm trying to love the name you gave me, but every time he uses a stupid palace name, I'm transported back to high school. All the insecure feelings come rushing back, and it just makes me furious!"

"Oh, my baby," Marie cried dramatically on the other end of the line. "Do you want me to fly up there and give 'em what for?" Kensie laughed lightly, and her mother's voice softened. "In all seriousness, nobody gets to change your name without your permission. Do you remember why I named you Kensington?"

Kensie sniffled, wiping the wetness from her cheeks. "Because it's associated with royalty, boldness, confidence, and resilience."

"And because I knew you would embody all those qualities, baby girl. You are a force to be reckoned with, unlike your old mother."

Stiffening, Kensie sat up straight. "You're a force, too, Mom. What makes you think that you're not?"

Marie was silent for three long seconds before she breathed deeply and replied, "Don't worry about me, Kensie. I'm just growing senile as I age."

Though she wanted to push her mother more, Kensie didn't have the energy. Instead, she told her mom that she would continue to work on loving her name—yet again—and that she would handle Nick. Everything would be fine. Just. Perfectly. Fine.

Chapter Ten

Nick

"Not in the face!"

Cooper, a sophomore who rivaled Nick's height but was skinny as a stick, hurled another red dodgeball at Trey, an oversized junior who constantly picked on Cooper. When the ball collided with Nick's star quarterback's face *again*, Nick covered his mouth and turned his head away, pretending he didn't see it that time. Trey was a good kid, but Nick had that same streak in him—not knowing when to stop jesting with someone. Maybe if Kensie had put him in place sooner, he would have stopped teasing and taunting her as much.

When Nick's father had said those unsavory things about Kensie, something inside of him, an innate protectiveness, rose to defend her. Kensington Smith was a lot of things, but she wasn't a whore, a bimbo, or after Nick for status reasons. Kensie's expression as she sat next to him in his truck while his father talked nonsense about her, stirred sympathy within Nick. Sure, Nick had endured his father for his entire life, but the last thing he wanted to do was put a target on Kensie's back.

And that's when he knew he would have to take a step back when it came to Kensie. To protect her from his all-consuming father, he'd have to step away from her. This was part of becoming a man worthy of her.

Nick liked Kensie. The thought of them together was plain as day since Wayne suggested it, and it was time to admit it to himself and stop pulling her pigtails like a little boy who couldn't express his feelings.

His terrifying, confounding, and ever-growing feelings.

Feelings he never thought he'd have again after his last Mississippi girl.

A high-pitched, feminine scream bounced off the gym walls.

"Coach! Help!"

Nick scanned the gym from his spot in the corner and saw Lovë, a sophomore student, lying on her side on the floor and clutching her right knee. Another pain-filled screech bounced off the walls as she cried out. Nick took off in a sprint toward the girl as the other students moved dodgeballs out of his way, clearing a path along the polished maplewood floor.

Within seconds, Nick was kneeling beside her and taking note of the injury as he calmly spoke. "Lovë, I need you to breathe. Focus on me and breathe."

Nick gently pried her fingers off her knee, and he fought back the natural wince that wanted to overcome his features as he saw the clear dislocation of her kneecap. Remaining calm, Nick said, "Trey, go get the nurse and Mrs. Lori."

Lovë took one look at her knee and lost her crap.

"Give her space," Nick commanded her crowding classmates. Everyone eased away except for two girls. Her best friends flanked her side and held her hands as Nick tried to hold her leg steady, and he allowed them to stay because it seemed to be helping Lovë. The more she moved it, the more pain she would experience, but he knew how scared she must be. He had once dislocated his shoulder in high school, and that pain was excruciating. "Breathe, Lovë. I need you to lie still, okay? The more you move, the more it will hurt. You're okay. Breathe for me."

Once Nick had Lovë calm again, he asked the other two girls what had happened.

They exchanged glances, and then they...*smiled?*

"Delen was trying to block her from getting hit," one girl replied, her smile growing wider.

The other added, "But his momentum to get in front of her was too strong. When the ball hit him, he fell and landed on top of Lovë. There was a sickening crunch."

All three girls grimaced and groaned, and finally, Nurse Hamilton arrived. Nick let him take over as he filled him and Lori in on what happened. While the two of them took care of Lovë, Nick gathered his class and told them to go ahead and pick up the game for the day. He pulled a sheepish and nervous-looking Delen aside.

"Dislocated knee," Nick told him. The curly-headed student's dark eyes tripled in size.

"I didn't mean to, Coach. I swear. I was only trying to stop the ball from hitting her face."

Nick chuckled and patted him on the back. "I know, kid. Good try."

"Chivalry is hard." Delen sighed, hanging his head. "I just want her to notice me."

Any remnant of laughter on Nick's tongue died. That was a feeling he knew all too well, unfortunately.

Acknowledging his feelings for Kensie was only step one. Now he needed to figure out what to do about it. Should he ignore it? That would be better than getting her involved in any way with his father. But just the thought of her fiery words, pretty face, and kind soul had him yearning for her. Would he be able to put away his old self in time to win her affections?

A ridiculous, immature thought occurred to Nick: If he stepped back from taunting and teasing Kensie, would she even bother to give him the light of day? Or would she allow him to redeem himself and weasel his way into her good graces? Would he become just another coworker she was polite and kind to? Or would she still stand up for herself if Nick did something to tick her off?

It was moments like this when Nick wished he were in God's good graces. Then, Nick remembered he was supposed to be helping a teenager out, not imitating one within the confines of his head.

Nick flicked his eyes to the anxious teenager, who looked ready to hear Nick's thoughts. "It's hard to be a man sometimes, Big D. But remember that it's always the

better option than cowering in the face of a challenge."
Nick recognized that he needed to take his own advice,
and through a grimace, he added, "Or a woman."

"They are complicated creatures."

Nick harrumphed in agreement, patting him on the
back.

"Yeah, they are princesses to be cherished. But that's
what makes them worth it."

Delen and Nick sat with that lingering statement like
age-old wisdom.

Was it time to switch up on Kensie? To start trying to
build a friendship instead of an enemy-ship? To make
the Princess of Crescent Cove his ally? Nick would have
thought frenemies was the correct term, but he remembered the way she spoke about him to Lori, and he had
no doubt that term did not exist in her head. Despite his
warring mind, Nick knew one thing for certain: He wasn't
ready to let Kensie out of his life, and he sure as heck
would not let his father get a hold of her. It was time to
put his boyish teasing and taunting aside. It was time to
attempt something genuine with Kensington Smith. It was
time to figure out who Nick Lancaster was when he put his
mind to something and pursued it with the same energy
he'd put into toying with Kensie.

As if he summoned her with his thoughts, Kensie ran
into the gym, her long, curly hair blowing behind her
as she rushed to Lovë's side. A worried but loving look
overtook Kensie's face as she knelt beside the student,
taking her hand. Lovë actually cracked a smile as she

recounted the events that led to her condition to Kensie. Then, both of the females looked toward Nick and Delen. Nick elbowed the kid and whispered, "Go check on your girl."

As Nick watched Delen approach Lovë, he noticed Kensie was still sneaking glances in his direction.

Nick felt like the Grinch. Specifically in the moment where the green creature's heart thumped, thumped, thumped as Kensie tried to be obscure in her curious observations of him.

There's hope, Nick thought to himself as a slow, genuine smile spread across his face.

Chapter Eleven

Kensie

Three days after having her brain rewired because of Nick's apology—*was it sincere, though?*—Kensie found that she could exchange niceties with him when she encountered him in the hallways. She never brought up his apology, and she never sought him out to elaborate upon her rushed one. Instead, she simply continued to pray. That's all she was able to bring herself to do.

But Nick Lancaster seemed to stop seeking her out, and Kensie noticed.

She didn't like that she noticed.

She didn't like that she didn't like the way he smiled and said hello cordially in the hallway instead of spitting off some flirty comment or engaging her in a rhetorical debate just to test her and rile her up.

Kensie observed Nick two days ago, watching as he handled the situation in the gym. One of Kensie's leadership students had come and told her about Lovë, so Kensie had Braelee step over and watch her class since it was Braelee's prep period. When Kensie entered the gym, she saw Nick sitting next to a former student of hers, consoling him, or so it appeared by the way Nick patted his back. Seeing him with the kids always stirred an uncomfortable feeling inside her. She had brief thoughts of what he would be like as a dad, and Kensie knew she couldn't think that way. *Good,* she thought anyway. *He would be a good dad. A dad who stayed.*

"Miss Smith, can you bring me some more tape?" Corey, one of her leadership students, asked, knocking her out of her unwarranted reverie. Corey was high on a ladder hanging stars from the ceiling. The dance would take place exactly a week from today, so the students were working on getting decorations up that wouldn't get torn down before the dance could even begin. Kensie grabbed a roll from her box of things—which included duct tape, packaging tape, double-sided tape, scissors, hot glue, you name it—and tossed it up to Corey.

"Need anything else?"

"Nah, I'm good."

Kensie smiled and encouraged him before checking in on the progress of the photo booth some students were painting in the Arctic entryway. The moment she stepped through the doors, paint fumes burned her nostrils and suffocated her lungs. "Did we paint the entire school?" she jested, waving her hand in front of her nose to no avail.

The three girls on their knees, spray-painting the sides of the booth, looked up and grinned. "How is it looking?" Katie asked, standing up and pushing black hair out of her face with her wrist. Her hands were spotted with a deep-green color from the paint.

Kensie raked her eyes over the explosion of bright color contrasted by darker tones; they did it. The girls painted the aurora across multiple pallets.

"Absolutely stunning, Katie." Kensie looked at the other two girls with the same face a proud, loving mother would wear. "Haley. Nakita. Great job! Everyone will be tripping over themselves to get a photo in front of this."

A chorus of thank yous rang, and the girls recounted to Kensie the plan for the rest of the photo booth before snapping photos to send to Lovë, who was currently on the way home from the hospital in Anchorage. The leadership class had all signed a card, and Kensie would mail it off later.

Kensie's nose was getting cold, so she decided it was time to check in on her indoor students once more. When she entered back into the commons area—where the dance would take place—in front of Crescent Cove High School's auditorium, Kensie caught sight of Josh standing midway on the smaller ladder, chatting sullenly with Nick.

Too nosy for her good, Kensie walked over to a small group of students who were on the floor creating props for use on the music stage. She acted as if she was checking in on them, but she was straining to hear what Josh and Nick were talking about.

"I don't know, Coach. My mom said we couldn't afford the fees for me to do more than one sport next year." Kensie's heart sank at Josh's admission. He continued.

"But I don't know how to choose between basketball and football. I'm doing basketball this year, obviously, but I may not get to do football come summer."

Kensie fiddled with a balloon as Nick responded. "Would she be open to having someone cover your fees? Because we can make that happen."

Josh sighed heavily. "I told her the office would do that, but she said something about having pride and stuff. Not asking for handouts or something like that."

Silence stretched between the two of them. The students in her balloon group continued to chat away, filling the void they had no idea was opening just to the right of them.

Finally, Nick said, "I get that. Sometimes it's hard for adults who have worked hard to pave their way to ask for help when life throws curveballs their way. But I promise you I will do everything I can to make sure you get to participate in any sport you want." Nick paused, and from the corner of her vision, Kensie saw Josh wrap Nick in a hug before clapping him on the back as if the two of them were best buds.

"It's been hard since Dad left us." Josh's voice wavered, and Nick didn't let Josh out of his grip.

"I know, Josh. I know."

"Does it get any easier having an absent parent?" Josh asked.

"I wish I could tell you that it did, but I'd be lying." Nick lowered his voice, and Kensie could no longer hear what he was saying to Josh. Her heart shattered for her student. She knew that feeling all too well.

Nick did, too, it seemed.

He never had a parent leave him, Kensie knew that much. But there was something there with his folks. Something that brought hurt to both of the Lancaster siblings. Kensie saw it clear as day when she asked Braelee about her dad's career yesterday while having lunch. Braelee shrugged and said, "They make sure we have everything we need, but yeah, they are gone a lot. It's been that way for a while, though we had a good childhood."

Add that to what Kensie overheard on the phone when she was riding in Nick's truck a few days ago, and one didn't have a pretty picture painted of the Lancaster parents. Kensie wondered if it was better that her father had left before she could remember and hadn't looked back. Would having parents who were still in one's life but not very present be worse?

Josh responded to Nick. "Thanks for the honesty. It's nice not to hear it's all going to be okay, you know?"

"I know," Nick stated just as Kensie thought it in her head.

What was with the way Nick was having a heart-to-heart with Josh? Nick was able to say the right things and in the right language for Josh to understand. Kensie struggled to talk to teenagers sometimes.

It was unbelievably attractive, and Kensie's heart was beating out of her chest as her stomach swooped and swirled.

"Hey, Kensie."

Kensie's thoughts were interrupted by Nick's smooth voice coming from beside her. She looked up from the balloon she was still toying with and met his eyes. They had a sad shine to them, but he still wore a stunning smile.

One that she found didn't have traces of smirk.

Genuine.

Beautiful.

Snap out of it, Kensie.

Wait—did he say her name?

"Hi." Brilliant. Just brilliant. What did this man do to her feisty energy just by smiling nicely at her and using her name? Was she seriously allowing one apology, heartfelt conversation, and recent Nick-to-student interactions to derail her every thought about him? He was still that nasty man who had sent her that awful email, called her by ridiculous palace names, flirted with zero intentions, and would run out of her life quicker than her father if she gave him even the hint that she found him attractive, and now, oddly compassionate.

"I came by to check the progress and see if you need any help." As he was talking, Nick stretched an arm across his chest and then rolled his shoulder.

"We're good, thanks." Kensie paused, debating whether she should even ask. She decided to give this friendly conversation thing a shot. "Are you okay?"

"Hm?"

Kensie dropped her balloon and pointed. "Your shoulder."

"Oh, yeah. Just sore from today's workout."

He was the one who brought up working out, so one couldn't blame Kensie for allowing her eyes to fall from his face to his fitted t-shirt and down to his black sweatpants. She had seen Nick in a variety of outfits before, but honestly, this was her favorite. Casual, comfortable. *Sexy.*

Goodness gracious! What was wrong with her? A man couldn't go from being her mortal enemy number one to occupying adjectives such as sexy within her brain. Unacceptable. She was better than that. Just because it happened in the books she read didn't mean it would translate to real life.

Nick had a knowing smile as Kensie's eyes landed back on his face, and she was quite afraid her thoughts were being broadcast on clear FM radio.

But Nick didn't comment, which was unusual for him. Speaking of unusual behavior, Kensie remembered that Nick hadn't stopped by her room to razzle her up in three days. And for some reason only known to God above, she blurted, "I haven't seen you in a while."

"Three days?" Nick raised an eyebrow and crossed his arms over his chest. "Do you miss me, Windsor?"

Kensie's foot was tasting bitter within her mouth, even as he went back to addressing her as Windsor. Why, why, *why* did she ask him such a thing? Blood rushed to her face as she stuttered over a single syllable word. "N-no."

"You know, it's okay if you do. I'm quite missable. But…" Nick stepped closer to her, and Kensie stood her ground, refusing to cower. Stuttering was bad enough.

This was it.

This was the moment where Nick would humiliate her because she let her walls down a teensy, tiny bit. Because she let her "find the best in people" mentality win out with him. Because she started to see a small snippet of back-story within his life. Because she attempted to choose friendship and take a block of her wall down in the name of understanding.

She couldn't let that happen, so she spoke before he could.

"I guess the war of words between us will resume." Kensie folded her arms to match his stance. Surprisingly, Nick flinched.

"I was going to say you were missable, too. Why do you hate me, Kensie?" He sounded…*hurt*.

Kensie, baffled, dumbly replied, "I don't hate you."

"You highly dislike me, then."

"Yes," Kensie said without hesitation.

"Why?"

"Because you're rude."

"Me? And you're not?"

Kensie blew out an irritated breath, reminding herself that she had been praying about this for days. She couldn't lose her cool. "I only am because you are."

Nick laughed in disbelief, and anger rose fast and wild within Kensie's veins at the sound. Without thought, she opened her mouth to say something, but was divinely interrupted by a student asking if Kensie could make a store run to grab more supplies.

She fixed her face into a calm smile. "Of course I can. Send me a message with exactly what you need."

Kensie stepped around Nick without meeting his eyes. But he wasn't letting her go. He matched her step for step as she walked across the commons to get her purse.

"I'm only rude to you because you are rude to me. So, we are at an impasse, Buckingham. Who started the war of words? Because I don't think it was me." Nick's tone was quipped and whispered, which was good. Kensie didn't want her students to see her arguing with Nick. Hopefully, they hadn't overheard anything already.

Kensie snagged her bag from the table and turned to face Nick.

"You started it." Great. Now *she* sounded like one of her high schoolers. Maybe she had been acting like them this entire time, but Nick Lancaster just *did something* to her. She inhaled courage and released her backlist of reasons to despise him.

"The email you sent me when I first moved here was rude and clipped, and you made fun of my name while demanding I address you in a specific way. When you offloaded cleaning your old classroom on to me, I wasn't impressed. You walk around the school like you are the hottest thing in existence. You ignored me for the first half of my first semester here, and then after I befriended Braelee, you made it your personal mission to tease and taunt and flirt with me as if you didn't ignore me or send me a scathing 'Welcome to Crescent Cove High School' email. I didn't like it. I *don't* like it."

Nick blinked, and Kensie saw when the words hit home. His face slipped into blankness as he nodded once, and then turned to walk away. But before he made it two steps, he spun on his heel and said, "You know, I don't remember that email, but I was going through a rough breakup at that time, which you would know if you would take the time to get to know me instead of hating me. I'm sorry I offloaded my responsibilities to clean my classroom on to you. That wasn't okay. My attempts to befriend you through humor and flirting hurt you badly, and I apologize and will put an end to it. But as for the rest? Maybe you should hold a mirror up to yourself."

Kensie's fight evaporated into thin air, leaving her heart hollow and her conscience convicted.

She quickly told her students she would be right back, and she held herself together until she was safely inside Sandra the Subaru. She flipped the visor down and did as Nick said. She looked in the mirror, and she could see why he would think her actions stemmed from conceit.

But he didn't understand.

He didn't know that she had to please everyone. Had to do her best to prove her worth. Had to always be kind and helpful so that she would be liked. *So that maybe her father would come back...*

Kensie thought she left that back in Mississippi, but it looked like her perfectionist ghost and father-wound found their way to Alaska. Something dark lingered beneath her surface, but she couldn't figure it out. All she knew was that she was angry, bitter, and distrustful of good intentions.

And poor Nick didn't realize that he was, for whatever reason unbeknownst to her, the only person Kensie allowed herself to get angry with.

Chapter Twelve

Nick

"Do you think they will accept me?" Big Bear asked, wiping his damp forehead with the back of his hand.

Nick set the last fork beside a plate at his table and straightened his shoulders. It was typical for them to have lunch together every Sunday afternoon, but Nick's parents would be in attendance today. He wasn't nervous, nor was Braelee, but Big Bear's sweaty shirt and brow reeked of his terror.

"As long as you keep your coat on, you're fine." Nick elbowed his friend, who scowled in return. "I may have an extra shirt lying around that might fit your overgrown body. I'll check."

"I'm not squeezing myself into one of your too-tight shirts, Nick."

"Suit yourself, sweaty pits."

The door swung open, bringing with it a gust of frigid air into the fire-heated cabin. "Sorry I'm late." Braelee walked inside, kicking off her snow boots. Big Bear rushed to grab the brown Safeway grocery bags in Braelee's arms as she shook the snow out of her hair. Once he had secured the goods in his arms, he kissed her chastely, bringing a glowing smile to her face. Braelee shed her winter coat and donned a sweaterdress underneath that matched Big Bear's t-shirt. Nick grinned at the two of them as they walked side by side into the kitchen.

"What are you smiling at?" Braelee asked, bumping into Nick playfully as she passed him.

"Just love seeing my sister and my best friend swapping spit in my house," Nick teased with a shrug. While it was true he didn't care to watch them kiss, he did think they were good for one another.

The crew spent the next hour cooking, chatting, and stoking the fire. It was an icy night, and Nick didn't want to risk having to rebuild the fire inside the cast-iron stove later. Right as Braelee took the moose lasagna out of the oven, a steady knock rapped on the door. His father.

Big Bear stiffened next to Braelee. She grabbed his hand and gave him a reassuring smile as Nick nodded once toward the nervous man and went to answer the door. James Lancaster and his wife, Stacey, stood on the porch under the glow of the yellowish light as snow fell in sheets behind them. James was a tall, slender man with sharp features, and while Stacey was still tall for a woman, she had softer, lighter features—much like Nick.

"Hey, Dad." Nick shook his father's hand before ushering them inside. James stepped around Nick as Nick hugged his mom and kissed her cheek. "Good to see you, Mom."

"It smells delightful in here," Stacey commented, kissing her son's cheek. She moved to stand by James, who had begun cataloging the cabin with a look of disdain, like he did every time.

It was why Nick wasn't keen on inviting him over often.

"Dad. Mom," Braelee said with surefire confidence in her voice as she looped her arm through Big Bear's and walked him over to the living room. "This is my boyfriend. Panuk Ivalu. We all call him Big Bear. He owns and operates The Siren's Call."

"It's a pleasure to meet you both." Big Bear stuck out his hand to James first. After the men shook hands and sized each other up—Big Bear was taller and stockier—Stacey opened her arms for a hug, which Big Bear stepped into willingly.

"I'm thrilled to see my daughter has found such an accomplished young man."

Nick didn't know if Big Bear could hear the sarcasm dripping from her voice, but when Nick and Braelee exchanged looks, he knew his sister had heard it.

Braelee grimaced, then smiled forcefully. "Food is ready. Moose lasagna. Your favorite, Mom."

To her credit, Stacey genuinely looked happy to be there, unlike Nick's father, who had barely spoken a word. That was unusual for him and potentially an adverse sign.

"I brought a new batch of brew that I developed with Kenai Brewing Company," Big Bear said, moving behind the counter and holding up a twelve-pack of bottled beer.

"I'll take one, thank you." James nodded once in Big Bear's direction as he received a bottle and sat down at the head of the table. Nick didn't bother trying to fight his father for the spot.

Nick helped Braelee serve everyone as James and Big Bear talked about the specifics of the brew. Nick didn't like that his father drank, but so far, he'd shown no signs of being an alcoholic like Grandpa. Nick, after what happened to Jesena and how he turned to the substance for comfort, vowed to stay away from the liquid.

"Yes, I can taste the hint of apple. Nice pairing." James took another sip of the beverage and hummed in approval. Big Bear and Nick exchanged glances, an invisible thumbs-up between them. Nick had told Big Bear that his dad was a beer aficionado, so he had brought the case in the hopes of impressing James. It seemed to be working.

Nick expected the conversation to trail into what got Big Bear into brewing and opening up his bar in Crescent Cove, but instead, his mom shifted the conversation. "So, Nicolas. Where's Kensie? Will we get to meet her?"

Braelee's attention snapped to Nick as Big Bear arched a brow in his direction.

"Why would the two of you need to meet Kensie?"

"She's your girlfriend, isn't she?" James asked after swallowing a bite of lasagna. "As we discussed on the phone the other day, the two of you have created a public image that must be dealt with."

"And as I said on the phone," Nick bit out, "Kensie and I are not together."

"Senator Garrett Keen is asking about the two of you, along with other prominent politicians. Word is getting around that Kensie is your plaything. What am I supposed to tell them? I have to tell everyone you are serious about that clout-chasing woman so they don't think you are with a—"

"Enough!" Nick shouted, banging his fists on the table and rocketing to his feet. His chair clattered to the ground as he took breath after breath in an attempt to calm himself. "Kensington Smith is one of the most respectable women I know. She, of all people, is not after me for money or status. She is a hard worker, intelligent, kind, and you do not get to insinuate she is anything less than a wholesome, beautiful woman who had the unfortunate luck of tumbling into me and catching the interest of the likes of you."

"Nicolas James Lancaster, you do not talk to your father like that. I raised you better." Stacey plastered her hand to her heart, appalled, but Nick knew it was only a front. If Big Bear was not in the room, Stacey would have pretended she didn't hear the argument happening and would let Nick and James duke it out verbally until James got his way, as he always did.

That was until Nick stood his ground and quit law school.

James stood and faced Nick from across the table. "The gala is Saturday. You will be there just like every year. And you will bring Kensie. The two of you will present as a loving couple and not as—"

Braelee's phone rang, interrupting whatever awful thing James had to say next. Excusing herself from the table, she walked, white as a ghost, into the kitchen and quietly answered the phone.

Nick focused his attention to his red-faced father. It did not complement his silver hair well. "Listen, Dad. You don't get to decide if I go to the ball, nor who I bring to it if I do decide to go. I've gone every year to support you and Mom, but this year, I think I'd rather stay home and sleep." Nick folded his arms and maliciously grinned as he proclaimed, "I'll have had a busy night with Kensie, after all." They didn't need to know CCHS's annual Winter Solstice dance was the night before, and that was the real reason he would be exhausted come Saturday.

Stacey shot to her feet. "Nicolas!"

"Uh, Nick. Can you come here for a second?" Braelee called from the kitchen, her hand over the phone. Nick, burning in his anger, strode into the kitchen to meet his sister as his parents gawked after him.

"Can you believe them?" Nick was exasperated, but Braelee shushed him.

"Kensie's on the phone. She's stuck in a ditch and needs help."

Nick's anger froze as a sense of urgent duty filled him. "Where is she? I'll go help her."

"Big Bear and I can—"

"No. Stay here with Mom and Dad," Nick snapped, already stomping toward the door and putting on his jacket and snow boots. "I've got her. Tell her to text me a pin with her location."

After gathering a tow strap, extra blankets, a couple jugs of hot water, and a few other emergency items, Nick was in his truck speeding toward the location pin Kensie had texted to him. He had forgotten the heated conversation happening with his father only minutes earlier, his thoughts now full of images of Kensie freezing to death in a dark, deep ditch. Her location looked to be on Paul and Tarin's road, and Nick wondered what she was doing out that way in the middle of nowhere. Was Paul okay? Did he reinjure his leg? Kensie was the kind of woman to help him out.

As he flew across an ice rut, he bounced an inch off his seat and fought to keep the truck on the road. How would he help Kensie if he went and got himself stuck in a ditch?

He continued to drive, thinking over the last interaction he had with her. Kensie didn't hold back in her assessment of him. She had her list of reasons Nick had offended her, and at the moment, it felt like nothing he could do or say would change her mind. Standing in front of her as she listed his faults and failings without pause infuriated him.

Nick didn't know how to make Kensie change her mind about him. He still didn't fully understand where she was coming from. Who held a grudge this long over a quipped email (he had email reports pulled later that evening and winced as he read it), a little harmless flirting, and such? There had to be something deeper going on. Would Kensie allow him to dig for it?

Maybe.

If he started first...

A few minutes later, Nick turned onto Paul's road and drove until he came upon red taillights sticking up from the ditch, which, *thank God*, wasn't too steep. Nick breathed deeply for the first time since Braelee said Kensie was stuck out here in this frigid, icy darkness.

Putting the truck in park, Nick hopped out, holding his to-go container full of hot coffee that Braelee made while he packed the truck, and carefully made his way through the piled snow. The blanket of white glittered under the moon and in the headlights of the truck, and he thought it would be pretty if the woman he was falling for wasn't trapped in its clutches.

Freezing in his tracks over his thoughts, Nick became as cold as the air around him. *Falling for?*

The door of the Subaru opened begrudgingly, pushing snow out of its way, and Kensie fell out of the car and face-first into the snow. Sobs rang out in the silent night as she struggled to get up, and Nick snapped out of his daze, dropped the contents in his hands, and ran to her. He slipped down the bank as he took giant steps, but sheer willpower held him upright. Within breaths, he was by her side.

Her body was heaving with uncontrollable sobs as he lifted her out of the snow bank, dusted off the flecks stuck to her face, and carried her bridal style back to his truck. She threaded her arms around his neck and shoved her face into his chest as she cried. With every single over-sized step Nick took, holding her as he climbed their way out of the ditch, his thoughts played like a broken record in his head.

Nick was falling for Kensie.

He had been for a while, he supposed, but was too afraid to admit it to himself, much less her. He had hidden his affection for her behind his humor and flirtations like a man-child, as Kensie would say. Toying with her just to keep her attention on him. Relishing in every snarky retort and vicious glare she threw his way. Like a bone, and Nick was the dog.

It was clear as the night above him, and it terrified him. Nick didn't know where to go from here, but he knew he wasn't telling her that he was falling for her. Not yet. Not until he knew she was ready—and willing—to hear it. Not until he could fully understand it himself.

Nick had a difficult time opening the truck door with his hands full of Kensie, but he managed, and he gently eased her into the passenger seat. She refused to let go of him, so he continued to hold her against his chest, using one hand to pull the blanket that was sitting on the console around her shoulders. Every atom in the air screamed at him to take care of her, to protect her, and to comfort her. "You're safe, Kensington. I'm here. You're safe. Do you hear me? You're safe with me. Let's get you warm, yeah?" Her car had still been on, so thankfully, she wasn't too cold. But that fall into the snow bank and trek up the knee-deep snow had taken its toll.

Kensie mumbled unintelligibly against his chest as he continued to ramble on autopilot about how she was safe with him.

What happened to shake her up this badly?

Running into a snowbank, especially in the dark of night, wasn't anyone's definition of fun, but it happened all the time. One of the perks of living in a frozen paradise. It wasn't anything to freak out over.

Continuing to hug her as her sobs lessened, Nick thought of all the possibilities. Maybe a moose trekked up to her and scared her? Maybe she thought she saw something of legends lurking in the woods, like skinwalkers or Bigfoot? Nick didn't necessarily believe in those things, but maybe Kensie did. As little as Kensie knew about him, Nick realized he still had much to learn about this woman. But he was looking forward to that journey. If she'd let him embark on it, that is.

"Um, Nick?" The sound of his name coming from Kensie's stuffy, tear-stained voice jerked him from his head. He pulled back from Kensie, who was now sitting up with her hands dropped to her lap instead of around his neck. Her flushed face was puffy, with mascara stains down her face. She looked a mess, but Nick couldn't deny that even in this state, she was stunning. He'd always thought she was beautiful.

"You said my name without being angry at me," Nick dumbly stated, his hands lifting to her face in an act to wipe the liquid from her cheeks. She flinched, and he dropped his hands and took a step back.

"You rescued me." Kensie laughed, but there was no trace of humor in the sound. "You at least deserve me using your name. So, thank you, Nick. For helping me out. I'm sorry I—"

Kensie dropped her speech, looking away from Nick and tugging the blanket tighter around her.

"You don't have to apologize for crying. You don't have to apologize for being scared. Is anything hurt?"

She shook her head.

Nick took a step toward her, his thighs hitting the edge of the lifted truck, and when she didn't lean away, he slowly lifted his hand. Her gaze snatched on the movement, but she sat still as an ice-carved statue and let Nick rest his palm against her cheek, his thumb rubbing underneath her eye to clear away the wetness. Nick tensed at the feel of her soft skin underneath his calloused fingers, and Kensie locked eyes with him, which set a flood of warmth into his chest that countered the biting chill of the night.

"Nick." The breathless sound of his name rolling off her tongue was a symphony of happiness in his soul. "You called me Kensington."

He couldn't help but laugh as he dropped his hands and took a step back to keep himself from pulling her face to his and kissing her. "You scared me, Windsor. I spoke without thinking. Forgive me."

Kensie narrowed her eyes, but a smile pulled at the edges of her lips. "We should probably get my car. Do you have a tow strap just in case something is damaged?"

"I do. But you wait in here and warm up. I have a canteen of coffee for you, but I dropped it on the road. Let me grab it."

Kensie began to protest, but Nick was already walking around the truck. He gathered the things he had dropped and brought the dented canteen to Kensie. "Here. Drink this while I get your car pulled out. Turn on some music and relax." Nick reached for her face again—where he was gathering the audacity, he didn't know—but he must have moved too quickly because she flinched once more.

Had someone hurt her? The thought brought a roaring red to Nick's vision, but now was not the time to go into a conversation like that. Nick swallowed the anger and went to shut the door so Kensie could stay warm, but she shot out her hand and stopped him.

"It's my car. Let me help you. You don't have to do it alone."

Nick stared at her, his mouth opening and closing as he searched for a response. He knew she didn't mean that he never had to do life alone, but her words took his thoughts there. He could imagine it. Him and Kensie going to work together. Eating lunch together. Him stopping by her room for quick smooches and her sneaking away to his office in the weight room for lengthy make-outs. Going home together. Cooking together. Snuggling by the fireplace. Her reading a fiction novel while he read nonfiction. The bantering back and forth over which was better. Holding her when she had a hard, long day. Kensie consoling him when the football team took a loss.

"I—I," Nick began, but he couldn't shake the visions of forever dancing inside his head. "Thank you, Kensie, but let me take care of this for you."

Kensie swallowed, nodded silently, and Nick gently shut the door and went around back to gather his supplies.

Twenty minutes later, Nick had her car pulled out, but he wasn't comfortable letting Kensie drive it home without checking it out in the daylight first, which was why the two of them found themselves over the sentimentality from earlier and in another classic standoff.

"I'll be fine, Mr. Lancaster. Please, just give me my keys." Kensie held out one hand with the other placed firmly on her hip. She was dressed in all black, something Nick hadn't noticed earlier. Black leggings, a black parka, a black beanie, and gloves. Her auburn hair was down in perfect, tight spirals, and her cream face was highlighted by the moonlight that had made a grand appearance after the earlier snowstorm. Her freckles were the constellations. She was a dark, universal vision, but Nick wasn't backing down.

"No. Let me continue to be your knight in shining armor and make sure you get home safely." Nick puffed out a breath, visible in the cold. "It's freezing out here. Get your butt in the truck and drive us to my place while I direct the car."

Kensie looked back at the truck. The two of them stood in front of Nick's white truck, which was already turned around to head back toward the main highway. He had Kensie's car hooked to a tow, and when Kensie found out, she immediately went on the defensive.

"I can't drive that monstrosity. I'll wreck it, and then you'll get all up in arms." Kensie crossed her arms, cocking one hip. Nick shouldn't have followed the movement, but he did. Her all-black outfit paired with her feisty attitude made him think of things he shouldn't. Like keeping her at his place when they arrived. But his parents were probably still there, so that thought was a water hose dousing out the fire building in his stomach. He wouldn't be able to let her inside. They'd drop her car off in his yard, and he'd take her back to her place. Either he or Braelee could pick her up for work in the morning. It was the perfect plan, but Kensie, true to her nature, had to fight him on it.

"You're not going to wreck." Nick had to bite his tongue not to roll his eyes. "I don't want to, but I'll concede to this: You can direct your car, and I'll drive the truck, but it's being towed to my house so I can look at it after work tomorrow."

Kensie huffed. After a few beats of silence, she dropped her arms and slouched. "Fine. But Braelee needs to pick me up in the morning. Not you."

Nick bit out a laugh. "Noted, Buckingham."

"I'm sorry. That was rude," Kensie responded, not meeting Nick's gaze. "I'm just still worked up from tonight."

Nick softened his voice. "What happened? Were you at Paul's helping with something since his leg is broken?"

She shook her head. "I'm good friends with his wife, Tarin. I was visiting with her."

"Huh, I didn't know that," Nick commented. Of course, Kensie was one to spend her free time with a woman much older than her. It spoke a lot about her character that she sought out wise friendships. One more thing to admire.

Kensie shrugged. "Anyway, I slid off the road and into the snowbank on my way out. Mr. Paul obviously has a broken leg, so I didn't call him. Tarin doesn't need to be out in this weather. I tried to call a few other people from church, but none answered. I knew Braelee was introducing Big Bear to your parents tonight, so I didn't want to bother her. But then I realized I didn't know who else to call, so I called her anyway. That feeling of not having anyone, it..." Kensie trailed off, and Nick's chest ached with the same feeling. His heart felt hollow that she hadn't thought to call him, but how could he blame her? She was clear about the way she felt about him, and Nick hadn't had the appropriate opportunity to change her mind quite yet.

But he had one right now.

"You can always call me, Kensie."

"I did think to call you, but..."

"But what?"

"I didn't want to bother you."

Nick had a feeling that wasn't the real reason, but the temperature was steadily plummeting, and they needed to get off this road. Nick crept toward her and gingerly placed his hand on her shoulder. He moved like a sloth so she wouldn't flinch away.

"You are never a bother to me, Kensington." Then he tacked on with a cheeky smile, "And even when you are a teensy bit bothersome, it's never the kind of bothersome that makes me upset with you or makes you a burden to me. It's the kind of bothersome that makes me a little addicted to experiencing it more."

Kensie's jaw dropped open, and she blinked a few times as she comprehended his words. He didn't give her time for a rebuttal, however. "Here." He handed her the keys to her car, instructed her on guiding the car, when to softly brake, and how much distance to keep between the two of them when rolling to a stop. Then, the two of them were on their way back to his house, and the entire way, Nick found himself genuinely and wholeheartedly praying aloud for the first time in a long time.

"God, I don't know if I'm worth Your time and effort. I know I've fallen on the wayside during and after Jesena. I know I've grown calloused to You and have pushed You away. But, please, God. If You hear me, fix me. Make me a man worthy of Kensington. Soften my heart and break through the walls I've built. Give me understanding when it comes to her, and work on her heart toward me, too. Help her understand me. Grow me up. Open her up to

me. God, just...Please. I don't know why I hid this growing feeling for so long. I don't know why I resorted to
pulling her pigtails just to get her attention when there
were a thousand better ways to do it. Help me not to ruin
this—whatever *this* is—now."

Chapter Thirteen

Kensie

*G*od, *please take the memories away,* Kensie pleaded silently as she followed Nick, carefully navigating her car through salty tears as she was towed behind his truck. When she'd slid off into the snowbank earlier, she'd hit her head on the driver's side window, and an army of memories viciously attacked her. Memories from before her father left. Memories of him hitting her mom as Kensie watched from a dark corner of a room, shrunken, confused, and distraught. *But I had to be quiet, or else it would have been worse for Mommy.* Red and blue lights, sirens, blood. *So much blood...*

Kensie now remembered vividly why she didn't grow up with a father, and why she flinched or froze in close, unexpected proximity to a man. The memories were real, but she couldn't wrap her head around the truth. How could he? Why didn't her mom tell her? What else was missing from her mind?

More memories continued to replay, and with each one, Kensie grew livid. She'd spent her entire life trying to do good. To be perfect. To not mess up. To walk the straight and narrow. All in the hopes that her father would come back to her and accept her. She had thought he'd left because *she* wasn't good enough.

No, *he* wasn't good enough for her and her mom.

From wherever that abusive, evil man was in the world—if he was still alive—he had been unknowingly pulling the strings of Kensie's life, dictating her every thought and move. Nausea crawled up her throat.

Kensie lay on the horn to get Nick's attention, but after a moment, she flung her door open and retched onto the highway. She was grateful they were going at a turtle speed, and she vaguely remembered to press on the brake as she saw red taillights illuminate in front of her. Once they stopped, Kensie felt another rumbling in her stomach, and she threw the car in park and emptied the squash casserole from earlier out onto the ice-slicked road.

Nick's caution lights made Kensie dizzy, and when she started to topple out of the car—thank goodness for her seatbelt—Nick was right there to catch her. "Kensie! What's wrong?"

"Nauseous and dizzy," she responded before shoving him out of the way so that she could throw up again. When she finished, she struggled to find her buckle, her strength waning with every passing moment. The weight of the evening, the memories, the cold, the dark... It was pressing upon her with pressure that could not be stopped. Talking with Nick earlier had distracted her, but she was alone now, and the thoughts were too loud. Bitterness seeped in as she questioned God—*why? Why? Why?!*

No, I'm not alone. Nick's here. Right here. He has me. Kensie kept herself from focusing on the new memories by focusing on the absurdity that Nicolas Lancaster was her knight in a snowsuit right now.

Hands reached around her, unbuckling her seatbelt. Nick helped her out of the car, and the blast of cool air wrapped around her like an ice bath, ushering in clarity and calmness. She could breathe again.

"I, uh—" Kensie began, embarrassed, but Nick pulled her into a tight hug, cutting her off, her cheek against his chest. He had one hand splayed against the small of her back, and the other pressed into the side of her head as he held her close. Kensie didn't try to squirm away out of anxiety or fear, and she didn't know why.

Nick's chest rumbled as he said, "Don't you dare try to apologize or explain yourself."

Kensie, for once, relented. "Okay." Then, if only for this moment, she sought refuge in his arms.

Safe.

Nick felt safe.

When they finally arrived at Nick's house, Kensie had numbed her thoughts enough to function without anger pangs or waves of nausea. She didn't want to be mad at

God, but she just didn't understand. She was exhausted, craved sleep, and had become a zombie as she climbed out of her car and shuffled to Nick's truck. He had already unhooked the tow strap from his truck and had the vehicle turned around, ready to take her back to her blessed place of permanent safety—her apartment.

"Do you need your purse or anything?" Nick asked as he met her at the passenger door.

Oh. Yeah. Kensie sighed, bone-tired. "One second." She shuffled the short distance back to her car and grabbed her purse from the back seat. Right as she shut the door, the one to Nick's cabin opened, revealing a tall man who was clearly Nick's father, judging by his uncanny, though sharper and darker, looks to his son as he stepped under the porch light. Kensie froze. She didn't have the energy to deal with whatever was about to happen if the scowl on Senator Lancaster's face was a warning. Braelee popped her head from behind her father and gave Kensie a quick wave before she gently pulled her father back inside.

Kensie relaxed. She'd have to tell Braelee everything later, but for now, she was glad her best friend had a handle on the man who would undoubtedly only make Kensie's night worse.

Nick already had the door open for her as she approached, but he wasn't looking at her. His glare was fixated on his house, probably waiting to see if his father would make another appearance.

His intuition must have been working overtime, because right as Nick closed Kensie's door, she watched from inside the truck as Senator Lancaster busted out of the light-brown door and marched down the few steps until he was only inches from Nick.

"Nicolas James Lancaster!" His father yelled, then a train of expletives erupted from his sour mouth. Kensie only caught parts of it, but the jist? She was a nobody and was clout-chasing, and words she didn't want to repeat.

Kensie plugged her ears as tears streamed down her cheeks. She rocked back and forth in her seat, humming the first song that came to mind, which happened to be one of her favorite hymns, "It Is Well With My Soul." She clung to the words, hoping they would erase the unwanted memories of the past and the present. Somewhere in the depths of her psyche, she remembered her mom singing it to her while they both cried rivers into their pillows. Kensie didn't know how much time had passed, but she'd hummed and silently sang all the verses and the chorus twice over before Nick yanked the driver's side door and flung himself into the truck. Wide-eyed, Kensie stared at his twisted face as he cranked the truck, revved the engine, and shifted gears, the tires spinning on the ice of his driveway.

"Nick!" Kensie shouted as the force of the vehicle moving pressed her flat against the seat.

"What?" Nick snapped, his chest heaving with silent, deep breaths. Kensie felt herself growing smaller, sinking into her bones to become nothing more than a skeleton. Then Nick looked at her.

The anger evaporated from his clenched jaw and pressed lips. His eyes softened in the second he met hers. He turned his attention back to the road and let off the gas. Nick's voice was gentle and laced with concern when he spoke, either pleading to God or taking His name in vain, before apologizing. "I'm sorry. I didn't mean to—" He shook his head. "Just hang tight. We're thirteen minutes away from your apartment. Focus your breath and hang tight." Kensie thought he might be talking to himself more than her at this moment.

The rest of the drive was unspoken words enunciated by the rumble of the tires and the hitting of the occasional ice rut in the road. Silent streams of tears continued to cascade unbidden from her eyes, soaking the collar of her coat and seeping down her chest. Her thoughts were a whirlwind, and she couldn't focus on a singularity if she tried. Instead, she sought mindlessness. She listened to the purr of the engine, the force of the heat flowing from the vents, Nick's breathing steadying out with every passing mile. She watched a wall of black through her window, broken up by the moon illuminating freshly fallen snow glistening on the trees. A beautiful sight if she wasn't hollow inside.

A million years later, or maybe it was in the blink of an eye, Nick pulled into her apartment complex. But he didn't drive in front of the door to drop her off. He parked in one of the unmarked spots as if he was staying for a while. Kensie wiped her tears as Nick shut off the truck and opened his door. "Nick, I can—"

Nick leveled her with a "don't fight me on this" look that might have sent shivers down her spine. Or maybe it was the cool air rushing in to caress her face. "I've got you, Kensie. You're not okay. I'm not okay. Let's be 'not okay' together for a while."

She sat with that for a second, contemplating if it was a good idea to let a man into her apartment. But it was Nick, and moments ago, her brain told her that Nick was safe. She had to trust that.

Kensie picked up her purse and went to grab her door handle when Nick beat her to it. He helped her out of the truck and looped her arm through his as he walked her to the apartment complex entrance. She didn't know who was holding who up. Nick didn't let go even as they entered the building and took a flight of stairs down to the first floor. He held her close even as she fished her keys from her purse and unlocked the door to her apartment, number eight. The two of them crossed the threshold together, and when Kensie flicked on the light, she knew she'd never see the entryway to her living space the same again. Not now that Nick Lancaster, in all of his vulnerable, broken features, haunted the area. The instinct to mother him back into his roguish smiles and melodious laugh was strong, but Kensie barely had the energy to mother herself back into loathing Nick tonight.

Tears began to fall again as she put her purse down on the stand next to her door and thought of how she wished it wasn't so late. She wanted to call her mother. To be in her arms. To cry and scream and hold her tight. The two of them against the world.

How did she talk to her, though? What did she say?

Hey, Mom. So, Dad beat you, and I forgot about it. I'm sorry I went twenty-two years acting like nothing tragic ever happened. I'm sorry I forgot he existed in our lives when I was only five years old.

Maybe that was exactly what she was supposed to say, but she couldn't. Not yet. No matter how badly she wanted to hear her mom's voice. Kensie would break into fractals the moment her mom said, "Hey, baby girl."

Kensie shrugged her jacket off and took Nick's from him, storing them in the coat closet. They kicked their snow boots off and Kensie padded across the wooden floor into the kitchen. "Do you want some tea?" Maybe giving over to the urge to mother him would tape her together.

"Kensie." Nick's raspy, strained voice was right behind her. She hadn't even heard him following. She spun and stared at his chest, so she lifted her head. Their proximity made her heart thump in a good way, but she was too tired to think much else other than mentally noting the reaction. Nick cleared his throat. "Come sit with me. Let's just sit, yeah?"

Kensie didn't argue. Nick gently grabbed her hand and led her to her brown couch. Once he set her down, he grabbed a pink blanket from her stack against the wall and turned off the living room light, plunging them into darkness. Kensie could barely make out his frame from the dim light floating in through the living room window. Nick sat next to her, their thighs and shoulders touching.

The silence in the room was ear-splitting, but Kensie wasn't scared. Not of Nick. Not anymore. Not when he was the only thread holding her together.

She took his hand.

And then Nick Lancaster, the cockiest, most smart alec, sunshiny, annoyingly charming man she'd ever met, collapsed into her lap in a heap of sobs.

The sunlight pouring onto Kensie's face was too bright for the darkness brimming within her soul. Her body, however, was pressed against something warm and hard, though she knew nothing on her bed should be feeling like a—

Human.

Kensie's eyes flew open, and she stared into the dark-chocolate eyes of Nick Lancaster, crinkling in the corners as he smiled brilliantly, as if he didn't have red veins saturating them.

"Hi, Windsor."

"Nick!" Kensie threw herself backward, plummeting to the carpeted floor and bumping against the coffee table. That's when she realized she was in her living room, and she had been snuggled up with Nick on her coffee-brown couch.

And the sun was up.

"Sunlight! Work!" Kensie shouted, scrambling to her feet, untangling herself from the patchwork quilt she now remembered covering up with after Nick had retrieved it off her bed last night. She remembered him crying. Her crying. No talking, but still understanding one another on some spiritual level. Him offering to bring her to her bed. Her telling him to stay. The way his arms were a net of safety. The way his tear-stained voice coaxed her into sleep.

Now it had to be at least noon, because the sun was up, and it was December in Alaska.

"I called Lori." Nick sat up and stretched out his arms. His voice still had a morning raspiness to it, and the sound impacted Kensie more than she'd care to admit. "We both have subs covering for us."

"Get ready!" She snapped her fingers at him.

"I see you've evolved to two connective words now. Positive sign." Nick laughed, reaching for her waist. Kensie stepped back before grumbling about Nick's work ethic under her breath and stomping off to the bathroom.

When she flipped on the light, she was greeted with a monster in the mirror: Smudged mascara and eyeliner, frizzy hair, swollen eyes, and a full face of freckles on display. "He saw me like this," Kensie groaned to herself, mortification settling into her stomach. "Here," she mimed, handing a box to the person in the mirror as she spoke in a sarcastic, sleepy tone, "let me arm you with more ammo to take shots at me with."

A knock at the bathroom pulled her from her one-person skit. "Kensie? Do I need to come in there? You're talking ammo and shots and such. It's concerning."

"Go away, Nick."

Nick chuckled and plainly stated, "Three words." The voice on the other side of the door went quiet, but she knew he was still there. "It's morning, and you're still calling me Nick. I like it a lot." There wasn't a trace of sarcasm in his tone. Kensie, against her judgement, opened the door.

"Thank you," Nick said as he leaned against the doorframe, eyes soft and sincere, coaxing Kensie into their depths. She swallowed back the desire to sink as Nick ran a hand through his messy waves. "I think I've needed to cry for a long time."

Love him like Jesus.

Kensie pegged Nick for many abominable things, but she missed the other half of him. The half that might have been as broken as her.

God, forgive me.

Her frustration with God didn't denounce her surrender to Him; she had bitterness to work through, but she still clung to God as her Lord and Savior—cried out to Him in her soul. That was the only way she'd make it through this journey.

"You always have a place to break apart. Right here. With me." Kensie's heart shattered for the man in front of her as it wept over the way she'd treated him for so long. How had she misunderstood him so deeply? How had she not seen through his happy mask and into the pain and anger simmering under the surface? How had she not realized that he had deep-seated father issues just like her? Abuse came in many forms. She knew the signs; she'd trained for it. How did she miss it in Nick? *In herself...?*

Not wanting to go there right now, Kensie shook her head clear and continued to gaze upon a blank-faced Nick. She arched her brow, inviting him to respond. Nick cleared his throat and crossed his arms, a smirk forming across his face. "Looks like I've finally gotten you to come around to me."

A snarky retort danced on Kensie's tongue, but she cut off the music. The cocky, flirty, happy-go-lucky demeanor was Nick's defense. Just as people-pleasing was hers. *Had been yours,* her brain reminded her. *No more. Not now that I remember.* By golly, she was going to shred Nick's cracking mask to pieces. At least around her.

Yes, show him My love, a voice inside her head whispered. Wasn't this exactly the moment she'd been praying for? What she'd been striving for yet failing so desperately at?

It was time to pass the test. Focusing on Nick and his daddy-issues would put hers at bay. Someone to help. A way to be useful.

Kensie rolled her shoulders back and dared to look him in the eyes, a challenge painting her vision. "Yes, you have, Nicolas Lancaster." Kensie tilted her chin even higher. "And you're going to regret it."

Nick arched his brow, leaning in closer to Kensie. "Am I?"

When he was breaths away, Kensie placed her hand on his chest and rose to her tiptoes. A smidge of fear rose in her throat, but she shoved it down because Nick was safe. She would say it a thousand times until she no longer had an inkling of doubt. "Because I'm not going to let you live in Fake Land anymore. Together, we are going to tackle your demons."

"What about your demons, Kensington Smith?"

Evil hands clamped her throat. So much for bravery and determination. She preferred to be the fixer, not the one in need of fixing. But if she was going to help Nick, she'd have to let him in. *One day.* She nodded.

Chapter Fourteen

Nick

"**W**indsor, I want you to meet someone," Nick hollered as he stomped the door to his cabin and kicked off his snow boots, finding Kensie curled on his plaid couch with her hair in a messy auburn bun. She sported reading glasses as she flipped the page of the novel she'd brought over to read while Nick fixed her car. Instead of scowling at the nickname per usual, her lips twitched upward. Then, as if she'd caught herself slipping, the scowl made a wondrous appearance.

She set down her book and tugged at her hair. "Who is it? I look a mess."

Nick snorted. "Don't worry. He looked a mess on my couch for a while."

"Actually, I found him in quite a similar situation as you," Esme said from the doorway. Her husband, Noah Prewitt, stood behind her with his hand on her hips, grinning from ear to ear.

Noah shrugged. "Yeah, it was a bad time for me. But Nick was gracious toward this stranger in need of a reset."

"Kensie, this is Noah and Esme Prewitt." Nick waved them farther inside. "I met Noah over the summer, and he stayed with me for a bit. They're in Crescent Cove on their honeymoon and stopped by to say hello."

Kensie unfolded her legs and stood to her feet, patting down her frizzy flyaways unsuccessfully. Nick had to bite back the grin over how adorable she looked in this state.

"Hi, I'm Kensington Smith, but everyone—" She shifted her eyes to Nick. "—except Nick, of course, calls me Kensie."

"What does he call you?" Esme asked, a twinkling in her eyes. "If you don't mind sharing. I'm an author and am always looking for unique nicknames."

Kensie narrowed her eyes, but she relented through a sigh and turned her attention back to Esme. "He calls me Windsor when he's attempting to flirt. Buckingham when he's aggravated or mad. Starjna when he's trying to catch me off guard. If it's a palace name, it's fair game, apparently."

"Because your name is Kensington!" Esme laughed and looked up at her husband. "That's so cute. We totally have to use that."

"Yeah, cute," Kensie huffed. But then she quickly transfixed a smile onto her face as Nick vowed to get to the bottom of her aversion to the nicknames. "So, I hear you two are here on your honeymoon. That's exciting! How did you two meet? I enjoy a good love story."

"We should sit down for this one," Esme said. "We're authors. This could get long-winded."

Esme and Noah exchanged a knowing glance, laughed, and after moving everyone to the kitchen table, dove into a story that had Kensie entranced the entire time. Nick knew this because he was watching the woman who was stealing his heart one brilliant smile, one soft gasp, and one wide-eyed gaze at a time.

"Which is how I know God is always with us, even when we don't feel Him there. There's beauty in the bramble of life." Noah's ending statement jarred Nick out of his Kensie-ridden reverie. *Is God really always with me?*

"I need to read your book when it comes out!" Kensie said breathlessly, her eyes alight with excitement. "God works in the utmost mysterious ways. Wow. Just...*wow*."

Nick took advantage of the silence. "I've never seen you at a loss for words, Wind—er, Kensie."

"Because you're not capable of having that effect on me," Kensie snapped back, but her tone was...flirtatious? If Nick wasn't reading it wrong...

"Ooooooh!" Noah shouted with his hand over his mouth, while his wife clapped and said, "Good one."

"Challenge accepted." Nick winked and leaned back in his chair. But his confidence was too high, and he crashed to the ground, eliciting the howling laughter of those at the table with him.

Esme spoke up as Nick gathered himself. "What other books do you like to read?"

"I'll read just about anything," Kensie responded. "But *Jane Eyre* is my emotional support book. And the movie. I love the movie."

"Jane Eyre is a gripping read," Noah added, him and Esme leaning toward Kensie.

Nick sighed dramatically and folded his arms. "I'm surrounded by lovers of fiction. Take me now, Reaper."

Three pairs of eyes bore into his skin. Nick had fallen into the lion's den.

Kensie was the first to bite. "Fiction, as I've said before, Mr. Lancaster, is just as important as nonfiction. You can learn just as much."

Esme clamped down next, her fingers tapping the table. "Fiction is the lens into which we see outside ourselves. Into which we grapple and battle with ideas, worldviews, and religion."

"Seriously, Nick," Noah began, though not as fiery as the ladies. His voice was more of a warning. "You've got to quit dissing on fiction. It's not just me and you in this cabin." He grinned at the two women before challenging Nick with a raised brow. "You're outnumbered."

Nick held up his hands. "I hear you, I do. But I just don't see how you learn from something that isn't real."

Kensie straightened. "Because regardless of if you're reading about characters slaying dragons, meet-cuteing in a coffee shop, or battling an ancient Roman army, readers can identify with the emotional struggles or the conflicts and resolutions. Fiction displays timeless truths about humanity. Truths you might not confront if told in a factual, nonfiction format."

"What if I read your favorite book and report back to you? If I find these so-called truths, I'll acquiesce. If not, you'll stop hounding me about not liking fiction. Deal?" Nick held up a pinky, inviting Kensie to wrap hers around it. Kensie stared for a moment before hooking her pinky around his. The touch wasn't electric. It was coming home and slipping into your pajamas with a steaming mug of tea as the snow feathered down outside your window.

"Deal. I'll bring you the book tomorrow."

Nick brought her hand to his and kissed it. "Can't wait to find out why *Jane Eyre* captivates you so much."

Kensie's answering blush-ridden smile was all the motivation he needed to read the story.

Later, after Noah and Esme left and Nick finished fixing Kensie's car, the two stood a bit awkwardly on Nick's front porch. Last night changed everything. Nick didn't see how they could go back to the *before*. But he also didn't know exactly how to navigate the *now*.

He tucked his hands into the pockets of his snow pants as he averted his gaze from Kensie, who was busy looking effortlessly lovely in her oversized Crescent Cove High School sweatshirt, leggings, and snow boots. Nick knew he was down bad, but he didn't want to break the fragileness of the new. Or scare her away from coming on too strong. For real this time. Not childish flirting.

"So, what's your plan this evening?" he asked, rocking back and forth on his feet before looking back at Kensie. She was wringing her hands together and watching the movement.

"I need to go to work to check on the dance decoration progress, and it would be nice to make sure my room is put together from the sub today. I always hate when I come back to a mess, so I'd rather go this evening to make sure everything is..." Kensie trailed off, meeting Nick's gaze. Her face reddened. "I'm talking too much."

Nick held his hands up. "No, no. Not at all. I think it's smart that you want to make sure everything is good to go the night before instead of starting your morning off on a bad foot."

"Really?" Kensie narrowed her eyes, probably wondering what had gotten into Nick.

You, Nick thought. *You've permeated every inch of me.*

But he couldn't lose his edge, right? Not just because he was falling for a woman. Nick closed his eyes, reset his brain, and smirked. "Need some company? Someone to make you laugh in case you're mad over the condition of your room? Someone to hold your hand in case the school ghosts try to get you?"

"You're so full of yourself." Kensie placed her fists on her cocked hips. "I go to that school late at night all the time on my own."

This was familiar territory. But Nick needed to navigate it as a man, not as a boy pulling pigtails. How to flirt, but like a man? Nick was ready to figure it out.

"I know you're capable, Kensie," he started, slowly pulling one hand from her hip and into his hand. She allowed him to take the other one quicker. "But what if you didn't have to go at it alone?"

She searched his eyes, and he mustered all the sincere smolder he could. He really hoped he was doing it right.

When her lips parted just a breath, he had his answer. She relented. "Yeah, you can come keep the big bad ghosts of Crescent Cove away from me if that's what you *really* want to do with your evening."

Nick grinned victoriously and squeezed her hands. "Yes, that's how I *really* want to spend my evening. Let's go."

While Nick wanted her to ride with him, he knew she'd have to go back to her apartment afterward, so they took separate vehicles. Nick had eight minutes, so he called Wayne on his way. He got his voicemail.

"Hey, Wayne. So, I just wanted to update you on the Kensie situation. I don't know what happened, but somehow, someway, we found ourselves in each other's company during some pretty dark stuff, and it forced us to lean on one another. I haven't told her I like her in as many words, but I'm trying to show her. I want her to believe my words when I finally do tell her point-blank. I don't want her to think it's a joke or me being silly. Just, uh, continue to pray or whatever. God listens to you. I don't want to mess this up."

Nick hung up and rode in silence for the remainder of his trip. He pulled in beside Kensie in the parking lot, and he followed her inside the navy doors nearest to the English wing. It was dark in the hallways sans the floodlights, making the navy and silver lockers look menacing. Shouts, screeches from shoes on the gym floor, and dribbling sounded from basketball practice happening at the other end of the school echoed down the way.

Following close behind Kensie, Nick accidentally ran into her when she stopped in front of her door. "Oof, sorry." He took a giant step backward. *Real smooth, Nick.*

She tossed him a look over her shoulder, silently questioning if it was truly an accident or not. Nick shrugged sheepishly, and she shook her head, a small smile tugging at her lips as the floodlight acted a beacon from heaven shining down upon her. "It's okay."

Kensie turned her attention back to unlocking her door as Nick peeked into Braelee's room next door. Her desk was a mess, and he knew Kensie's was going to be pristine. Everything had a place in her room. If it didn't, then it didn't belong within the walls.

The door opened, and she plugged in her lights instead of turning on the overheads. Nick loved that about her room—how cozy, inviting, and settling it was.

She had her tables in a square around her room. Nick wondered if the kids ever got tired of looking at one another across the room, but as much as he pestered Kensie over her class, he never heard a student say a bad thing about her. They loved her, even if they didn't always love her subject.

Nick thought he ought to tell her that, but when he went to open his mouth, he snapped it shut. Kensie was standing at her desk, fists clenched, with steam rising from her head.

He kept his distance, speaking from across the room. "What's wrong?"

She picked up a note and held it like evidence in a courtroom. "My third hour was awful to the poor sub. I get that they're my heavy IEP and 504 class, but still. I've never received a note like this. Ever. I'm so embarrassed, Nick."

Nick released a breath and made his way to her to read the note. When he tried to take it, she pressed it against her chest with her hand on top.

"No. You can't read this. You're going to think I'm an awful teacher and don't know how to train my kids to be good for substitute teachers." The fear in her eyes was palpable. Nick laughed despite himself. It was so like Kensie to fret over this.

"Let me see it. Surely it's not as bad as you think. Trust me, I've had my fair share of bad sub notes. It's not on you; it's on the kids."

Kensie eyed him with suspicion, but when Nick held out his hand, she slowly set the paper into it. As Nick read, he had to bite his tongue from bursting with laughter. When he finished and met her stormy eyes, Nick's restraint broke. Through his laughs, he managed to get out, "This is nothing to be mad over. The kids wouldn't stop saying six-seven and other brain rot terms. So what?" Nick looked at the sub's signature again. Of course it was the bitter woman who hated kids. Nick never allowed her to sub for him.

"They should know better. Not every teacher or sub can handle curbing their affinity for brain rot. If they're asked to stop, they should."

Nick handed her the note back and sat down on the table closest to Kensie's desk. "Don't let Mary sub for you again. She's unnecessarily mean. I don't condone this behavior, but I understand why some of the kids wanted to push her buttons. You know how they don't like hammer-down authority. That's what Mary brings to the table. She doesn't know how to calmly negotiate, explain her reasons, and redirect. She just gets all riled up and explodes." Nick paused, thinking about all the times he'd seen Kensie explode. The difference was Kensie only exploded for him, and that thought had his skin heating as he gazed at the look she normally reserved for him and not for sub letters.

Great, he was turned on by her anger. Not cool.

Guess he had done it to himself at this point. Trained himself to respond in this capacity.

"Anyway," Nick continued, attempting to cool himself down. "Don't let it get to you. You're a great teacher, and the kids love you. Trust me, they'll be going on and on tomorrow about how much they missed you."

Kensie's face relaxed, and she set the note down. "I hear you, but I'm still giving them a stern talking to. And the names she took down will get detention. Actions have consequences."

"See? This is why they love you. You'll explain that to them, they'll understand, and hopefully they won't repeat the actions." Nick swung his feet as he folded his hands in his lap. It was strange being in Kensie's room and talking her down instead of rage-baiting her.

He liked it.

"Yeah, you're right." Kensie looked around her room. "At least the room is still tidy. I appreciate when subs take time to organize at the end of the day."

"Look at you, finding the good." Nick clapped dramatically for her, and Kensie rolled her eyes, taking a seat in her chair.

"I always find the good."

Nick hopped off the table and stood beside her desk. "Even in me?"

She spun to face him, her stark blue eyes widening as he leaned close, placing his hands on either side of the chair on the armrests.

Their faces were inches apart, and Nick had half a mind to close the distance and find out how she kissed, but Kensie leaned away, a trickle of fear in her features. *Too far*, Nick thought, and created distance between them, though he didn't move from her desk.

Finally, she answered his question as she stacked papers and binder-clipped them. "Yes. I think I'm starting to."

Nick's heart warmed as Kensie grabbed a thick book from the other side of her desk. "Here. *Jane Eyre*. You can write in it, but don't tear it please. It's what I call my journaling edition." Her cheeks pinkened. "You can read my margin notes if you want."

"Those might overshadow the story." Nick took the book and thumbed the pages. He didn't expect the book to be this big, and he was starting to regret promising to read it. Regardless, he'd do it. For her. And he wanted the insight into her heart and brain that the notes she'd written would provide. What did she find exciting? Sad? *Romantic?*

Kensie interrupted his thoughts. "Oh, it looks like Janet asked me to cover tutoring for her again tomorrow." She scrunched her nose in thought before adding, "I'll have to stay later than I was wanting to make sure I get some essays graded if I cover for her. But, I guess it will be okay because—"

"No." Nick's voice was firm as he stopped her mid-sentence. Kensie looked up at him with a slight frown.

"What do you mean, 'no'?"

Nick grabbed a red chair from against the wall and sat down. He splayed his legs to get comfortable and placed his forearms on his knees, steepling his fingers underneath his chin as he stared Kensie down. She was going to hear this whether she liked it or not.

"I mean, no. You're not taking tutoring for her again. You've taken it at least once a week for the past few months. You have a dance coming up at the end of the week that you need to finish preparing for, and you have end-of-term papers to grade. So, no. You can't tutor for her again."

Kensie's brows were furrowed, like she couldn't possibly consider saying no. "But, she—"

"No," Nick said again as Kensie tried to argue. "It's okay to say no, Hampton Court." Nick hoped the nickname might rustle her up a bit and light the spark of battle within her. She pursed her lips and leaned back in her chair, folding her arms. It worked.

"You don't get to tell me who to say no to."

Nick fought back his grin in hopes to win this round. "Think of this as practice. You're practically telling me no right now. If you can say that one syllable to me, you can say it to other people."

"That's a hasty generalization," Kensie snapped. Nick rolled his lips into his mouth in order to not laugh. He loved volleying with her. He couldn't give this up in his pursuit of being the man she deserved. But this time, riling her up was for a purpose, not for his own amusement, though he was certainly amused.

Nick sat back, grinning. "Oh? So you can't say that word to other people. It's only reserved for me? That's actually romantic, Windsor."

She rolled her eyes. "Either/or. Now you're proposing that I can either say no to you and no one else or that I can say it to everyone through your generalized statement."

"Then answer me directly. Are you physically capable of saying no to someone other than me?"

Kensie leaned forward, and he met her across the way. The eye contact fried his brain; he desperately wanted to taste the argument on her lips. Slowly, Kensie answered. "Yes, Mr. Lancaster. I am capable of saying no to people other than you."

Nick raised his brow. "Prove it. Tell Janet that you can't watch tutoring tomorrow."

Kensie worried her bottom lip, and Nick had to put distance between them and look away. He puffed out a breath as he distracted himself from his desire, counting the seconds ticking by while Kensie calculated her conclusion.

"Fine."

Snapping his attention back to her, not genuinely believing what he heard, he watched as Kensie responded to Janet's email with a wordy reasoning as to why she couldn't watch tutoring tomorrow.

Nick laughed to himself as he read the two paragraphs—full of flowery, appeasing language—over her shoulder. It was a start. At least she said no...poetically.

Chapter Fifteen

Kensie

Three days until the dance.

Kensie sat criss-cross applesauce on the cool, tiled floor, grading literary analysis papers while her leadership students continued to decorate the dance area. Between correcting bad grammar and fetching more tape or scissors, Kensie found herself getting lost in daydreams.

Occasionally a nightmare.

Nick's smirking face as he dusted off his hands from fixing her car.

Her dad's smirking face as he backhanded her mother.

Braelee's knowing laughter yesterday when she walked in on him and Kensie having lunch together in her classroom.

Streams of tears running down her mom's hollowed cheeks, while red and blue lights and roaring sirens flashed and sounded from the front yard.

Nick inches from her face, looking like he wanted to devour her where she sat in her chair.

Her father in a drunken rage.

Kensie decided she would never drink again.

"The demons are back at it, aren't they?" Nick's voice shook Kensie out of the memories. She met his gentle eyes, flinching only a little when he reached out at a snail's pace and wiped a rogue tear from her cheek. *Nick is safe.* "Tell me about it."

"Miss Smith! We need more..."

Nick's hand still palmed Kensie's face as he squatted in front of her. Kensie leaned to look over his shoulder and saw Katie standing slack-jawed, holding a can of paint in her hand.

Kensie snapped her eyes back to Nick and whispered, "Get up. Now." Kensie wasn't sure what her relationship status was with Nick. She was busy loving him like Jesus, but in the process, she thought something more *romantic* was developing. She sure as heck wasn't ready to share whatever *this* was with her students. She needed to figure it out for herself.

Nick didn't seem to share the same convictions. He slowly rose to his feet, never removing his gaze from Kensie. Hovering over Kensie at his full height, he held his hand out to her. She hesitated, and Nick relished in the moment, sporting a winner's smile. "Come on, now. Don't let these kids see you reject a gentleman's offer. Jane Eyre wouldn't approve, and what kind of example would that set?"

"Jane Eyre would very much approve. I can see you haven't read it yet." She set her papers to the side and grabbed his hand; he pulled her to her feet.

But he didn't stop there.

Nick tugged her right into his side and threaded his fingers with hers; their backs were to the students.

"What are you doing?" Kensie growled through her teeth, reminding herself that Nick was safe, even if he was being a nuisance at the moment.

Nick chuckled and squeezed her hand. "We've agreed to tackle demons together. I think that makes us a couple, don't you think?"

"I never agreed to that—"

Nick didn't give Kensie time to finish her response as he turned them around to face the students, who at this point, had all stopped their tasks and were staring. Some were smiling, others were shocked, and a brave few whistled.

"See, Windsor?" Nick whispered into her ear, sending an unauthorized tingle down her spine. "They're rooting for us. Let's give the people what they want."

Kensie ripped her hand from Nick, took a wide step to the side, and fought a losing battle against the redness tainting her fair skin. She cleared her throat, but her words still warbled when she spoke. "Yes, Katie? What do you need me to pick up for you?"

Katie shook her paint can, unable to hide her knowing smile. "We need more paint."

"Can it wait until tomorrow? I can run to the store after work."

Katie nodded, her short blonde hair bobbing with the movement.

"But Miss Smith," Corey started, the only one with a normal expression on his face, "we also need more of those tulle things."

"Walmart was out of them, Corey. I'd have to make an Anchorage trip."

"Please, Miss Smith," another girl pleaded. "We really need more to execute the aurora look we're going for."

Kensie sighed. "Yes, yes. Okay. I will make a late-night trip."

"There's a big snowstorm blowing in tonight. I don't think that's a good idea," Nick butted into the conversation.

Kensie waved him off. "I'll be fine. I'll drive slow."

"But the snow is supposed to pile—"

She shifted her gaze to him and interrupted. "Snow is easier to drive on than ice. I'll be fine. I want these kids to have everything they need."

Nick set his jaw. "Fine. You want to be stubborn and not practice saying no like I thought I'd taught you, then go ahead. I'm going with you, though. And we're taking my truck."

Kensie raised her brows and rubbed her temples. "No. I've got this."

Nick ran a hand through his dark golden waves. "See? You say no to me like it's your favorite pastime. But I'm your co-director, so I'm going. Period."

"Put that foot down, Coach!" Delen shouted from a little ways down the hall, emerging from behind navy lockers.

"Go to class, Delen!" Kensie hollered, wondering how he'd maneuvered his way down into the Commons with enough time to catch this unfortunate exchange.

"I have to talk to Coach," he responded, making his way over to them.

"Make it quick." Kensie felt a little bad at her snippy attitude, but when she turned to Nick, the guilt disappeared. "And you and I will talk about this later."

"You tell him, Miss Smith!" Lovë, who was back from the hospital and sitting on the floor, painting, yelled.

"Hey! You have to be on my side now that you're my woman." Delen ignored Nick and went straight to Lovë.

"The guy did it." Nick laughed in disbelief as he watched Delen sit next to Lovë on the floor, retrieving a brush she couldn't quite reach. "I didn't think he had it in him after he accidentally injured her."

Kensie watched the two in a state of disbelief. She would have thought Lovë hated Delen based on the way the two interacted. Kensie then peeked at Nick, who was walking away from her to talk to the seniors.

She guessed the same could have been said about her and Nick, but that was the thing: Kensie didn't hate Nick. In fact, she wasn't sure she ever had. Just like Lovë was harboring a deep, secret crush on Delen, maybe Kensie had, this entire time, wished Nick was hers. She secretly relished in every sharpened encounter, waiting for the next moment the snake would strike her. She craved his attention, and now that she had it in a shimmering new capacity, Kensie needed to make up her mind. Was she going to let herself fall for him? Nick had her backed against a metaphorical electric wall, and she was humming with energy as she awaited what his next move would be. She knew, at the very least, she wouldn't make the first move to initiate something more than mutual understanding and friendship.

Kensie silently took it to the Lord as she sat back down with her papers and flair pen.

God, make this clear, please. Shove the instructions of how to proceed into my face. How can I even entertain the idea of a relationship when I'm still processing what my father did to my mother? When I'm just now realizing where some of my issues stem from? God, it's just not the right time. You know this, right? Or...is it the perfect time?

"Make sure you pack an overnight bag." Nick sat on Kensie's brown couch, right where she'd left him, waiting for her to finish getting ready for Anchorage.

"Why would I need an overnight bag? I'm not staying anywhere overnight with you." Kensie, from her room, stripped out of her plaid flowy skirt and white blouse, put on warm leggings and a bookish sweater that read *All I Want for Christmas is Books*, and changed into a new pair of wool socks.

"Because there is a massive snowstorm rolling in, and we may very well get stuck in Anchorage!" Nick exasperated from the other room.

"We're going to be fine. I checked the weather. The system is staying mostly to the west." Kensie threw her coily hair into a thick messy bun and walked into the living room to stand in front of the man who had changed from his khaki pants and dress shirt into sweatpants and a football sweater. Kensie's stomach knotted over how casually sexy he looked, but she shoved the thought from her mind as she crossed her arms over her chest. "You don't have to go, you know. If you're that scared we'll get stuck, then stay here."

Nick stood up and stepped forward, invading her private bubble. "And miss roughly five hours with you in a vehicle? No way. We're discussing demons tonight whether you're up for it or not. You're mine for the night, Windsor."

Kensie swallowed the budding fear as she looked up into his sincere eyes. The thought of fully opening up to Nick terrified her, and she still wasn't sure she would be able to. Nonetheless, she vowed to help him, and she meant it. "Yeah, okay. Well, let's get going then. We have to stop by Sea Siren for coffee first."

Kensie walked around him and headed toward the door to slip into her snow boots and grab her Birkenstocks for the truck.

"Yeah. I figured as much. You can't go without that wretched dirt water you call good coffee." Nick began to put on his boots.

Kensie stopped mid-tie and looked up. "How do you know I drink iced Americanos? Or that my kids call it dirt water?"

Nick shrugged as he tied his laces. "I pay attention to you. And your students are extremely vocal about their distaste of it."

He finished putting on his shoes while Kensie gathered her wits. Did she know what kind of coffee he drank? Did she know his favorite color? His favorite food?

No, she didn't.

"What's your favorite color?"

Nick plucked his keys from the holder on the wall. "Aurora green."

"Mine is—"

"Red." They both spoke at the same time, locking eyes. Nick added, "But like, deep maroon. Not the screaming color. You like sultry, not loud."

He continued as Kensie stared at him with confoundedness. "And your favorite adult beverage is an Old Fashioned. You enjoy anything involving potatoes, and your favorite book is *Jane Eyre*. I venture to say it's your favorite movie, too, judging by the amount of times you've made my sister watch it with you."

As he opened the door and walked out into the apartment building hallway, Kensie scurried after him. "How do you know these things? It's not like I go around talking about them all the time."

Nick stopped, turned, and leveled her with a knowing look. "Like I said, I pay attention. I have for the past two and a half years since I met you. I've learned some things over that time."

Kensie squirmed under the heat of his gaze. Nick bit back a smile then looked past her, raising his eyebrows. "You left your door wide open, Kensington Marie."

Thirty minutes into the drive, Kensie knew she'd made a mistake.

Even in the darkness of four p.m., the sky somehow darkened more, blocking out the stars and the near full-ness of the moon. She tried to check the weather, but her phone didn't have signal.

She was mentally preparing to eat crow, and she re-gretted not having grabbed an overnight bag like Nick suggested. She could tell him to turn around right now. They could make it back home before it began.

But when she glanced over at his frame, one hand on the wheel and the other lazily resting on the center con-sole, palm open, she had to fight the smile attempting to crawl up her face. If she were honest with herself, she didn't care where they ended up tonight. Nick had said she was his for the night, and Kensie wanted that. Whatever was going to happen, she'd let it.

Besides, she now knew he drank disgusting, flavorless lattes. It was a step to cracking him open the way she used to sit on the porch and crack pecans with her mom.

"Tell me more about who you are." Kensie adjusted herself so that she was angled toward Nick. She tucked one foot underneath her and took a sip of her iced Americano.

"What do you want to know?"

"What was it like growing up with a state senator as a parent? How was your relationship with Braelee as children? Why did you quit law school? What really went down with your ex?" Kensie paused, wondering if she should ask the next question. She decided she might as well. "Why did you stop going to church?"

Nick took a curve gently, then turned down the radio. "Whew, Windsor. Where do I start?"

Kensie opened her mouth to answer him, but Nick beat her to the punch. "Braelee and I have always had a close relationship because we had similar pressures placed upon us by our parents, so let's start with why I quit law school. I think it ties into my parents and will bleed into my ex."

She didn't miss how he ignored the church question.

As a light dusting of snow began to fall, Nick launched into his backstory.

"I went to law school because it's what was expected of me as Alaskan State Senator James Lancaster's son. To be frank, I enjoyed my time there. The law is interesting, and I do love a good debate." He tossed a wicked smile in Kensie's direction, and she laughed softly. Nick continued as he slowed their speed to accommodate the light, floating snow.

"During my third year, which was the final year, I realized that while I loved learning about the law and arguing with people, I didn't love the massive amounts of paperwork, how time-consuming the career was—and would continue to become—and how I was missing time spent with my friends back home.

"I was volunteering what little time I had at a youth football camp during fall break that year, and it dawned on me that I was doing what I genuinely loved—coaching kids. I loved teaching them football, but even more, I loved the connections I made and the impacts I had on their lives during that short time. It was as if God said, 'You can do this all day, every day,' and I was all in. I never went back to school and opted to get my teaching licenses through an alternative route, while taking on the head coaching position that had miraculously opened up at that time."

The raw joy and integrity in Nick's voice had Kensie pushing back emotions she didn't want to name. Whoever Nick used to be—that man who followed God's leading—was still the same man she sat beside now. Tainted by life, but still there. He just needed a reminder that God was still for him.

Kensie took another sip of her coffee, relishing in the tart taste. "How did you meet your ex? What was her name again? Jenessa?"

"Jesena." Nick corrected, but his voice wasn't sour or bitter like Kensie expected. It was leveled, factual. "Jes was in Alaska with her brother, Chase Hayes, who is a political scientist, news commentator, and author."

"Oh, wow," Kensie commented, maybe just a tinge of jealousy poking its head into her heart. "He's huge in the political arena. You dated his sister?" If Nick dated women like her, did Kensie even stand a chance?

Nick shrugged as if it were no big deal and continued his story. "He was covering the so-called Red Wave that swept Alaska four years ago. Anyway, she instantly caught my eye, and I caught hers. It was one of those lust-at-first-sight situations, if I'm honest. She stayed even when her brother left. I grew to love her outside of her looks. She's a brilliant woman, and she's had her fair share of bad parenting stories. Despite what she did to me, she really is a nice and kind—"

"Okay, I think I get it," Kensie interrupted, fighting the growing jealousy. Why was she writhing with envy right now? Nick wasn't hers. Regardless, this woman was in the past. But again, Kensie questioned if a woman like herself was remotely in Nick's league.

Nick snuck a glance at Kensie, who had her jaw set, holding back the things she wanted to say but wouldn't. He laughed. "Don't worry, Windsor. She's in the past. You're the present. My future."

Kensie's stomach tumbled. "We're just friends."

"Call it what you want for now." Nick continued his story, a victorious smile painting his handsome face as Kensie's head swam with the words he'd just uttered.

"I was preparing to propose to her, and then I found out she'd been having an affair with my dad's senator friend. A man I sort of considered a friend. It wasn't a long affair, but cheating is cheating."

Nick's smile faded, and his leg bounced. "In my desperation, I gave her the option to call it off with him and commit fully to me, or she could choose him."

"She chose him," Kensie surmised, a sadness soaking her voice. She couldn't imagine being cheated on, especially by a person she was hoping to marry. Her heart broke for Nick. All that time, he was suffering, and she was spewing her sourness all over him.

"She chose him." Nick breathed deeply in the silence. "I don't know why I even gave her the option. I loved her that much, I guess. Regardless..." He pulled into the typical first bathroom stop on the road to Anchorage, Cave Man's. "I'm glad everything worked out the way that it did. That's what I was walking through when you reached out to me via email, and I rudely responded to you, which I'm sincerely sorry for, by the way. After you told me about it, I had the school pull email reports from that timeframe, and I read over the exchange."

Kensie swallowed her pride, pushing back tears. "You don't have to say sorry. I'm sorry I've held a pointless, childish grudge over that exchange. I'm sorry I allowed that one encounter to paint you in a bad light and never really gave you the chance to show me who you really were."

"Looks like we both had things we needed to apologize for." Nick turned the truck off, and they both went to use the bathroom and grab snacks for the remainder of the trip.

When they were back on the road and the snow started falling harder, Kensie spoke up. "I've never been in a relationship before, you know. I don't know what it's like to be cheated on. I don't really know what it's like to love a man and to be loved by a man. I don't know what to do or how to act because..." Kensie took a deep breath and closed her eyes, preparing to give Nick an inch, hoping he wouldn't reach for a mile. "Because my dad left when I was just a little girl."

Nick waited patiently for her to press on, and when he set his water down in the cupholder and placed his palm face up once more, Kensie slipped her hand into his. She wasn't ready to tell him the total truth. She still needed to process it with God, with herself, and with the counselor she'd set an appointment with.

She could give Nick her hand, though.

Nick squeezed her hand. "I'm sorry, truly. He missed out on watching you become the amazing, kind, and stubborn woman you are today. Do you want to talk about it?"

Kensie shook her head even as she stifled a laugh at his throwing "stubborn" into the mix of adjectives to describe her. "No, that's enough for now. I don't want to dwell on it too long, or I'll fall apart."

"I may not be able to put you back together, but I promise I'll hold your pieces," Nick whispered, barely audible above the rumble of the tires on the road. "You're not alone, Kensie. Just as you promised to be there for me, I'll be there for you."

Kensie felt one single tear fall before she sniffed and wiped it away. "Thank you, Nick." She squeezed his hand back and attempted to let go, but he didn't allow it. "It's because of him I'm no longer drinking. I remembered some things, and—" she cut herself off, unable to give him any more. He didn't ask. Instead, he changed the subject to another game of, "What's your favorite..."

Contentment settled in her soul at the feel of his warmth in the palm of her hand.

Chapter Sixteen

Kensie

"What do you mean you only have one room left?"

Kensie placed her palms on the concierge's desk at Midnight Sun Inn, leaning over the counter. They had made it to Target on time to get the tulle and other materials she needed, but the weather had become an outright blizzard with no sign or forecast of slowing up for the next several hours.

She admitted that Nick was right, and the smug man wouldn't let her live it down.

"Come on." Nick nudged her, and she shot fiery glares in his direction. He wasn't fazed. "We are not about to go find another hotel in this weather. It was bad enough getting here. We are taking the room and waiting this storm out."

"Is this you putting your foot down again, Mr. Lancaster?"

Nick didn't flinch. "Yes, it is, Buckingham. I'm the one driving, so I'm making the decision."

Kensie scrunched her nose in frustration. "Fine. I'll drive us to another hotel."

Nick laughed. "Cute. You're not wrecking my truck the way you wrecked your car."

"Um, guys? Do you want the room or not?" The wide-eyed young lady behind the desk visibly shrank as Kensie turned her stare onto her.

"No."

"Yes." Nick threw his card down. "We are taking the room. Now stay here and get the keys while I park the truck and get our things out."

"I didn't even bring an overnight bag!" Kensie shouted at his retreating frame.

"Good thing I had the sense to pack one for you!"

Nick disappeared into the blizzard, leaving Kensie staring after him in disbelief. How in the world had he managed that under her nose? When she finally turned around, the young woman was biting back a smile. "Whose name should I put the reservation under?"

"Nicolas freaking Lancaster," she grumbled.

Five minutes later, Nick and Kensie were standing in front of Room 12, holding a key with a Santa keychain attached to it, and glaring at the mistletoe above the door.

Kensie was glaring, that is. When she snuck a glance at Nick, he was smirking through the icicles forming on his scruffy face. The sight softened her heart, and she said a little prayer to ease her frustrations. *Love him like Jesus.* Nick was no longer a man she should fight. He was good. He was kind. He was caring. He didn't deserve the almighty wrath of Kensie.

"Let's get you inside." She plunged the key into the keyhole. As the door creaked open, she was greeted with the smell of sugar cookies and bright, white Christmas lights blinking slowly on a rotund, ornately decorated Christmas tree. The room was covered in shades of traditional Christmas-color plaid, reminding her of home back in Mississippi. Her mom was adamant that Christmas should maintain its integrity and steer clear of pinks, blues, and other non-festive colors. Kensie had the deep urge to call her mother, but she wasn't ready. She'd send her a Snapchat of the room later.

Nick kicked off his boots and strode past her into the room, humming "Deck the Halls."

She followed him in, removing her shoes, and as he dropped the bags on the heated floor, they both looked at the one, singular bed in the room before looking at each other. His humming ceased.

"You can have it. I'll take that mighty comfy-looking chair over in the corner."

Kensie followed his gaze to the armchair that did not look comfy in any definition of the word. "You have to drive us home in the morning. How are you going to sleep on that chair?"

Nick shrugged and walked over to it, his snowpants swishing with the movement as they'd yet to shed their added layers. He plopped onto the chair, which had a back-breaking bounce to it. He man-splayed and wiggled, and then set his arms down firmly on the rests. "See? I can sleep like this. Or..." He readjusted to where he was curled into a ball on the cushion, but because of his size, half of his legs dangled from the edge. Kensie, even in her smaller frame, didn't think she could fit in that chair well enough to sleep soundly.

Laughing at the goofy smile coloring his face, she blurted, "We can share."

Kensie froze, realizing what she had just spoken and wondering where in the heck it came from. She scrambled to justify her response. "I mean, it's a king-sized bed. We can have our own sides and our own blankets. You'll be driving us home in the morning, and you need sleep. Besides, it's not like we haven't accidentally fallen asleep together before. What's one more time, right? Two friends sharing a bed. No big deal."

Nick untangled himself, stood, and made his way to tower over Kensie. "Right." A smile crept across his face as he slowly lifted a hand to cup her face, her cheeks warming at his touch. "I love this change of attitude, *friend.*"

Kensie stepped away from his touch and busied herself by taking off her jacket and pants, followed by snatching her bag from the floor. *Friends. Friends. Friends.* Nothing more. Nothing less.

She still couldn't believe Nick had somehow packed a bag for her. When did he have the time to do that while they were at her apartment? Is that what friends did for each other?

"Go shower and warm up," she commanded Nick, desperately needing space from him and the thoughts he preempted in her head—the complicated feelings he made her feel.

"Yes, ma'am." Nick leaned in closer. Kensie was rock solid, not even blinking. "Our little impromptu date just keeps getting better and better."

Kensie came to her senses. "This isn't a date! I call mind projection fallacy in your argument."

His brown eyes were dancing. "I'm not arguing with you, Windsor. Therefore, reason states a fallacy doesn't exist."

"Oh, now you're just flat-out lying." Kensie couldn't help the smile that tugged at the corner of her lips. Tarin was right; she loved this tit-for-tat game between them. A little too much. "You're always arguing with me."

"Because it's the way to your heart." He winked. Laughing to himself, Nick grabbed his bag and disappeared into the bathroom adjacent to the bed, talking to himself under his breath about friend-dates or something. Kensie released a long, languid breath and turned to face the bed.

The bed is big, Kensie thought to herself. *There's enough room for both of us to sleep soundly without ever coming in contact. If all else fails, I'll sleep on the floor.*

Kensie sent a picture of it to her mom before taking a moment to send a voice memo to Tarin, letting her know the situation.

It wasn't long before she texted back.

Guard your heart. Even the mildest of temptations can lead to big mistakes.

The text was followed by a cute picture of her dog, Vixen, in reindeer horns, eliciting a chuckle from Kensie. Her phone rang, and when she saw it was Braelee, she answered.

"Please tell me the two of you are hunkering down in Anchorage?"

Kensie sighed. "Yes, we are. We are at the Midnight Sun Inn. Has the storm reached Crescent Cove?"

"Yep. Big Bear is staying over just in case the power goes out."

Kensie opened her mouth to protest, but Braelee was quicker. "And no, we aren't staying in the same room. He's just worried about me since Nick is gone. You know I'd typically stay at his place."

"Okay, good. No infringing upon your morality, you hear me?"

Braelee laughed. "Loud and clear."

"Kensie, I left my phone sitting on the counter downstairs. Can you run and get it for me?" Nick hollered over the running water.

"Excuse me, Kensington Marie Smith. Is that my brother in the background? Are the two of you sharing a room?"

Kensie's silence spoke volumes.

"Kensie?"

"Yes," Kensie replied to Nick in a gravelly voice. "Going now."

On the other end of the line, Braelee was howling with laughter. When she caught her breath, she threw Kensie's words back at her. "No infringing upon your morality, you hear me?"

"Bye, Braelee." Kensie hung up the phone, but she couldn't help the twitch in her lips, coaxing them to form into a small smile. *Friends. Just friends.*

Once Kensie was back with Nick's phone, she slipped it under the door to him and started the process of digging through what he'd packed for her. It didn't take long for her to realize the clothes belonged to his sister, but since the two of them were roughly the same size, it would work. He'd also stuck an unopened toothbrush and travel-sized toothpaste into the bag, along with mini versions of the very expensive hair care products she used.

"How did he..." She spoke aloud to herself, wondering how he knew what she used. Then she remembered he had been to her apartment once before this trip. He must have snooped around her bathroom. He truly did pay attention.

Kensie's heart melted toward the man in the bathroom, and she took the moment of solitude to allow herself to cry softly, asking the Lord to once again forgive her for the hatred she once held in her heart. Hatred that was transitioning rather quickly to something akin to affection.

Nick's phone rang as Kensie heard the shower cut off. He answered it at seemingly the last second, his voice coarse. "Hey, Dad."

Kensie tiptoed over to the closed door and pressed her ear up against the redwood, trying to make sense of his whispered tone.

"No. I told you that I'm helping with a school dance. I'm not attending your event."

Clinging and clanking sounds like items dropping on a counter sounded before Nick spoke again.

"Fine, yes. The dance is on Friday and the gala is on Saturday, you're right. I could come. But I don't want to. I'll be too tired from the night before anyway. And so will Kensie. I'm not dragging her into your mess, and I will not subject her to your cruelty. Goodbye."

Kensie darted away from the door, but it was still a few minutes before Nick emerged. One look at Kensie's face, and he asked, "You heard all that?"

Nodding, Kensie offered him a sympathetic smile. "If my being seen out in public with you is so unreasonably important to your father, I can handle it. Take me to the gala. I'm a big girl."

Nick shook his head, exhaling as he plopped onto the world's most uncomfortable-looking chair. The springs creaked. "You don't understand. He's trying to force us together for PR purposes. If I'm going to be with you"—Nick sat up and looked into her eyes—"I'm going to be with you on *my* terms. Not his."

A chill that had nothing to do with the blizzard raging outside rippled through Kensie at his words. The furnace in his gaze warmed her right back up. She wanted to say yes to him desperately, wanted him to lay out those terms of his, but she had to know...

"What happened to pull you away from church?" They could have been going to the same church this entire time. Braelee went there, and she said Nick used to go but had stopped. She wouldn't tell Kensie why because it wasn't her story to share, and, quite frankly, she wasn't interested in knowing why at the time. She didn't care.

Now, she cared. She cared deeply.

Nick motioned to the other chair in the room that was identical to the one he was in. Kensie dragged it across the floor, cringing at the screeching noise it made, then settled it in front of Nick and sat down. She motioned her hands to say, "Go ahead."

"I believe in God. I believe Jesus is the Son of God. I believe the Holy Spirit completes the Trinity. But I've had a difficult time believing that any of them truly care about me." Nick paused, looking up to the ceiling as he sat back in the chair. "I'm saved, but over the past few years, I've wondered exactly what that's supposed to mean for me. Yeah, sure, I'm going to heaven when I die, but what's the point of spending an eternity with God in heaven if He doesn't care about me enough to protect me here?"

Kensie softened, shoulders dropping. Nick knew how to be a man, be tough, be useful. He knew how to be a boy and act on his playful impulsiveness. But underneath it all, he had a well of emotions. Emotions that had broken him and healed him. Emotions that made him believe he was too far gone for God to care about.

God, give me the words, Kensie thought. She took a breath. "I've had similar thoughts. I've wondered why God in all of His supposed goodness would allow my dad to...do what he did."

Nick placed his elbows on his legs as he leaned closer. "You don't strike me as the type to question God."

A frozen silence choked Kensie as she thought of the freshly wounded past. She had a litany of questions for God. Why would He allow her dear mother to be tormented by that sorry excuse of a man? Why would He make Kensie forget about it and go on living her life alongside her mother as if everything was as perfect as a sunset on a beach despite her father "leaving" them? She snorted at the irony of it all before answering Nick.

"You'd be surprised, I guess. This instance wasn't the first time, and I'm sure it won't be the last." She didn't miss Nick's tilt of the head in question, but she kept on talking. "When those questions start invading my headspace, I make myself recite scripture. I remember that He says I'm fearfully and wonderfully made. That He knows every hair on my head. That He will take care of me more than He takes care of the birds. That He will never leave me or forsake me. That He knows my appointed days." Kensie held his stare, willing him to hear her as tears overwhelmed her. "That He sent His son to die for my sins.

I mean, what more can God do to reassure me that He cares and that He's with me?"

Dear God, help me to believe it right now. Even in my questions and bitterness.

Water pooled in his beautiful eyes. "Dang it, Windsor. You're making me cry. Again." He sniffled and sat back in his chair. Kensie mimicked his actions, tears marching through the barricades of her eyes as she reflected on the words she'd said. She willed herself to believe it and gazed upon an unraveling Nick.

He fought back more drops of emotion, releasing a masculine groan as he surrendered. "You're right. He's here. He's with me. Everything I went through led me to this moment. With you. And if you're here in front of me, He has to care. Because He knows I don't deserve you. Not after how I've treated you and how I've lived my life these past few years."

Kensie took his hands between hers. "This isn't about me, Nick. Even if I wasn't here in this moment, God still cares about you, and He's waiting for you to run back to Him."

I'm waiting for you, too.

Nick's tears fell freely, and Kensie pulled him to his feet and wrapped him in a hug. He smelled like the forest after a rainstorm, and his still-wet hair plopped onto her shoulder as he squeezed her tighter. "Thank you."

Then he stepped back, took her hands, and began to pray. "God, Kensie says You're listening, so here goes nothing. Thank you for her. Thank you for her faithfulness and her goodness. Thank you for her directness. God, I'm sorry. I'm sorry I've been running and living life according to my own terms as I tried to overcome a heartbreak and family issues by myself. I'm sorry for the anger I've held over the situation and that I allowed it to fester and build within me to where I shoved everyone out and masked my pain with smiles. Forgive me, Father. Show me the right way forward. Teach me to trust in You without wavering, just like I used to."

Kensie prayed after Nick, asking God to strengthen them both and grant them wisdom moving forward, not only with each other, but with their respective familial situations. Privately, she lifted her bitter heart of her loss of memories and dad.

They hugged and cried and laughed, continuing to swap stories late into the night over cups of hot chocolate before both falling soundlessly asleep on their respective sides of the bed, a fort of pillows between them for good measure.

Chapter Seventeen

Nick

Nick's alarm went off at three in the morning. He groggily reached for the device and silenced it before rotating and wrapping his arm back around Kensie. He enjoyed the warmth of her body against his, the way they fit together. He inhaled, smelling the addictive scent that was uniquely hers. The darkness was a comfy blanket, lulling him back into sleep—

His eyes shot open, and he haltingly pulled one arm out from underneath Kensie's head and propped himself up. He wasn't supposed to be touching her, much less cuddling her.

Kensie wasn't on her side, but he wasn't completely on his, either. They'd somehow managed to meet in the middle during the night. The pillows they'd carefully placed between them were nowhere to be found.

She stretched, a little noise escaping her lips as she exhaled before wiggling back into a sleep position. Nick was awestruck over how at ease, comfortable, and beautiful she looked—a sight he wanted to wake up to every morning for the remainder of his life. *God, give me strength.* Nick still felt uneasy calling out to God again, but if Kensie showed him anything last night, it was that God was listening, He was there, and He wanted a relationship with Nick. So, Nick vowed to pursue it no matter how his emotions and thoughts got in the way. He owed it to himself and to her. Definitely to her.

As gingerly as he could, he slipped out of bed and went to Kensie's side, kneeling. He brushed auburn curls out of her face with his fingertips and traced the constellation of freckles spattering her cream complexion. "So beautiful," he whispered, and Kensie stirred once more.

"Open your eyes, Windsor." Nick daringly pressed his lips to her forehead, and as he pulled away, he stared into her wide eyes. Smiling, he said, "Good morning."

"Good morning," Kensie replied through a sleepy voice, then she hurriedly covered her mouth, eyes wide. "I have morning breath. And my hair probably looks like a lion's mane."

Nick laughed quietly, enjoying this whisper war they were in. "I don't care."

They hadn't talked about them last night, but Nick knew they'd crossed an unspoken line. The former unknown feelings between them, demonstrated by years of verbal sparring to avoid them, were crystal clear. He could see it in her smile, in her eyes. Nick leaned in to kiss her, but she stopped him with the hand that was just covering her mouth, now covering his.

"No. Not here. Not right now."

Nick grinned underneath her hand. "So, later then?"

Kensie ignored him and got herself out of bed, effectively shattering the quiet coziness of the early morning as she turned on a lamp. Nick missed the feeling of her in his arms, the scratchy whisper of her morning voice, but they needed to get back on the road so they could make it to work in time.

After gathering all their things and dressing back into their travel clothes, they found themselves trudging through unplowed parts of the road and taking advantage of the parts already cleared. Nick missed her hand in his, but he needed both hands to drive in these road conditions. Instead, they blasted Christmas music and sang along. He'd never seen Kensie so carefree and loose, and he soaked in every broad smile, off-tune key sung, and loud laugh. Once they passed Cave Man's, Nick finally got the nerve to ask her *the* question.

"Why do you hate the palace nicknames so much?"

Kensie, to his surprise, laughed breathlessly and covered her face. "It's so stupid, Nick. I honestly can't believe I've let it get to me all this time."

Nick took his hand off the wheel for a second to pat her thigh. "Come on, tell me."

She pressed her head back against the seat, and Nick put his hand on the wheel and fixed his eyes into the dark abyss that was five a.m. "Okay, fine. When I was in high school, boys would make fun of my name by calling me palace names. It wasn't flirty or from good intentions. It was straight-up bullying."

Nick's heart dropped. "I'm so sorry, Kensie. Had I known, I—"

Kensie waved him off. "Seriously. After our talk last night, I remembered that no name-calling could ever rewrite who I really am. And I know you didn't mean it maliciously like they did."

"I didn't," Nick echoed. "I meant it as a means of flirting with you, even if my reasons for flirting weren't right. Even when I call you Buckingham in my frustration, it was never out of hate. I've always kind of thought of you as the princess of Crescent Cove."

"Confession time." Kensie rolled her lips into her mouth before breaking out in a broad smile. "I'm starting to like the way you call me palace names. I like that I know your mood by which name you choose to use."

Nick still hesitated. "But I will stop, Kensie. Say the word, and I will never use any of those terms again to address you."

"Listen, Coach." Kensie leveled a look at him, which Nick saw briefly before focusing on the road. His body hummed; she'd never called him Coach before. "Listen closely, because I'll only say this once. Call me Windsor when you're flirting with me. Call me Kew when you want to be silly. Call me Hampton Court when you wish to jest. Call me Buckingham when I get under your skin. You've successfully redefined the terms to mean something special, not hateful. But you're the only one who gets to use them."

Nick's smile was that of a champion. He sure felt like one at the moment. "I'm hearing you loud and clear, Kensington." He said her name as if it were another palace term of endearment to add to the list.

She caught on. "And call me Kensington only when you have that look of adoration in your eyes like you do right now."

He slowed and pulled over on the side of the road, flashing his hazards. When he glanced at her confused expression, his eyes softened. Adoration was indeed pouring out of him. "Can I kiss you now, my princess?"

Kensie laughed freely and swatted him away. "No, you may not. You're getting us back to my kingdom safely."

"Coach, you look like Santa brought your Christmas present early," Delen said, taking a seat on the bench next to Nick as a game of volleyball ensued during the P. E. class.

Nick raised his brows at the senior, but he couldn't shake his smile. Hadn't been able to all day. "He did."

"So, you and Miss Smith are officially dating?"

"You'll have to ask her," Nick relented. He wasn't going to risk starting a rumor she'd want to stamp out. He would let her lead how they interacted here at work from now on.

Delen grinned, his mop of dark-brown curls bouncing on top of his head as he bounded to his feet. "I'm going to do that now."

"No, Delen, wait—" But it was too late. The kid was sprinting across the gym floor, and Nick was too tired to chase him down. A write-up would be sufficient.

Unless Kensie said yes. Then maybe he'd forego the discipline.

The dismissal bell rang, and Nick wondered if he'd ever get his answer.

Delen walked back into the gym just as Nick was packing up.

"Are you gonna ask her to the dance?"

Nick scoffed. "What am I? Your age?"

Delen shrugged. "Don't matter what age a woman is. She likes to be pursued and treated like a princess. You taught me that." Then off he went, catching up with Lovë and taking her backpack for her while she hobbled on her crutches.

"Our students are wise occasionally," Lori chuckled.

Nick whipped around. "Where'd you come from?"

"I'm everywhere. You know that."

"You're right about that." Nick grabbed his bag and walked with Lori back to her office.

She shut the door behind him and dropped her smile. "Are you serious about Kensie? Because if you're not, Nick, so help me God, I will—"

Nick threw his hands up. "Yes, I'm serious. Back down, School Mom."

"I'm serious, Nick. She is not a woman you play with. She's the type of woman you marry."

Nick bit his lip to fight back a smile. He was glad Kensie had people like Lori, who cared so deeply about her. "I know. She's the type of woman I want to marry."

"Nick, are you sure?"

He lolled his head back and ran a hand through his hair. "Yes. How many times do I need to say it? She is genuine, intelligent, kind, loving, gorgeous, hardworking, and loves the Lord. What more could I want? I'd be an idiot to throw a woman like her to the wayside. As long as she'll have me, she's mine."

Lori relented and smiled. "Treat her like you mean those words."

He went home to Alexei and Big Bear starting a fire in his backyard pit.

"What in the world is going on here?"

Big Bear offered him a toothy smile. "Braelee said you and Kensie shared a room."

"So you both show up unannounced at my house?"

Alexei swept his arm around the yard. "We plowed the yard. You're welcome."

Nick shoved his hands into his pockets, staring at his friends. "You two are worse than the girls."

Thirty minutes later, Nick found himself sitting by the fire and sipping on green tea. "Look, guys. It's simple, really. We talked a lot about personal things, laughed a lot, and I think I'm starting to get back right with God, so I'll be at church on Sunday."

The fire crackled and popped as Nick waited for one of them to respond.

Alexei met the challenge, standing and drawing Nick into a bro-hug. "Praise God."

Big Bear was next. "He's answering our prayers, Alexei."

"You guys were praying for me?"

"Of course we were," Big Bear said. "What kind of friends would we be if we didn't take our broken friend and lower him through the roof to Jesus?"

Nick swallowed back his emotions. "Thank you, guys, really."

"You'd do the same for us." Alexei sat down, and the other men followed suit.

Would I? Nick wondered. *The man I've been over the past few years definitely wouldn't have, but this version I'm seeking? Yes. I would. Starting now.* "Can I say a prayer for the two of you?"

Chapter Eighteen

Kensie

"My gosh, Braelee. It was extremely difficult not to let him kiss me!"

Kensie and Braelee sat in Kensie's apartment, a movie paused in the background as Kensie gushed about Nick.

"Okay, girl. I don't think I want details of how you almost kissed my brother."

Popping up to check the kettle, Kensie teased. "Don't even lie. You want all the details because it's me."

Braelee surrendered, tossing a throw pillow at Kensie's backside. "Yeah, but like, don't give me descriptions and stuff when you finally do kiss him. Besides, when are you going to put the poor man out of his misery?"

The water wasn't ready, so Kensie sat back down and tugged her Christmas tree-themed blanket to her chest, lost in thought of exactly how she would kiss Nick. *When* she would kiss Nick.

The images were replaced with static interruptions of her mother kissing her father, and then her father slapping her mother across the face. Kensie pulled the blanket to her chin as if the shield of the soft spread would serve as a terminating force to the scratched film flickering in and out in her mind.

"What's wrong?" Braelee straightened, worry lines forming on her forehead as she leaned her face closer into Kensie's view. Kensie clutched the edges of the blanket, forcing her breath out in slow seconds. She looked at her best friend, at the genuine concern in her eyes—the ones that looked too much like Nick's.

She hadn't talked to anyone about this yet. She was still waiting to get in with the therapist. Maybe Kensie should tell Braelee as a trial run of sorts. Then she could talk to her therapist. She'd save her mom for last. Kensie hadn't a clue what to say to her or even how to bring it up. She couldn't begin to fathom how her mom would react, especially since Kensie was reacting the way she was, and she hadn't even been on the receiving end of his abusive blows. Just the observer, losing her childhood innocence, one foul word, death threat, and beating at a time. In the meantime, she'd continue to just send texts and Snapchat.

Kensie, knowing she could trust her best friend with this and needing to tell *someone*, lowered the blanket. "You can't tell Nick, okay? I'll tell him when the time's right."

Braelee tilted her head, one corner of her lip lifting. "Girl code. Duh."

Attempting a failed laugh, Kensie stopped herself from hiding her emotions. Her face crumbled as she dared herself to say the words. "I don't know where my father is. I don't know if he's in prison. I don't know if he's run off. If he's dead." Kensie paused, willing herself to say the sandpaper words grating her tongue.

"You've mentioned before that he left when you were a kid and your mom raised you. I know that couldn't have been easy." Braelee's gentle reassurance that she was listening emboldened Kensie's courage.

She wrung her fingers as she opened her mouth. "When I ran off into the ditch on Sunday, I hit my head, and I think amidst the loud sounds and fear-driven adrenaline, memories I had repressed came back." Kensie met Braelee's eyes for a second, and her friend nodded her head in encouragement. "My dad abused my mom. I used to sit in a dark corner behind the couch so that I wouldn't become a target. As far as I know, I was never"—she gulped—"beaten, but I saw it happening. Often. And afterward, Mom, sometimes bleeding and sometimes limping, would carry me to my bed and sing 'It Is Well With My Soul' through her tear-stained smile to lull me back to sleep."

Kensie was crying now, the nightmares crystallizing in her mind as she put them into words. Braelee wrapped her arms around Kensie, and the warmth and presence of Kensie's best friend was a signal that she would be okay. Maybe not right now, but one day.

"In the mighty name of Jesus, I pray peace and comfort over my friend..." Braelee launched into a powerful prayer over Kensie, and Kensie wept into the strong arms of the woman who'd quickly become someone she couldn't imagine living without. She silently thanked Jesus for Braelee's unwavering friendship.

When Braelee finished, Kensie laughed at the luckiness of her life. Things weren't great right now, but they were *good*. She had her best friend, knew the truth of her father, and had the grace of God poured out upon her. Back in Mississippi, she had her lifelong best friend, Frankie, and a strong mother who had endured much to raise her.

And Tarin, Kensie reminded herself. Thank God for her. Kensie would tell her next. Another person she could trust and open up to. Kensie took a deep breath of gratitude, thankful for the two communities she had, even though they were worlds away.

"Okay, okay. I don't want to cry anymore." Kensie wiped her tears and sniffled, feeling like a feather freed from underneath a boulder. "Let's finish watching *Jane Eyre*. You know I love that movie."

Braelee laughed. "But the book was better, right?"

"Duh." Kensie cut her eyes to Braelee, who was still snuggled close to her. "But the movie is still pretty darn amazing."

After making two mugs of hot chocolate, the women resumed their movie night. Another interruption came only twenty minutes later when Kensie's phone rang.

"It's Nick."

Braelee rolled her eyes but stood up. "Answer it. You're making him wait for a kiss; don't make him wait to talk to you."

"I've never talked to him on the phone." Kensie shot to her feet, pacing the living room as the phone continued to ring.

Braelee shrugged. "First time for everything. I'm going to the bathroom. It'll be a while because of the hot chocolate. Take your time and talk to my brother." With that, Braelee snatched Kensie's phone, answered the call, and shoved it back into Kensie's hand before bounding down the hall.

With a trembling hand, Kensie lifted the phone to her ear. "H-hello?"

"Hey, Kensie. What're you up to?"

Kensie stared out the living room window into the dark evening, breathing deeply to steady her shaking voice. "Oh, you know. Just watching *Jane Eyre* with Braelee. A typical girls' night."

Nick hummed on the other end of the line, and the sound stirred the symphony of swallowtails in her stomach, harmonizing with the hastening beat of her heart.

"What about you?" Kensie unintentionally squeaked the words.

"The guys were over for a fire. They just went home, and I wanted to hear your voice."

The symphony swelled. "Oh."

How does one talk to a man over the phone? Is there a rule book? A how-to guide? Kensie wondered.

"I also wanted to see if you're free tomorrow night. I know the dance is on Friday, so a classic Friday night date is off limits. So how about a Thursday night date?"

The symphony silenced.

"You want to take me on a date?" Kensie's dumb response had her physically facepalming herself. Why couldn't she be normal? Charismatic? Why couldn't she just say, "Yes, Nick. I'd love to go on a date with you. What time and where?"

Nick chuckled. "Yes, Hamilton. I want to take you on a proper date. What do you say?"

Gulp. "I, uh—That's a new palace name."

"Mhmm. It is. I'm expanding my options. So, what do you say? Join me Thursday night?"

Kensie froze, the moment too big. Too real. Too everything she secretly wanted but never admitted to herself.

Braelee waltzed back into the living room and hollered, "She says yes, Nicky."

Something about Braelee's dazzling smile and bright eyes gave Kensie the confidence boost she needed. She grinned at her best friend before responding to Nick. "Yes, Mr. Lancaster. I'd love to go on a Thursday night date with you. Pick me up at five, okay?"

"Wear something warm, Windsor." Nick paused, and Kensie could hear smugness infiltrating his voice even through the silence. "Or don't. I'll keep you warm."

She laughed, thrilled she knew him so well to read him over the phone. "Goodbye, Nick."

"Sweet dreams, Kensington. I'm off to read *Jane Eyre*."

Kensie ended the call, her face burning with excitement for the date and over him reading her favorite novel. Then she turned to her best friend. "You knew that's why he was calling, didn't you?"

Braelee winked. "I want you as my sister, not just my best friend. I've just been waiting for the moment you two idiots woke up and realized you're perfect for one another."

Chapter Nineteen

Nick

Nick held a bouquet of winter roses in one hand while he wiped his sweaty palm down his navy plaid, tailored dress pants before switching hands. It wasn't often he wore anything other than khakis, gym pants, or jeans, but tonight, he wanted to make a different type of impression on Kensie. He knew she'd be wearing plaid—Braelee informed him of Kensie's outfit, saying she'd fretted over it all night—and he wanted to surprise her.

Tugging at the turtleneck of his white, warm underlayer, which was mostly covered by his matching navy plaid blazer sporting gold buttons, he knocked twice on the door to apartment eight.

"Just a second," Kensie called. Nick calmed at the sound of her voice. Then he heard the sound of footsteps approaching, and the nerves spiked once more. He'd have to look at his watch later to see the jump in his heart rate. He cleared his throat and glanced down at the roses as she opened the door.

"Hi."

Nick lifted his eyes to her face, but they fell right back down her body. She wore maroon chunky-heeled boots; navy tights; a navy, gold, maroon, and white plaid skirt that sat mid-thigh, and a navy long-sleeved turtleneck tucked into her skirt. A golden bow necklace with matching earrings was a nice touch. Her hair was in its naturally curled state, pinned back to reveal her beautiful, pale, freckled face. "Gracious, Kensie. I, uh, I mean, you—"

Kensie smirked. "Looks like I've got you speechless now, Mr. Lancaster."

Nick brought his hand to his heart. "You can render me speechless anytime you want, baby." He meant every word.

"Ew." Kensie scrunched her nose. "I can't believe I'm saying this, but I think I prefer the palace names to 'baby.'"

"Noted."

Nick had momentarily forgotten about the hellebores in his hand. He gave them to Kensie. "I got these for you."

Kensie's fingers brushed his as she took the bouquet and lifted it to her freckled nose, closing her eyes and inhaling softly. "Roses are my favorite."

I know, Nick thought. But he didn't want to sound cocky. Not tonight.

"Hellebores are resilient little things. Bloom in the winter. Just like you." Nick met her eyes, and he swore he saw adoration flash across her midnight-blue irises.

"Thank you. Let me go put them in a vase, then we can go."

Five minutes later, Nick opened the truck door for Kensie to slide into his passenger seat, a mundane action he looked forward to getting used to doing. Once he was secure in the driver's seat, the truck roared to life, and he drove through the few inches of snow that had fallen during the day.

"Do you want to listen to Christmas music, or would you prefer something else, like country?"

Kensie drummed her painted fingers on her knee, and Nick had to rip his eyes back to the road once he realized he was staring at the rhythmic movement.

"Hm. I'm sort of in an *Apple Orchard Vows* mood."

Nick glanced her way and arched a brow. "Is that an artist?"

"You know, Fable Fox's album. *Apple Orchard Vows*."

"No way," Nick scoffed.

"Why not?"

"Because I'm not listening to that silly, poppy music."

Nick's gaze was straight ahead, and at Kensie's prolonged pause, he had the sinking feeling he'd made a mistake.

Finally, Kensie spoke, cool and collected. "First off, it's not just 'silly music.' That album has lyrical masterpieces on it. Secondly, this is her folklore-vibed album. Why did you even ask me what I wanted to listen to if you had zero plans to accommodate it?" Kensie snorted, then answered her own question with a sarcastic bite. "Oh, right. Because you teach P. E. and don't understand how to accommodate someone."

Nick gripped the steering wheel and spoke through his teeth. "Students have P. E. accommodations all the time, Buckingham. Don't speak to things you know nothing about."

Snow crunching under the tires occupied the silence building around them like fortified walls being reinforced.

With every passing heartbeat, Nick grew ticked at himself for not playing the stupid music from Crescent Cove's own pop star. And just as he was about to relent, Kensie spoke in a still, quiet voice. "I'm sorry. I shouldn't have said that."

"I'm sorry, too. I should have just played the music." Nick's grip on the wheel began to loosen as he pulled into The Hydeaway's moonlit, glittering, snow-covered parking lot. The hanging lights across the building's A-frame provided the extra illumination needed to navigate.

Kensie's deep exhale had Nick fully breathing again. "It's okay. It's not cool to force you to listen to something you don't want to. I guess I'm so used to firing shots at you when you say things I don't like."

Nick parked the truck and unbuckled, turning to rest his arm on the folded-down middle seat center console and giving the beautiful woman his undivided attention. "Seems we both have some adjustments to make. But I'm willing if you are." Nick slowly reached his hand to cup her smiling face.

"I am," Kensie whispered. Then, in a move that had Nick's brain frying, Kensie rested her hand over his before removing it from her face and kissing the inside of his palm. Her eyes were brighter than the Kenai River in peak summer. "Ready and willing, Mr. Lancaster."

"I can't wait anymore." Nick slipped his hand around her neck and drew her face to his, but at the last second, Kensie jerked backward, her chest heaving in panic. "I'm sorry, Kensie, I—"

"No, no." Kensie was breathless, but she forced a smile. "I'm fine. Just..." She shook her head, attempting a smile. "I'm scared to kiss you. I've never kissed anyone before."

Nick's worry eased, and a sweet smile crept across his face. "Kensie, honey." Kensie cringed, interrupting Nick to tell him how he sounded like her mother, and Nick laughed before finishing his statement. "Kiss me when you're ready, then, Windsor. Because I'll be waiting, *dreaming*, about the moment."

"Let's go eat," Kensie squeaked out, opening her door. "I'm starved!"

"Let me get the—" Nick hollered, but it was too late. Kensie had already bolted and shut the door behind her. Nick released a breath, lolled his head back onto the seat, and laughed. "Thank you, God, for this woman." Solemnly, he added, "And help me to keep her."

Moments later, Nick opened the door to the local "fancy" restaurant, if sporting taxidermied moose heads on the wall and Grizzly bear skins on the floor could be considered fancy. However, soft Christmas music played through the speakers in the corners, candle flames danced on every table center, and the few couples having a Thursday night outing were all dressed to the nines. It wasn't New York City, but it was home.

"Table for—" the hostess, a senior named Ciana, dropped her pen. "Oh my gosh. Lovë was right. You two are together!"

Nick took Kensie's hand, and for once, she didn't attempt to pull away. He looked down at her. "As long as she'll have me, we are."

Kensie met his gaze, and something flickered within her eyes. She grinned. "I'll have him if only he'll listen to Fable Fox with me."

"Ha. Ha. Ha." Nick squeezed her hand as he shook his head.

Ciana commented, "Oh, Coach. I'm with you. Maybe you should run away now if she likes Fable."

"Hush, Ciana," Kensie retorted as Ciana gathered menus in one hand. "I saw you bopping your head along to my Fable instrumentals while you were in my class two years ago."

Ciana swatted the air. "I'll deny it."

The group laughed, and Nick followed beside Kensie, hand-in-hand, as Ciana led them to a corner booth. "No kissing or getting handsy back here, or I'll use Miss Smith's teacher voice. I mastered it."

Nick watched as Kensie raised her brows, amused. "Unlike you teenage heathens, who I know I'll have to bust making out in corners at the dance tomorrow night, I don't do PDA."

Ciana dropped her gaze to where Kensie's hand was one with Nick's. "Mhmm. Sure you don't. I'll be right back to take your drink orders."

Nick and Kensie were left standing in front of the cherry oak table with maroon, cushioned seats.

Neither made a move to drop the other's hand.

"Here, you take this side." Nick pointed to the right entrance of the connecting booth. "I'll slide in here."

Reluctantly, he dropped her hand, then he met her in the middle of the booth, leaving enough space for elbow room when eating. Nick opened his menu, his body vibrating with Kensie's proximity, yet he wasn't touching her at all.

But he wanted to. He wanted to rest his hand on her thigh. Lean into her space. Kiss her forehead. Her cheek. Her lips...

"I'm going to get the fourteen-ounce ribeye and loaded potato with broccoli. What about you?" Kensie's voice snapped him out of his fantasy.

He cleared his throat. "Uh, yeah. Probably the same thing. The sixteen-ounce. Rare, of course."

Kensie gagged. "Omophagic. You disgust me."

"Huh?"

Kensie scrunched her nose. "Someone who consumes raw meat."

Nick nudged her shoulder and found he'd unintentionally slid a little closer to Kensie. "And you like the cow to turn into chewy rubber before you consume it, don't you?"

"Better than blood." Kensie grimaced. "I can't believe I'm about to watch you drink blood."

Nick chuckled, and as if he had done it a thousand times, slipped his arm around her shoulders. Their thighs touched, and Nick felt as if he'd walked through the doors of his home and put on his pajamas. "And here I thought you were the vampire of the night. Turns out it was me."

Ciana returned, took their food and drink orders, and Nick eased into conversation he never thought he'd have with Kensie as the food was brought out and they began to eat.

"So, tell me what it was like growing up without your dad?"

Kensie had just finished chewing, which Nick continuously poked fun at her for, saying she was getting a jaw workout. Her eyes widened for a breath of a second before she masked it.

Nick added, "Unless it's not something you want to talk about right now."

"No, it's not that." Kensie smiled gently. "The question just caught me off guard. Not many people are bold enough to ask."

"I'm nothing if not bold," Nick said with a tinge of self-deprecation. Kensie nodded in agreement, dabbing at her lipstick with a white napkin.

"My mom is one of the strongest, bravest, and most loving women that I know. I guess everyone says that about their mothers, but I truly mean it." Kensie's eyes took on a glassy look, as if she were fighting back tears.

"Raising a child on her own wasn't for the faint of heart. She played both mom and dad, was the primary caregiver twenty-four-seven. She wiped my snotty nose and cleaned up vomit, even when she was battling the same illnesses. She sang me to sleep when I was"—Kensie swallowed and closed her eyes—"when I was scared, even though she was scared herself. She's truly a superhero in my eyes."

Why would her mom be scared of the dark, too? Nick thought, but then he remembered Kensie didn't exactly say what they were scared of, so he asked.

A melancholic blue lensed her features. "There are many things for a woman to fear in this world."

Nick wanted to know more. He saw pain etching itself into her darkening eyes. But he didn't want to push her, and he definitely didn't want her crying on date one. So he decided to open up about his demons. "I was scared of the dark, you know."

Kensie's expression lifted. "Really?"

"Yep. Honestly, I still am a little. I sleep with a blue nightlight on."

To his surprise, Kensie didn't laugh or make fun of him. "What scares you?"

"You've met my father." Nick laughed, but it wasn't a merry sound. Kensie was quiet, waiting for him to continue. "There were many nights Braelee and I would fall asleep in my room because Mom and Dad couldn't stop bickering and fighting. Don't get me wrong. They weren't abusive to each other or anything. I think it was just early-marriage thawings or whatever. It stopped for the most part once I was like, seven, and Braelee was three."

He paused for a moment, lost in thought. "She'd take the bed, and I'd take the floor. We always sat in the dark, hearing the shattering of glass or clashing of furniture. One night, after the chaos ended, I went to check on my parents. As I was walking down the onyx-dark hallway, I stepped on glass and cut my foot. It's stupid, but I'm always afraid I'm going to step on glass when I get up and it's pitch black."

Kensie placed her hand on Nick's cheek. As her fingers lightly brushed his clean-shaven skin, a shiver rolled through him. Her voice was dripping with empathy when she spoke. "It's not stupid. Trauma from childhood haunts us better than any ghost could. Sleep with the light on. No one can tell you otherwise."

Nick clenched his fist off to his side, fighting the raging desire to kiss her. Not to taste her. Not to claim her. But to thank her. For listening. For understanding. For meeting him with knowingness instead of calling him immature like Jesena did the first night they'd slept together and she wanted the light off.

That thought punched Nick in the gut. He'd slept with Jesena. He'd slept with a few other women as well before her. Other girlfriends that he thought he might settle down with. He felt like a used rag.

Kensie deserved so much better. She'd never even kissed a man.

"Thank you," Nick managed to say as he held her gaze despite his whirling thoughts. Then, as quick as lightning and soft as a snowflake, Kensie pressed her lips to Nick's, effectively erasing her never-been-kissed status. He didn't even have time to compute what was happening before she created a girth of distance and shoved another piece of steak into her mouth.

"You kissed me." Nick blinked, attempting to clear his vision and process the moment.

"Thank you." Kensie swallowed her food and gingerly touched her bottom lip as her mouth curved into a waning moon smile. "Not only for being my first kiss, but for showing me the man no one else gets to see."

Chapter Twenty

Kensie

"**A**re you sure about this? It's a little cloudy."

"We'll still see some constellations. Don't worry." Nick winked at her, but she didn't miss the way his eyes searched her face and a struck expression overtook him before he turned back to the stargazing equipment.

Kensie and Nick stood knee-deep in snow in the open field across from Kensie's apartment building—both had put on their snowpants, jackets, and boots back in the apartment. The temperature seemed to be steadily dropping, and Kensie wished she had grabbed her beanie to go underneath the hood of her coat.

But no amount of shivering or icy fingers underneath gloves could erase the pure elation that radiated within her. *Nicolas Lancaster,* she thought to herself, laughing at God's sense of humor. Of all the men He could allow her to fall for, of course it was Nick. The one she swore she'd never entertain.

Over the span of two weeks, he'd rewritten every plan she'd carefully curated and chased down her heart.

Kensie watched him adjust the telescope. "What's your favorite constellation?"

"The one found in the freckles across your face." He looked back at Kensie—no, he devoured her in one glance, a hungry fire burning in his eyes. Then he went right back to his task at hand as if he hadn't just tilted her sky.

That look was no stranger to Kensie's senses. Longing, desiring, and needing.

She had kissed him, light as a snowflake drifting onto eyelashes, but the one moment of contact was imprinted in her mind. Kensie wanted more, but she wasn't sure if she could handle it. Not with her aversion to a man's nearness and touch. She'd been working hard at it with Nick. His arm around her at dinner was like personal protection equipment, but when he raised his hand too quickly or his face came too close, Kensie panicked while flashes of her father and mother replayed on repeat in her head. Should she tell Nick the truth about her father? After what he shared, she thought he'd understand. Maybe he'd have helpful tips for her regarding bringing it up to her mom.

"Okay." Nick stood and dusted snow off his gloves. "It's ready."

Kensie pushed the thoughts aside. Not tonight. Tonight was for romance and fun.

She shuffled through the snow, right up to Nick and the telescope. Kensie looked up, meaning to catch his eyes, but instead, she landed on his lips and shivered.

"Do I need to go get you another jacket?" Nick brought his hands to her arms, rubbing as if attempting to start a fire with sticks. She fought not to back away, reminding herself that he was safe.

Safe.

What a precious feeling to experience.

"No, I'm good." Kensie tore her eyes from him and bent down to the eyepiece of the telescope in front of her. "Show me where to look."

Nick's frame pressed against hers, his arm running the length of her own as he guided her hand to a resting spot on the black scope. Kensie shivered again, but Nick didn't question it. She felt him shiver, too, and that simple action had her careening over the edge of bliss.

"Tell me what you see." His voice was a whisper, as if he were afraid to wake the world.

Kensie watched the glowing dots dance, already wide awake. "I see the Big Dipper, but it's a little blurry."

Nick fiddled with a knob on her left, so now he had her completely caged in his arms. Kensie wanted to panic, but instead, she prayed silently, asking God to put her at ease so that she could thoroughly enjoy this moment. It wasn't immediate, but when the brightness struck clarity in the sky and Nick whispered in her ear again, the anxiety melted away. "Is that better?"

"Light-years better." *Thank You, God.*

They continued like that, swapping out who got to gaze upon the heavens and opening up about their journeys with finding their way into their reformed Christian faith, until Kensie shivered one too many times.

"Okay, we've got to get you warmed up. But first, will you walk somewhere with me? It's not too far."

Kensie nodded, dazed with images of planets and constellations inside her mind. "Mhmm."

Nick grabbed her hand and started leading her away, trudging through the snow.

"You're leaving your equipment?" Kensie asked, looking back.

"For now. I'll get it when we return from the walk and head to my place for the bonfire."

Kensie followed Nick down the familiar walking path a little way down from her apartment complex. But before they made it to the half-mile point, Nick led them off the snow-plowed paved path. "Where are we going?"

"Ah, so you haven't discovered it yet. Good."

"Discovered what? What's out here?" The woods were dark, lit only by the moonlight pouring through the trees and bouncing off the snow.

Nick laughed in response and squeezed her hand as he pulled her along. "Trust me, Windsor."

Minutes later, they came across a faded red fence with hanging locks all over it embedded in the ground, stopping people from venturing farther. Beyond it, a drop-off.

Nick placed his hands on the railing. "This is called Lover's Ledge."

"How did I not know this was here?" Kensie wondered aloud.

"A well-kept secret of the locals. It's an old tale. Fiction. Fable Fox sings about it on one of her earlier songs. I'm surprised you didn't know that."

"I'm surprised you know it since you only entertain nonfiction and don't listen to Fable Fox," Kensie pushed back in a playful tone.

Nick slipped his arm around her waist and pulled her into him, a wide grin spreading across his handsome face. "Hey, I'm reading *Jane Eyre*. And I have to know about Fable's music since she's from here. Doesn't mean I enjoy listening to it. Don't start with me."

"I like starting with you."

The inferno in Nick's eyes flared. "Are you prepared to finish it?"

Kensie redirected, certainly not prepared to finish anything. "Why did you bring me here?"

"Come this way." Nick led her to the farther end of the fence and pointed to a silver lock. Kensie moved to get a closer look and realized "WINDSOR" was written on it. She looked back at Nick, who was grinning like a love-drunk fool. "Keep going." He motioned his hand down the bridge.

Kensie set to work, looking over all the locks, trying to find ones that seemingly went with whatever Nick was up to. By the time she made it to the end, she'd found ones that read, "DANCE," "SAVE," "ME," "TOMORROW," "A," "YOU," and "WILL." It didn't take her literature degree to unscramble the phrase.

She turned to him, wearing an expression colored in shades of awe and disbelief. "But I don't dance."

Nick's face fell, and Kensie laughed softly before throwing her arms around him. "Gotcha!" She kissed his cheek in an act of boldness to match his show of thoughtfulness. "Of course I'll save you a dance. I'll save them all for you."

"Scared me for a second. I thought I was going to have to teach you how to dance in one night." Nick kissed her forehead, and that one small action, coupled with the pure adrenaline coursing through her veins, bolstered all the confidence Kensie needed.

"Kiss me, Mr. Lancaster."

Nick didn't even blink before his lips pressed fervently against hers, lingering for a moment before he began to pull away, but Kensie wasn't finished. She touched her forehead to his, their eyes locking in a winnerless war.

"*Kiss* me, Nick."

When his mouth met hers, it was in a meteorite collision of built-up tension, desire, and harbored feelings. Breaking apart and shattering throughout space. The kiss was an aurora painting the sky in vibrant streaks of love, happiness, and safety. And when they came back down to earth, Kensie was no longer concerned with the cold. She was thankful for the icy chill because Nick had lit her up from within.

An alarm went off, and the two jumped apart. Kensie looked all around her only to find the sound coming from Nick's watch. He checked it and laughed, shaking his head. "Well, Windsor. This is a first." He held up his wrist, holding back his jacket sleeve with one hand. Kensie read: *High heart rate. Your heart rate rose above 120 BPM while you seemed to be inactive for 10 minutes.*

"Oh my gosh!" Kensie howled with laughter, exponentially pleased with herself. She wondered if she could make it happen again.

Nick kissed her forehead as her laughter died down. "Yeah, yeah. You have a physical effect on me. This probably won't be the last time it happens."

Humming in agreement, Kensie kissed him again. Long and languid.

After they broke apart to catch their breath, Nick uttered, "I have one more lock." He reached into his pocket and pulled out a gold lock with "N + K" written on it. "Let's hang it together."

Chapter Twenty-One

Nick

The fire crackled and popped as Braelee laughed at something Big Bear said. Alexei was inside, and his wife, Margo, was chatting Kensie's ear off. Kensie had met Big Bear, Braelee, and Alexei before, but it was her first time meeting Margo.

"Trust me. You should have seen Nick in middle school. He hasn't always been the ladies' man you know him as today. Look." Margo showed Kensie a picture of Nick when he was acne-faced, shaved nearly bald, and sporting top and bottom braces. He wanted to snatch the phone, but the sound of joy threading Kensie's laughter stopped him. He'd sacrifice his dignity over and over if it meant hearing that sound.

Nick still wondered what secrets Kensie was hiding beneath that smile of hers, but when it looked as genuine as it did in that moment, he didn't want to be the one to rehash her history.

"Okay, okay. Enough teasing at my expense." Nick stood and stretched before checking his phone for the time.

Perfect. He'd have a little more time alone with Kensie if they left now. "Nearly ten. Don't you guys think it's time to go home?"

Alexei walked over. "Nope. It's time for a sauna."

"No way. It'll take an hour to heat up. I want you all gone by eleven." Nick smiled at Kensie. "Except for Kensie. She can stay as long as she'd like."

"Good thing I got the wood burning when I got here, then." Alexei was already grabbing Margo's hand. "Come on, everyone. Let's go. We need to sweat out any lingering diseases you three may have picked up from school."

Nick met his sister's eyes, and she shrugged. "I'm game. Big Bear?"

"Always down for a relaxing sauna. Do you have euca-lyptus with you?"

Braelee nodded.

"You guys don't even have clothes," Nick exasperated. He desperately wanted them gone so that he could have at least another hour alone with Kensie. Maybe kiss her again. Make his watch go off.

"Yeah, we do," Braelee called over her shoulder as she started toward the house.

"Always come prepared." Big Bear grinned and threw his hands up.

Kensie stepped beside Nick as they watched the other two couples disappear inside. "I didn't come prepared."

"We can stay by the fire or go inside to watch a movie while they sweat their brains out."

"No way." Kensie beamed up at Nick. "The only time I enjoyed coming over here in the past with Braelee was to use your sauna when you were supposed to be away on a hunting trip. It's heaven-sent. I'll go in my skirt and sweater if I have to."

Nick melted at the image conjured in his head, but forced it away as quickly as it came. He'd seen her use it once before when he'd come home early from a hunting trip and busted his sister. Kensie had been in a tank top and athletic shorts, looking a fever dream. He swallowed the growing lump in his throat before he finally responded. "You can borrow a shirt and gym shorts from me if you'd like. Braelee has some clothes lying around somewhere, too."

Her fingers interlaced with his, and she pulled him behind her as they made their way to the house. "Is it wrong if I say I want to wear your clothes?"

Nick couldn't stop his groan. "It's so very right, Windsor."

Ten minutes later, Nick was praying fiercely for God to help him maintain self-control. He hadn't faced temptation like this in a long while.

Seeing Kensie swallowed by his silver Crescent Cove Football t-shirt and navy gym shorts, which she'd rolled several times at the waist, had Nick's thoughts stuck like the hands of the dying analog clock in his office. Even as she sat beside him, their shoulders and thighs pressed together in the tight, dark space, he couldn't shake the image of her walking out of his bedroom wearing his clothes.

"See? This was a great idea." Alexei sprinkled eucalyptus oil into the bucket of water and then poured the mixture over the burning coals. The minty steam was a heated blanket smothering them. Coughs erupted from several people, Nick included.

"Yeah, fantastic," Braelee sounded from the dark, still hacking up a lung.

Once Nick calmed his cough, he inhaled deeply and slowly. The movement made him extra aware of the woman pressed against his side, and he moved his hand to rest on her thigh. He squeezed. So quietly, he hoped only he could hear it, she sucked in a breath, then it was her turn to cough loudly.

Grinning to himself, he patted her on the back. "There, there. Get it out, Kew."

She pushed against him as she coughed, then he wrapped his arm around her waist and tugged her closer. Her cough grew quiet, and while Big Bear made some non-funny joke, Nick whispered in Kensie's ear. "I'm starting to think Alexei is a genius."

Kensie turned her head slowly, and through the flickering coals, he could make out her lips excruciatingly close to his. "What do you mean?"

"The sauna. You in my clothes. Forced to nearly sit in my lap due to limited space." His forehead found hers.

Kensie laughed quietly, and the smell of cinnamon from her earlier tea mingled with the eucalyptus and left him dizzy. "And you said you weren't a philandering soul."

"I'm not. But I'm still a man, Kensington."

Nick lifted his free hand to her face, his fingertips kissing her balmy skin. The other couples talked to each other, and Nick had a feeling they were purposefully leaving them alone on the back bench of this homemade sauna.

"I'm waiting."

"I know."

He could barely see her eyes, which looked black in the low light of the orange coals. She was trembling despite the heat. "Don't break my heart."

Nick put his thumb under her chin and lifted her mouth mere breaths from his. "I'm more afraid of you breaking mine." He touched his lips to hers and spoke against them. "We both have scars. I'll love yours. Please love mine."

He kissed her tenderly. She sighed, long and slow. "Love?"

"Yeah." Nick fingered back wet hair from her face. "I think I mistook my affection for agitation. I've had a thing for you for a while. I adore who you are. I was aggravated to stand by and watch people take advantage of your kindness and your willingness to help. It made me sick to think about, and I projected it as a weakness onto you."

"Nick..."

"It's your strength." Nick breathed a laugh, unable to believe he was confessing it all to her. "Though I will continue to teach you how to say no sometimes."

She met his laughter and then kissed him. "I genuinely didn't like you. But I'm falling for you. Right here. Right now."

He hadn't blatantly said "I love you," so why did something in Nick's gut twist over the fact that she didn't say that four-letter word in any capacity as he had? He let it roll off his shoulders because, at the end of the day, what she did say was enough. It lit a fire of hope within him. One day, after he'd given her enough time to adjust to the idea of *Nick + Kensie*, just as he'd written on the lock via their initials, he'd boldly declare his love for her. Because he knew she was all he wanted.

"That's enough for me, Windsor."

The night drew to an end, and he parted ways with everyone. Nick lay in bed, reading. Rochester had just proposed to Jane, and Nick wondered why she said yes to such a man. There was a foreboding, dark feeling. Secrets left unspoken. And for the love of all good things, Nick found he didn't want to put the stupid book down.

Chapter Twenty-Two

Kensie

K ensie plopped down onto the sound stage and dropped her head into her hands before groaning, "This always happens!" It was a bit dramatic, but she *really* didn't want to climb a ladder to hang the decorative shiny stars back onto the ceiling. Especially not in her silky, deep-maroon dress. It was cinched in the waist, flowy elsewhere, and versatile. Plus, she was wearing her white, sparkly sneakers, but that didn't mean she wanted to climb up and down five times before the long night.

Nick sat beside her, his sleeves rolled in that hot, careless way men with great forearms can pull off, and took her hand. "That's why I'm here. You don't have to climb. You just need to hold the ladder steady so I don't die, yeah?"

Kensie's frustration dissipated, and she grinned. "Deal. I'm glad I like you now. If I still hated you, I would have insisted on climbing the ladder just to show you how independent and capable I am."

"I know how capable and independent you are, believe me. But you don't have to be when you're with me. Let me take care of you." Nick kissed her forehead, and she welcomed it, not flinching away.

Safe.

Nick stood and Kensie followed, lingering a little behind him to admire the way he walked. Or, more so, admire the way his black pants fit him perfectly. Don't get her started on the way he filled out that button-down that matched the color of her dress.

Kensie's phone rang from behind the stage. "Let me check that real quick." She left Nick fixing the ladder into place and answered her phone with a knot in her stomach.

"Hi, Vickie. Almost here? We could use a little help with some fallen decorations."

Kensie knew what this phone call meant, but she was still pleading for the best.

"I'm not going to make it tonight. I've caught a cold."

Kensie bit her lip in frustration but kept her voice pleasant. "Oh, that's all right. I'm sure I'll get it all taken care of. Thanks for letting me know."

Vickie went on saying something on the other end of the line, but Kensie was watching Nick climb the ladder, and she knew what he'd tell her to do. With a shaky voice, she interrupted Vickie's spiel. "Actually, Vickie, I really need you here. We need all the supervision we can get tonight, and you signed up specifically for this event at the beginning of the year. If you're not actively dying or running a fever, please show up for your simple hour and a half shift."

She ripped the phone from her ear and pressed the "end call" button ten times as her heart raced and hands trembled. Kensie simultaneously felt like crawling under a rock and shouting from the mountaintop.

"I did it!"

Nick looked down at her as she raced to the bottom of the ladder, beaming up at him with adrenaline coursing through her skin.

"Vickie called and was trying to back out of helping tonight, but I was firm and told her that I needed her here and that she'd signed up for this. I held my ground."

With the smile the size of her mother's when Kensie brought home her report card of all A's, Nick descended the ladder and wrapped Kensie in a warm hug, whispering in her ear. "I'm so proud of you, Windsor. I know that wasn't easy. Especially to Vickie."

Kensie laughed, squeezing him through her shot nerves. "I felt like a scared cat, but I did it anyway."

Nick ran his fingers down her back, and Kensie arched into his touch. They gazed into each other's eyes. "Thank you for being you." Kensie pressed a light kiss to his lips. "For reminding me that I can say no and that I can hold my ground."

"You've always been capable." Nick tugged her into him, holding her tighter as their foreheads pressed together. A mischievous grin crossed his face. "I'm living proof."

She pushed him away in her laughter, and they set back to work hanging stars.

"What were you like during high school dances when you attended school here?" Kensie asked as Nick hung one of the fallen stars.

"You sure you want to know?"

Kensie grimaced as she thought of the homecoming dance a couple of months earlier and second-guessed herself for a moment. "Yes, I do. I want to know exactly who you were then and who you are today."

"I warned you." Nick climbed down the ladder. "I was the testosterone-fueled teenage boy in the middle of the Grind Circle, trademark pending. And yes, we called it that even then."

He hauled the ladder to the next fallen star while Kensie scrunched her nose, willing images of a teenage Nick in the middle of the Grind Circle out of her head. Control-Alt-Delete, please and thank you.

"That doesn't shock me." She moved to hold the ladder again. "I never went to a dance at my high school."

"Why not?"

"Because I was never invited. I was too scared of what people would think if I went alone."

Nick looked down at her from the top of the ladder. "Tell me you had friends in school, right?"

Kensie nodded and smiled. "One. Her name is Frankie Sellers. She's a teacher and coach back home at Willow Bay High School now. We don't talk often since I moved, but I know she's only a phone call away. And when we do talk, it's like no time has passed at all."

"Why didn't you two go together?"

"She always had a date. She married her middle school sweetheart."

Nick descended and wrapped Kensie in a hug. For some reason, she wanted to cry for the girl who craved to go to dances but allowed her fear of people to stop her. But she pushed back the tears. She didn't want to ruin her makeup before the night officially started.

"That's sweet for them, but I'm sorry you never experienced a dance." He pulled away, but his hands lingered on her bare arms, his thumbs rubbing circles into her biceps. "I'll have to help you make up for it tonight."

"I'm not grinding against you."

Nick chuckled and pulled her close. "We don't need to dance dirty to dance flirty, Miss Smith."

Kensie's knees went weak. It was the first time he'd ever called her that after two and a half years of mandating it, and she wanted to record it in her heart and press replay again and again.

Nick started to lead Kensie in a dance to a tune only meant to be heard through the rhythmic beating of their hearts. But then, Kensie had an idea. She broke away from him, holding one finger up as she bounded backward. "Give me just a second." She rushed to turn off the big lights, flicked on the light that would reflect off the spinning disco ball, and turned on the various fairy lights within the space. It truly felt like an aurora night by the time she hooked the old iPod up to the sound station and clicked on the first slow song she found. As the opening chords to "Chasing Cars" by Snow Patrol sounded, Kensie placed herself right back into Nick's waiting arms.

"I used to practice steps alone. Be my first dance."

When Nick didn't immediately start leading her, a shyness seeped in. Just when she meant to pull away and say never mind, Nick yanked her into his chest. "I love this song."

Kensie tossed her head back, her curls bouncing against her back. "*Grey's Anatomy?*"

Nick spun her around, and she felt like a princess as her dress billowed around her. She was extra thankful she wore her biker shorts underneath. When he tugged her back into him, he kissed her. "Yes. Braelee forced me to watch it with her and Mom."

"Ah, so you do have good memories with at least one parental figure."

"I have amazing memories with both. Deep-sea fishing and hunting with Dad. Gardening with Mom." Nick sighed reminiscently, and Kensie dropped his hands in favor of wrapping her arms around his neck. "It's not like it was always bickering, fighting, and screaming."

Nick slid both hands around her waist. They officially resembled the classic, awkward couple.

Except nothing about the moment was awkward.

She once thought working with Nick would be like dancing with the devil. No, dancing with Nick was like floating in the particles of light itself. Glowing. Twinkling. Blinding.

"Tell me all the *good* things about your father."

As they swayed back and forth, Kensie fingered the budding tears from his eyes as he recounted the time he caught his first salmon, was given his first truck, and all the times he helped his dad fix things around the house. "But ever since he stepped into public office, it's consumed him. Consumed our family. All he seems to care about these days is image."

Kensie pushed back the water pooling in her eyes. Did she have any pleasant memories of her father that she could recall?

Not really. Only drunken rages, the smell of soiled carpet, and thick clouds of cigarette smoke. What had her mom been thinking about getting involved with a man like that? Kensie resolved to call her mom tomorrow. If for nothing else but to ask her about her father, as she did often as a child, but never as an adult.

And she was going to do whatever it took to help restore whatever Nick and his father had lost. "Let's go to the gala tomorrow."

The song slowed to an end, but Nick didn't let go. "Do what?"

Kensie steeled herself. "Let's go to the gala. I want to prove to your father that I'm a woman worthy of his son. That what you and I have isn't fleeting or fading, but has been brewing under layers of buried feelings for a long time."

"It has been a long time coming, hasn't it?" Nick smiled and pulled on a curl. It bounced back into position when he let go. "I love your curls. I don't think I've told you that before."

Kensie preened, and she tucked away the comment to relish in later as she fell asleep. If anyone could make her love her curls, it would, of course, be Nick. "I rather like yours, too." Kensie tugged at a piece of hair on his neckline, teasing. Dragging her finger down his neck and across his shoulder.

Nick groaned and closed his eyes before clearing his throat. "Okay. Let's go to the gala. But if he says one negative thing or compliments you underhandedly even once, just know I'm not responsible for whatever comes out my mouth."

Kensie laughed. "I'd expect nothing less out of you."

He kissed her cheek before his fingers slid up her back and around her waist, resting right below her ribcage. Nick gave her a squeeze, a sly smile stretching across his face. "I remember seeing a butterfly tattoo right about here." His fingers burned through her dress.

"I, uh, yeah." Kensie was lost in his touch.

Nick relented, slipping his hands back around her, a winner's smile showcasing the dimpled trophy. "Tell me about it."

Bringing her hands to his chest, she stepped in pace with him. "It's a butterfly with the colors of the sunset on the beach. Mom has one, too, on her wrist. We got them when I turned eighteen as a symbol of new beginnings and freedom." Kensie swallowed back heavy emotion, now fully understanding exactly what her mother wished to be renewed from. But she wasn't telling Nick about that tonight. Instead, she fingered a strand of honey-brown hair that had fallen in his face and softly pushed it aside. "She loves the beach. She loves butterflies. I was officially an adult, and it'd always been the two of us, so I said, 'Why not?'"

"Breaking in the dance floor?" a feminine voice called from down the hallway.

Kensie turned to see Lori approach, wearing her classic black pencil skirt and white top. It was the same outfit she wore to all the dances.

"It's good to see you two not at each other's throats," Lori continued as they broke apart and the song slowed to an end.

"I'm always at her throat," Nick commented before tossing a wink at Kensie. She blushed, embarrassed. Mostly because nothing like that had even happened outside of the vampire incident at the Christmas parade.

But right as she opened her mouth to object, the next song on the playlist roared to life, drowning out her protests as DJ Casper belted, "It's time to get funky!"

Lori placed her hands on her knees and...

"Oh my gosh!" Kensie covered her mouth, but it wasn't enough to stop her boisterous laugh at the sight of her head secretary twerking to the beat of the song. Nick, to absolutely no one's surprise, joined in. They beckoned Kensie, but she backed away, waving her hands as if to say, "Absolutely not."

"Don't let fear of people's opinions stand in your way of having fun, Hampton Court," Nick shouted above the thumping bass. "Remember who you are: Kensington Marie Smith! Princess of Crescent Cove!"

"We aren't judging," Lori echoed, throwing her hands in the air and spinning.

Kensie bit her bottom lip, indecisiveness bouncing around her brain. But when she saw Nick hold a hand out to her, she took it, and the three of them completed the "Cha Cha Slide" before guzzling water, finishing putting the fallen stars back up, and dragging out the snacks for the night.

An hour into the dance, Kensie was sweating bullets.

"How in the world did we fit four hundred kids in here?" She hung her head out of the door for a breath of wintry air. Outside felt like a freezer, and she'd never been more thankful for it than in that moment.

Lori, sitting in the arctic entryway and stacking all the tickets she'd received, shrugged her shoulders. "I don't know, but every year, we're getting bigger and bigger."

"We're going to have to relocate this shindig to the armory or something next year."

"I like it when your Southern slips out." Lori chuckled. The song inside switched to something slower, so Kensie thought she'd take the opportunity to make another round through the dance floor to pick up any trash that might have been accidentally dropped.

"I'll be back to breathe soon." She waved and entered back into the dance.

The energy was palpable. Dresses were glittering like the disco ball hanging in the middle of the roof, faces were flushed, but the smiles were miles wide. Kensie couldn't help but feel a sense of pride. She might not have appreciated the dirty dancing in the middle of the floor, but she was grateful she could play a part in providing a memorable, fun experience to the students of Crescent Cove. In a short two and a half years, this place had become home.

Home.

Kensie thought about Mississippi. Something inside her pushed her to call her mom. Kensie hadn't spoken on the phone with her since her memories had resurfaced. She'd texted and sent Snapchats, but she hadn't heard her mom's voice. She had an overwhelming urge to pick up the phone.

Navigating through the couples remaining on the floor, enjoying their moment with their significant other, she picked up a few paper cups and fallen decorations. Yes, another star had fallen.

And now it was trash.

"Miss Smith!" a few of her students collectively hollered. They did this every time she passed them, and like every other time, Kensie waved. "Hi! Having a good—*agh!*"

Kensie looked to her left to see who she'd accidentally shoulder-checked. The most beautiful man in the world smiled down at her. Even with sweat rolling down his face and staining his pits, she still thought no other man could compare to the perfection that was Nick Lancaster. *My, my, how my thoughts have shifted,* she laughed to herself.

Aloud, she said, "I'm sorry. I didn't see you there."

"May I have this dance, Windsor?" Nick was already slipping his hand around her waist. Kensie panicked.

"The kids are watching."

Nick pulled her close and whispered, "Let's show them how to really dance."

He spun her once, just as the song transitioned to the title track of *Apple Orchard Vows* by Fable Fox. "You didn't!" Kensie exclaimed, bliss rolling through her as Nick led her into a Western swing.

"Lovë helped me sneak this on there earlier today."

If she wasn't still frightened by the idea of the kids watching her dance with Nick, she might have cried. But instead, she allowed herself to be spun, dipped, and swept around the circle the students had formed. She danced with Nick until everyone else faded from her mind, and all she could see was his contagious smile and one small dimple on the left side. "Thank you," she mouthed as Fable sang the last line of the song and Nick brought them to a slow sway.

Without warning, he kissed her, and she lost herself in him for the smallest of moments before a roaring cheer brought her back to reality. She pushed Nick away and wiped her lips, but the glee on the students' faces told her she had nothing to be embarrassed about. She was a grown woman. Nick was a grown man. They were a couple. And the kiss was a mere lingering press of lips.

Kensie reached for Nick, and he took her hand, leading her toward the front doors. Good. She needed fresh air.

They passed through the arctic entryway and waved to Lori before throwing open the door and stepping into the frigid night. She followed Nick a few steps to the edge of the awning cover, where a thick layer of snow from today's weather had accumulated, separating the school from the parking lot.

"Ah, that's nice." Nick threw his head back, eyes closed. Kensie mimicked the action, except she hadn't closed her eyes, and when she met the sky, an explosion of vibrant green greeted her overhead.

"Nick! The aurora's actually out!" She pointed to the sky with one hand and slapped his arm with the other, giddy with happiness. "Thank You so much, Jesus!"

They stood in amazement, staring at the show.

"I've seen the aurora a thousand times, and it's always different. Just like my athletes running the same plays over and over, yet somehow, they always find a way to mix it up."

Kensie laughed and leaned into Nick's side. He lazily draped his arm around her hips and tugged her closer. She'd seen the aurora a few times since moving here, and she often wondered what it would be like to gaze upon its majestic hues as it danced and sang tunes only the heavens could hear with a man by her side. When she tore her eyes away from the show to gaze at Nick, she caught sight of a moose eating from a tree, but thankfully, it was far enough away and minding its own business. She loved it here. This moment. This sky. This moose.

This man.

"Should we go tell the kids?" Kensie asked.

Nick shook his head and kissed her forehead. "Let's have this moment for another minute. Besides, you need to explain to me why you gave me a book to read about a mad wife, traitorous spouse, and morally conflicted woman."

"Do you love it?" The hope in Kensie's voice was buoyant.

Nick shook his head. "I kind of hate these characters."

"But that's why the story is so good. It makes you feel and experience and search."

He snorted. "No lie. I was up too late reading. But I'm not finished yet, so I don't have a conclusive answer for you."

"Fair enough." She wouldn't push him, but she smiled knowingly to herself.

Kensie looked to the performing sky and then back to the man who'd stolen her heart. Every impish remark. Every time he called her on her crap. Every moment of loathing that led to here. The aurora was dazzling, but Nick was mesmerizing. She clung to him as colors permeated the night, while a shrouded voice in her head taunted, *All shows come to an end.*

"I can't believe it actually showed. Judging by the weather earlier, I thought it was a lost cause."

Nick nodded. Kensie turned her attention back to the sky as Nick spoke. "Thank you, Kensie. For pointing me back to Jesus. You know, my friends had been praying for me. I had no idea. But earlier, when you said that I was exactly what you prayed for, I wished I could have said the same thing back." Kensie rested her head on his shoulder but remained silent. The wobbling uncertainty in his voice told her that he wasn't finished.

Plumes of hot breath from their breathing rose, and Nick continued. "I want to be the man who prays for you. For his friends. For his family." His head rested against hers. "I will be that man. I promise you. I just..."

Kensie heard the surrender in his voice. "Yeah?"

"I just wanted you to know that. I won't become like my father. *Ever.* You never have to worry about that with me, okay? I vow it. Tonight's the solstice—a time of new beginnings. This is *our* beginning, Kensington. Despite the past. Despite our upbringings."

A shiver ran through Kensie at that moment, and Nick pulled her closer. "Shoot. I don't have my jacket to give you. Let me go inside and—"

"No, it's okay." Kensie lifted her head and gazed into his eyes as she placed her palm on his chest. "I'll grab both of ours." She needed a moment to process not only what he had said, but how he had said it. As if the words were a binding agreement he was scared he would break, despite his strongest intentions. As if he had to reassure himself.

As she turned to walk inside, her thoughts spun with the sincerity in his voice and the fire behind his commitment. This was real. Kensie wasn't a passing phase for him. The more she'd gotten to know the heart of the man who tormented her days and occasionally her sleepless nights, the more she understood him, related to him, and felt for him. She was beginning to love him. *God, what are You doing? Is this my forever? It's what I've prayed for, so why am I scared to have it?*

But she didn't need a sign to tell her why.

She had a past in screaming red, telling her everything she needed to know.

Kensie snagged their jackets from behind the sound stage, and on her way out, she told Lori that the aurora was lighting up the sky and to send the kids out after the next song.

The cool night teased her skin, no longer the refreshing touch she needed. Now, with her thoughts in a tizzy, the frigid air was a foreboding knife.

"Look." Nick beamed at her and pointed toward the west. "Red hues are coming out."

Like blood pouring out upon the sky.

She stitched a smile onto her lips.

God, make the thoughts go away. Nick isn't my father. Spending forever with him doesn't mean I will end up like my mother or will put my kids through what I went through. He swears it. Dark forces whispered in her mind that Nick could turn out exactly like his father.

Kensie's phone vibrated, and she fished it out of her jacket pocket. She had three missed calls from her best friend back home, Frankie. *That's odd.* A blossom of panic for her friend bloomed. Before she could call her back, her phone was ringing again.

"Hey Frankie, everything okay?"

"Oh, thank God." Frankie was breathless. "Marie is unconscious in the hospital. She was stabbed by an escaped convict they're calling Roman. I'm still trying to figure out all the details. Are you able to come home soon?"

Roman.

The heavens glowed above Kensie as her world fell into a dark chasm. The ice from outside found its way into Kensie's veins as she tried to make sense of what she was hearing. "Wh–what?"

"Are you able to come home? I can pay for your ticket if you need the money. I don't know what's going to happen to your mom."

Kensie's mind went numb, rational instincts taking over. "I'll take the first flight out. Keep me updated. I love you."

She ran inside just as the kids were coming out. Stuck in a parade of heels and sequins, she finally forced her way through. In a voice that didn't belong to her, Kensie spoke to Lori. "I have to leave. It's my mom. She's in the hospital."

"Go. I've got you covered." Lori's saddened eyes were the last thing Kensie remembered seeing before she found herself being jerked backward as she tried to leave the school.

"Kensie, what in the world is going on?" Nick's grip on her forearm had her in a state of terror. When she met his eyes, they were pools of frustration. "You just ran away from me out there. Talk to me. Who was on the phone?"

His grip got tighter as he spoke. "Let me go," Kensie bit out.

Nick flicked his gaze to his hand and immediately released her arm. "I'm sorry, I didn't mean to hurt you."

Roman. Dad is alive. Dad attacked Mom. Mom is dying. Kensie's head was spinning, images of her dad's face merging with Nick's. "Leave me alone. I've got to go."

Nick stepped toward her, and she flinched backward. "Don't come any closer."

He froze long enough for her to run.

She bolted. Thoughts of her mother dying in a hospital bed while her father got the last laugh were pushing her through the long, sinister night.

Chapter Twenty-Three

Nick

The phone dug into Nick's palm as he white-knuckled the steering wheel with his other hand. He had tried to call Kensie a thousand times, and now, he was being sent straight to voicemail.

Nick cursed and hit the wheel as his life crumbled around him.

The woman he loved completely shut him out in a time of turmoil. He'd spoken with Lori, who said Kensie was heading back to Mississippi because her mom was in the hospital.

Images of Kensie's fear-filled eyes as she stared at him before she left haunted him. Why had she looked at Nick as if he were the cause?

Not much later, Nick pulled into Kensie's parking lot. Her car was still there. Good.

He cut the engine and made his way inside the complex. When he stood in front of apartment eight, he knocked twice. A minute later, Kensie opened the door, her now-makeupless face as white as a ghost and eyes rimmed with red. "What are you doing here? I said leave me alone."

"Don't shut me out, Kensie. Lori told me what was going on. Let me take you to the airport at least. You shouldn't be driving like this." Nick stepped forward, but Kensie hid herself behind the door, only her head poking out.

"Please don't force yourself inside." Her voice was littered with fear, and Nick's heart broke. What exactly had Kensie been keeping from him all this time? Did it have something to do with her father? The stuff she didn't want to talk—

Nick's blood went hot at the idea that her father had somehow hurt her in the past.

"Kensie, listen to me. I am not going to hurt you. I am not going to force myself into your apartment. But please, let me help you."

Tears welled in her eyes. "I can't. I'm sorry. I thought I was ready." She shook her head, the pile of hair in a bun flopping. "Please, leave. *I* need to leave."

"Kensie, just—"

She shut the door.

Nick wanted to rage. He wanted to bang on the door and demand she accept his love and his help, but he knew if she was coming from any semblance—most likely worse—of an environment he was a product of, that was the absolute last thing he needed to do.

Like a despondent ghost haunting the aurora night, Nick shuffled through snow, got into his truck, and drove to his cabin in the woods. He walked through the creaking door, walked across the creaking floor, and lay down in his creaking bed.

That's what life felt like for Nick at the moment—unstable, uneasy, and uncertain.

"God, Kensie says that You listen. My friends say that You listen. I'm working on believing that. I can say all day long that I'm fully on board, but right now, it's hard to keep that faith."

Nick rolled onto his side, unbothered by his fully dressed state. He briefly wondered if this was what his friend Noah had felt before the woman he loved came back to him. If so, no wonder it took him a while to find peace again.

To trust God again.

He closed his eyes and spoke aloud once more. "Help me to understand what You're doing. Because I have no clue, and uncertainty is terrifying in the face of losing someone you love."

Nick sighed, waiting for the peace that was supposed to fill him when he turned things over to God, but it was nowhere to be found. He checked his phone one more time, but there was no message. No missed call. Just a picture of the woman he hoped came back around, staring at him through tempered glass.

He picked up *Jane Eyre*, and Reader, he finished the novel in a heap of tears.

Nick awoke with a groggy start, hoping that when he opened his eyes, he'd have a message from Kensie telling him good morning, that she couldn't wait to see him at work, and then at the dance tonight.

But he knew that wouldn't happen.

Because that was yesterday's memory.

And days couldn't be rewound, no matter how many times you reset the clock.

He checked his phone, begging the device to show him a text message from Kensie, at least letting him know she was safe. Maybe she would have responded to his text about how he could relate to parts of Jane Eyre's redemption or her longing for a family life that felt so out of reach.

Only promotional emails, texts from his friends, and a message from his father reminding him of the gala tonight.

The gala.

"For the love of it all." Nick groaned into his pillow, throwing his phone on the other end of the plaid, quilted blanket.

He'd forgotten all about the stupid gala that Kensie made him commit to at the last minute last night. He wished he'd never texted his father to tell him that they were coming.

His phone rang, and Nick scrambled from the bed as if he was being attacked by a bear. He grabbed the device, which had fallen to the floor, and wanted to shatter it when he saw it was Braelee and not Kensie.

But he answered anyway. "Hey."

"Good, you're up. Have you heard from Kensie yet?"

"No. Have you?"

Braelee exhaled slowly. "No. Not since she told me she made it to Anchorage last night."

"And you didn't tell me?" Nick clenched his fist. His sister should have known to give him such a vital piece of information that Kensie had at least made it safely.

"I sent you a—" her voice faded before returning in full force. "Shoot. My text didn't send. Sorry."

Nick bit his tongue before answering. "It's okay. Thanks for thinking of me."

"Are you still coming to the gala with us tonight?"

Her tone was hopeful and expecting, and Nick didn't want to shatter that. What else was he going to do? Kensie was clear to leave her alone. If he had any shot of salvaging the mutual trust and respect he thought they'd built—and a semblance of hope to not have another woman he thought he might one day marry walk away from him—he had to honor her requests. So, he could sit at home and wait for a call, or he could sit at a gala and wait for a call and make his family happy for once.

"Yeah, but I'm driving myself still. Just in case..."

He didn't have to finish the sentence, and Braelee didn't need him to. "Yeah, okay. Well, I'll see you tonight. Let me know if you need anything."

There wasn't really anything for his little sister to do, but he was thankful for her nonetheless. "Love you."

"I love you, too."

She hung up, and Nick called Wayne, who immediately invited Nick over for counsel.

The gala felt like a grown-up version of the dance from last night. Glittering snowflakes covered the ceiling, ornate Christmas trees decorated the walls, and, instead of serving store-bought meat and cheese platters with water, they had tables of fruits, vegetables, and foods Nick couldn't even begin to pronounce, along with various champagnes.

The ballroom in the Dena'ina Civic and Convention Center was spacious; however, it was full to the brim with wealthy, prominent people from all over Alaska. Politicians, businessmen, investors, lawyers, doctors, you name it.

Nick felt suffocated in his tuxedo and quickly tugged off the bow tie. He didn't care what others thought. He wanted to make his appearance and then disappear. Wayne told him earlier that he should seek amends with his father before attempting to chase down Kensie, but honestly? Nick wasn't sure he was up for it.

"Son, I'm glad you showed up." Senator Lancaster, dressed to the nines with his golden-blond hair styled back, clapped Nick's back before pinching at his shoulder and offering him a glass of champagne from a waitress who passed by. "I was sorry to hear Kensie wasn't going to be accompanying you tonight."

His dad's voice didn't sound sorry at all. In fact, he sounded gleeful.

Nick's stomach soured, and he denied the bubbly liquid. "Yeah, it's a shame you don't get to meet her. I was hoping you would get to redeem yourself from your previous encounter with her.

Eyes the same dark-brown as Nick's, flashed with aggravation as his father clenched his jaw. To Nick's shame, he realized it was like looking in a mirror. When Nick was frustrated or angry, he looked just as terrifying as his father. No wonder Kensie pushed him away last night.

"No matter. I asked someone else to come." He motioned to a corner, and Nick followed. Out of a group of people stepped an icy witch he knew all too well.

"Dad. What are you doing?" Nick bit out as Jesena Hayes walked their way.

His dad whispered through a smile. "Win her back. We need her family connections. If we have her, then we have her brother on our side. You know just how much influence Chase Hayes has in the conservative media."

Nick was about to retort that he would never date a woman to bring his dad more influence, but Jesena, in a tight black dress with a plunging neckline revealing too much, had already approached and went in for a hug. "Hi, Nick. How have you been?"

"Jesena." Nick stepped backward from her attempt. "I'm well. And you?"

She flicked her eyes between Nick and his father, confusion shining through dark-blue irises as she dropped her arms. But she kept her bright white smile framed with vivid red lipstick intact. "Much better now that your father informed me that you were ready to work things out with me, though I expected to hear that from you, not him."

"I'll leave you two to it," his father said, spinning on his heel. Nick grabbed him by the arm.

"Tell her the truth." Nick yanked his father to his side. The action must have caught his mother's attention, because she joined them from another group, quickly taking her husband's arm from Nick.

His father remained quiet.

"Fine. I will." Nick grinned sardonically at his father before facing the woman standing still with shock. "Jesena, I'm sorry you've wasted your time. As I said before, I have no interest in dating you again. My dad thinks he can use you to get to your brother, which I don't agree with and won't participate in. I do wish you the best in life, but it won't be a life with me."

He turned to his red-faced father just as Braelee and Big Bear joined the party. "And as for you, I will not allow you to disrespect me, Kensie, Jesena, Chase, or our family in this capacity. You are not a puppet master; you do not get to pull the strings of our lives for your political advancement."

Though conversations and laughter filled the room, Nick's world was silent as he stared into his father's raging eyes. Years of good and bad clashed in a cacophony of memories, warring over whether to walk away or to beg his father to change.

Nick finally found words to continue. "If you want to keep a relationship with me after this moment, you will stop. You will change. You will not use your family for your own advancement, and you will be the father I once knew before politics consumed your soul. The one who taught me life skills and took me to church and taught me about the Bible. I'll gladly have a relationship with that man, but not the one you've become."

Having nothing more to say to his father, Nick nodded once to Jesena, hugged his mother and whispered that he loved her, waved to his sister and best friend, then walked toward the exit. His heart was bruised in many places, and he felt as if his bones were breaking from the release of pressure. He had needed to say that to his father for a long time, and now that he had, he was simultaneously relieved at getting it off his chest and anxious about what his father would choose—Nick or his career.

This was the best he had to offer, and Nick was sickly at peace over it.

"Nick, wait up!" Big Bear hollered from somewhere inside the ballroom after Nick crossed the threshold into the foyer. His friend came bounding out the door in his khaki pants and button-up shirt—the definition of "dressed up," according to the bartender. Braelee followed on his heels, wearing a pretty yellow dress that had looked wonderfully out of place in the sea of white, black, silver, and navy inside the ballroom.

Leaning against a wall, Nick waved them over.

Braelee launched herself into his arms, and he heard her sniffle against his neck. "Thank you for saying what I've wanted to say for a long time. That wasn't easy, I know. Are you okay?"

Nick hugged her close, inhaling that floral perfume she'd worn for as long as he could remember. "Yeah, I'm okay. I feel relieved, actually."

Big Bear stood off to the side, watching the siblings, but when Nick caught his eye, he smiled, inviting him into the conversation. Braelee stepped away from Nick and grabbed Big Bear's hand.

"That took guts," Big Bear remarked, patting Nick on the back. "I don't think I could have ever stood up to my dad like that, but I'm glad you had the chance to before it's too late."

They all nodded in sympathy with Big Bear, who had lost his father years ago to suicide after his father's long battle with substance abuse. It always shocked Nick that Big Bear would own a bar and make his own brews, but

Big Bear had always just said that the alcohol wasn't the problem; it was the person and their demons.

Thinking of people and their demons brought Kensie back to Nick's mind. "Have you heard from Kensie?" Braelee had messaged Nick at lunch to tell him that Kensie was with her mom. He had felt his chest ease, but now, everything was wound up again.

Braelee shook her head.

Unsure of whether he should ask the next question plaguing his mind, he decided it was better to know than not to know. "What do you know about Kensie's father?"

Big Bear and Braelee exchanged knowing looks, and when they turned their sorrowful expressions onto Nick, he didn't need her to answer to know the truth. The way Kensie had had a hard time adjusting to his nearness at first, the way she had reacted last night, the vague comments about her father and how she didn't want to talk about him...It all pointed to the signs Nick knew to be abuse. He had had years of training on it as an educator, and Kensie demonstrated all the mental turmoil of a broken childhood.

Nick released a breath, running a hand through his hair as he tapped his foot.

"I'm sorry, Nick. She asked me not to tell you. Please don't be mad." Braelee pleaded.

Nick nodded, dragging his hand down his jaw. He pegged his sister with a determined look. "Tell me this. Is her dad the reason her mom's in the hospital?"

Braelee, with doe-eyes filling with tears, nodded once. "And according to Kensie's last message, her dad took some wounds, too, and is at the same hospital currently."

"Forget Kensie's request, I'm going after her," Nick muttered under his breath as a savior-switch flicked on within him. All he could think about was Kensie in the hands of her wretched father. Louder, he demanded, "What hospital is she at?"

"St. Ann's in Willow Bay, Mississippi. Let me bring you to the airport. Big Bear can drive your truck home."

Nick hugged his sister. "Thank you. Don't tell her I'm coming. I don't need her freaking out before I even get there. I'll handle the fallout."

He was at the airport thirty minutes later, purchasing the earliest ticket he could and paying extra to avoid more than one short layover in Minneapolis. Praise God, Nick thought as he learned the flight he would board had been delayed due to maintenance. If it hadn't been, the only other flight would have been one leaving in three hours. Nick didn't have it in him to wait that long.

He hadn't bothered to bring anything but the overnight bag he always kept in his truck for emergencies, his phone, and a charger. He even left his sanity back with Braelee, apparently, as he knew he was most likely digging his own grave with this grand show of affection for Kensie. But he didn't care. He needed to know she was safe, and he needed to be that safety for her.

After securing the ticket, he began to make his way toward TSA. As he took the stairs, something reflecting light caught his attention. He noticed a deep ruby gemstone set inside a golden band lying on the floor off to the side of a step. He paused; it looked expensive, and some woman was probably missing it. However, he was crunched for time, so he stuck it in his pocket with intentions to return it to the front desk whenever he found his way back to Alaska.

Once through TSA, he ran to his plane, which was already boarding, and sent a silent prayer of gratitude up to God.

Chapter Twenty-Four

Kensie

*B*eep.
 Beep.
Beep.
Her hands were cold.

Kensie sandwiched her mother's hands and breathed. "I've asked them to bring another blanket," she whispered. "They're coming soon. I promise." She brushed her finger down the shallow wrinkles in her mother's forehead and took to memorizing her features once more. An action she'd done over and over since arriving in room 212 early in the morning hours after they took her out of the ICU yesterday. Thankfully, Frankie was around when they made the switch, so her mother wasn't truly alone while she waited for her only child to arrive. Kensie held so much gratitude for her childhood friend. Especially because she didn't make it in until after lunch on Saturday.

It was now Sunday morning, and Kensie was desperate for her mom to wake up. Angry bruises had blossomed under her mom's eyes. Her nose was set in a stint, and her bottom lip busted. Purpling fingerprints were embedded in her neck. Even doctored up, the sight was gruesome.

That was just her face.

If Kensie were to lift her mother's sheet, she'd find a stitched, swollen abdomen, bandaged. Thank God all vital organs were left unscathed. Now, it was up to God to wake her mother up and prevent her from developing an infection.

All she could do was pray and recruit the help of others to pray. Kensie texted Tarin, letting her know there wasn't an update, before relaying the same information to Braelee.

Thinking of Braelee brought Nick to mind, and Kensie couldn't bear the thought of his haunted eyes as she closed the door in his face. The whole way home, all she could think of was what a massive mistake she'd made in closing him out, but it was done and over with now.

He'd read and loved her favorite book. For nothing.

Kensie traced the sunset beach-colored butterfly on her mother's wrist. "So much for new beginnings. It looks like we keep returning to old patterns, don't we, Mom?"

A knock sounded at the door, and a kind, older nurse poked his head in. Kensie smiled at the elderly man who reminded her so much of Mr. Paul, with his snowy-white hair and rounded cheeks, from back home.

No. Back in Alaska.

This was her true home. Right here next to her mom.

"Hey, Kensie. I've brought a blanket like you request-ed." He stood over Marie's bed, a sympathetic smile slip-ping across his face. "Let me check her vitals while I'm here. How are you faring?"

She stepped away from her mom's bedside as the nurse, whose name she sadly couldn't remember at the moment, did his thing. "I'm well. Tired. But my friend is going to bring me lunch and coffee soon."

"Take care of yourself." He tucked the blanket around Marie. "Get plenty of rest and keep yourself fed."

"Yes, sir," Kensie replied, mustering the smallest of smiles. "Thank you for the blanket."

They exchanged a few more words before he left Ken-sie and her mother alone with that stupid machine that blared like a warning signal that they weren't out of the woods yet every time it beeped.

"Goodness, Mom," Kensie cried, gently lifting her mom's hand so that she could place her own underneath it. She rested her forehead on top of their hands, tears falling like shattered diamonds. "Why didn't you tell me about Dad? I could have protected you had I been here."

Silence.

"One iced americano for the zombie, and one sug-ary-sweet crème brulee for the bestie of said zombie."

Frankie Sellers, who used to be Frankie Matson, set down Kensie's go-to drink order in front of her. Kensie took a long, slow sip before sighing.

"You are my literal lifeline right now. Thanks, Franks." Her friend sat beside her on the hard sofa. "What's in there?" Kensie pointed to the lunch box.

Frankie grinned and began to pull out containers. "I made you red beans and rice and sweet cornbread. Figured you would need to eat like you were home while you were home."

Kensie salivated just thinking about one of her favorite foods as a child and took the glass container from Frankie. "I really, *really* love you. I hope you know that."

"Oh, and Mom is tidying up Marie's house today, by the way. She'll probably come visit after. But anyway, how're you holding up? Like, for real." Kensie made a mental note to reach out to Gayle, Frankie's mom and Marie's best friend, to thank her.

Kensie shoved a spoonful of spicy beans, rice, and sausage into her mouth while she thought of how to answer Frankie *for real.*

"I should have been home." She set the spoon down and looked at her friend, who was encouraging her to go on. "If I had known about Dad before I ever left, I would have never left. I could have protected Mom."

"I know you won't believe this right now, but Kensie, it's not your fault. Logic tells you it's not; your emotions are lying to you, honey."

"Ugh," Kensie groaned, throwing her head back and fanning her watering eyes. "I'm trying to believe that. I know God has a plan and that everything works for His good and according to His timing, but I don't understand this."

"You don't have to understand it. You just have to have faith that He is who He says He is."

"It's hard right now, Franks. It's hard to believe that He's working this for His good."

Frankie wrapped her friend in a hug after removing the food from their laps. "I know, honey. I know. You're not alone. Okay?"

"Kensie?" a voice like sandpaper called. "Is that you?"

"Mom!" Kensie jumped to her feet and was at her mom's side in two strides. Wet, hot drops of liquid sprinted down her face and dropped onto her mom's blanket. "Thank You, God. Thank You. Thank You."

"He's always good, Kensie baby." Marie coughed several times, a pain-stricken wince etched into her face. But she kept talking. "No matter what. Never doubt Him."

"Yes, Momma. Now, shh. Let me call the doctor and tell her you're awake."

The next few hours were a whirlwind of doctors, nurses, and even the police. Since her mom was unconscious when she got to the hospital, they'd been waiting to take down her statement. Kensie listened in horror as she, in her gritty voice, explained how her father had burst through the door yesterday evening, drunk and screaming about how Marie had been the reason his life was a living hell. She tried to fight him and even managed to dial 911, but he ended up getting the upper hand. Not before Marie had landed a few blows and cuts herself, though. And apparently, Marie's mixed-breed dog, Pepper, got a few chomps in herself.

She was so darn proud of her mom.

"He's secure, right?" Kensie asked, regarding Roman.

The policeman nodded. "Yes. He's cuffed to his bed, and there's an officer standing guard."

"How did he escape?"

"It's an ongoing investigation, but I will let you know as soon as I have answers myself."

Kensie nodded. "Thank you, Officer."

When the room was still and quiet, outside of the blasted beeping machine, Kensie pulled up a chair next to her mother's bed. "I'm so proud of you, Momma. And I'm so sorry I wasn't there to protect you."

Marie looked up at Kensie, remnant tears in her blue eyes, and smiled. "You did protect me, baby. I was thinking of you the entire time. I was praising Jesus that you weren't there. That you were safe."

"Why did you ever get involved with that man?" Kensie had to ask. And then she added, "I was in a little wreck six days ago, and when I hit my head on the window and steering wheel, I remembered memories I'd suppressed. Bad ones, Momma. Of you and Dad."

Marie's lips trembled. "You got in a wreck and are just now telling me? Are you okay? Come here, let me—"

"I'm fine, Mom. Truly. It wasn't really a wreck. I just ran off the ice and into the ditch. I wasn't going fast at all."

"But still—"

Kensie grabbed her mom's hand. "Please, Momma. I have to know."

Beep.

Beep.

Beep.

Marie rolled her lips into her mouth, her eyes clouding over, then she squeezed Kensie's hand. "I didn't know, Kensie. He was such a gentleman when we met. Had a stable job, was attractive, and kind. He showered me with love." Her eyes darkened into storms. "But after we got married, it was like a switch flipped. It started with him telling me not to see my friends. Then he isolated me from what little family we had left down here. He controlled every part of my life. Then he became addicted to alcohol, prescription painkillers, and, I suspect, the way it felt to make me cry and bleed. When I realized, after the night he was arrested, that you had seemingly woken up and forgotten about it all, I thought it better you didn't remember."

"Oh, Momma," Kensie wept. "Why didn't you run sooner?"

Marie smiled. "Because I had you to look after. And regardless of what he did to me, he never laid a hand on you. He loved you for the five years I allowed him to know you. It was when he lunged at you, though never touched you, that I finally called the cops. That was the night he—"

"I hate him!" Kensie screamed through her tears. "How dare he! How dare you stay, Momma! You're worth so much more than that."

Water brimming in Marie's eyes fell over, and she lifted her hand to Kensie's face and wiped at her hot, swollen cheeks. "I'm so sorry I kept it from you all this time, baby."

"I'm not mad at you," Kensie choked out. "I'm mad at him. At God for letting this happen."

"What did I tell you earlier?" Marie chastised. Kensie sniffled and tried to catch her breath.

"To never doubt Him."

"That's right. Listen, baby. I know you know this, but you seem to need a reminder. The Good Lord doesn't promise us a perfect life. He promises to be with us through the sin-ridden world. If He had called me home, I would be with my Maker. And there's no better place to be."

Kensie sniffled some more before wiping her nose with the back of her sleeve like a toddler. "I know, Momma. But who do I talk to if you're not here? Who do I run back to? I know it's selfish, but what do I do if I don't have you? You can't leave me, especially not because of that wretched man."

"I'm here, Kensington. God still has me here."

"I'm staying here," Kensie blurted. "At least through the rest of the school year. I'm not going back right now."

Marie's dark brows pinched. "You can't do that, baby."

"I can, and I will," Kensie demanded. "You come first, Momma."

The two women spent the next hour talking and crying, and laughing on occasion. Kensie told her about the school dance and had caught her up on how the end of the semester had gone. Gayle had popped by for a little bit and brought dinner for Kensie.

After the nurses brought dinner for her mother and Gayle had left, Marie asked Kensie, "And what about that Nick guy you used to complain about all the time? How's seeing him through God's eyes treating you?"

Kensie remembered that the last time she'd spoken on the phone with her mother was when she'd confessed her conflictions surrounding Nick, who, at the time, had just started showing Kensie who he truly was under the layers of baited flirting and cockiness.

"We, uh," Kensie really didn't want to talk about Nick, but she wasn't going to lie to her mother's face. "I'm his girlfriend now. Or, I was." She grimaced, recalling the madwoman she'd become after hearing the news of her mother. She couldn't stop seeing the repressed memories, and Nick's face had begun to blend into them. Kensie pushed him away out of roaring fear and fickle uncertainty.

It's for the best, she thought, *since I've made up my mind to stay. He can find someone with less baggage and is less crazy.*

"Was?"

"It's a long story. Why don't you try to get some sleep for now?"

Marie looked like she might protest, but a yawn overtook her. "Fine. But we're talking about this in the morning."

Kensie forced a tired smile. "Yes, Momma. Sleep well. I'm right on the couch if you need me."

"I love you, baby."

Kensie waited for her mother's heart rate to slow, telling her she was asleep, before she released her hand and went to use the restroom. After tidying up the room, she noticed her phone was dying.

And that she had more missed calls and texts from Nick.

Her heart felt like a punching bag. Every text was a right hook. Every missed call was a jab. The unopened voicemails were a sequence of punches.

Fishing her charger out of her bag, she groaned when she saw the port had broken. Maybe she had one in her old car? Frankie and her husband had driven Kensie's old car from high school over to the hospital in case she needed something, and no one was around.

Throwing a light jacket and her sneakers on, she fixed her matted bun on top of her head and headed for the elevators.

She hated the smell of hospitals now. She would forever associate the smell of sterilizing chemicals with her mangled mom. The elevator ride to the first floor was short. She exited, waved at the tired-looking woman at the front desk, and slipped through the automatic doors.

The balmy coolness of Mississippi in December took her by surprise. She knew she wasn't in Alaska anymore, but she still half-expected to have her teeth chattering when she stepped outside, not just hugging a light cardigan close. Alaska. She missed the frigid, fresh air and the mountains greeting her every morning. She missed the glittering snowfall and how time felt like a lazy stroll through the woods. She missed how the world looked like it was close to Christmas.

But as she gazed at the vivid sunset, she took pleasure in the colors Alaska often lacked during this time.

She reached her car and dug around a bit. No luck. She'd have to break down and buy one. Though she needed to be frugal until she figured out a job. She was also going to have to call Lori tomorrow to tell her she needed the semester off.

Kensie wasn't quite ready to say she was never going back. She'd have to see how these next few months panned out.

As Kensie shut her door and began to walk through the lot, she saw a rather large man in a hospital gown hobbling toward her, clutching his side.

"Sir, are you okay? Do you need help?" she called. The man didn't reply but kept steadily wobbling forward. "Sir?" Kensie took a few steps to meet him, and that's when she saw a metal cuff hanging around his wrist.

Time stopped.

Kensie dragged her eyes to the man's face.

His eyes were blacker than night. Soulless.

But Kensie still saw her nose on him. The shape of his lips matched hers.

An alarm blared, and Kensie momentarily looked for the sound on instinct. The hospital.

Her father snarled as Kensie turned back. "You ruined my life, Marie."

He lunged, and hot hands wrapped around her neck.

Chapter Twenty-Five

Nick

The ocean looked like white diamonds where the setting sun reflected on its surface.

Nick was driving with his windows down, enjoying what he would consider late summer weather in Alaska. Even in waning light, the world around him still held color, unlike Alaska in the winter. The coast of Mississippi in December was something he might enjoy if he weren't rushing to St. Ann's Hospital to be with the woman he loved.

He had a lot of time to think on the plane. To worry. To stress. To conjure worst-case situations in his head.

And he prayed. He doubted. Then he prayed some more.

Braelee called, and he answered through the car's system. "Hey, I'm five minutes away from the hospital. Have you heard from her?"

His sister sighed. "I'm glad you made it safely. I talked to her a couple of hours ago. She said her mom woke up."

"Thank You, Jesus." A morsel of stress left his body. Maybe Kensie would be more open to talking to him, knowing her mom was going to be okay. One prayer answered. A million left undetermined.

"Be safe, Nick. I just...I have a bad feeling. We are praying."

Nick's gut twisted, and he didn't know what he was doing.

Why was he chasing her down when she said not to?

He was going to push her further away.

The urge to turn around was strong, but a small, still voice inside of Nick whispered for him to go.

A few minutes later, the hospital came into view. Nick's nerves soared, but still, he was going to do what he had set out to do. He navigated to the front parking entrance, his knee bouncing up and down. Red and blue lights flashed from the lot, and when Nick turned in, he saw several police cars. Blowing out a frustrated breath, he muttered, "I can't deal with this right now." He was too anxious to see Kensie to try and navigate whatever was happening right now.

As he looked for a parking spot, he caught sight of a man in a hospital gown being cuffed onto a stretcher as he thrashed and tried to escape. Blood poured from his side, soaking through his gown. Across from him, a woman was lying on the ground.

Medics clamored about, shouting various orders. "Help them. Go—"

Nick paused and threw the car into park. Looking back, he saw that familiar heap of auburn curls bouncing as she was lifted from the concrete.

"Kensie!" he shouted, throwing open his door and fighting with the stupid buckle. Once he was free, he ran toward the scene with only thoughts of getting to her side.

Two officers swarmed him. "Sir, stop. Sir, I'm going to need you to stop."

He heard the officers, but he was watching as Kensie lay still.

Too still.

With panic in his eyes, he told the officers. "I need to see her! That's my Kensie." He pointed as his heart beat out of his chest. Pain seeped into his ribs, a pang like nothing he'd ever known. "Please, Officer. Please. She's my everything."

Nick didn't know if it was his desperate pleas, the tears welling in his eyes, or his pitiful expression, but one of the officers said, "Okay. Okay. Let's go check, but you can't fight me."

"Thank you." Nick willed himself not to try and break free and move quicker. But in exactly thirteen steps, he was at her side, walking beside them as they crossed the lot toward the hospital.

Her eyes were closed, and red welts the size and spacing of fingers were on both sides of her neck. Nick broke at her side, his upper half collapsing on top of her. "I'm sorry I'm late, Kensington. I'm sorry. I'm here now." He wept.

"Sir, we need to get her into the hospital," a man in scrubs and a white coat said.

Pull yourself together, Nick, he chided himself, sitting up. But how did a man hold it together when the one who even dares to make him a man lies unconscious on a stretcher?

The doctor spoke again. "Are you her spouse or family? Because if you aren't, I can't let you into her room if we determine we need to keep her after we run tests."

Nick remembered a certain item in his pocket and blurted, "I'm her husband." He dug the ring out of his pocket. "This is hers. She's been staying here with her mom, Marie Smith, and she forgot her ring at home and asked me to bring it."

At the moment, Kensie's eyes fluttered open as tears ran down her cheeks. She tried to open her mouth to speak, but no sound came out. Pain painted her face. As the doctor paused to take vitals, Nick clutched his stomach. He felt a lump in his pocket, and a crazy idea hatched to make sure he could be in her room when they brought her back. Because there was no way he was leaving her side.

While the doctor was occupied, and the police were busy tending to what Nick surmised to be Kensie's father, he slipped the ring onto Kensie's ring finger. *A perfect fit. Thank You, Jesus.* He pleaded with Kensie to understand as he stared into her terrified eyes.

"Is this man your husband? Blink once for no and twice for yes."

Nick waited with bated breath.

Kensie blinked twice, never taking her eyes off Nick, and as they started moving again, Nick whispered, "I love you,

Windsor." With a minuscule movement, she tilted her chin down. Nick took that to mean everything was going to be okay.

Everything has to be okay, God. Do You hear me? I can't lose her.

Nick had no choice but to trust Him as they wheeled her into the hospital, and he had to watch her disappear through medical-staff-only doors.

"I'm Nick Lancaster, Kensie's boyfriend." Nick's attempted smile flatlined. He added in a low voice, "But between us, they think I'm her husband. I wanted to be able to get into her room if they have to keep her."

Marie Smith might have been in her hospital bed, but even from her horizontal position, she appraised Nick from head to toe as he stood beside her.

He kept his hands folded in his lap and willed the redness in his eyes to miraculously disappear. But it was no use to try and present himself as put-together right now. His hair was a disheveled mess, he was sleep-deprived, and he probably smelled from long, overnight and day travel. It was hard for him to believe it was Sunday evening, and he was supposed to be going back to church for the first time. Instead, he was busy finding Jesus in the midst of the atrocities of life.

Finally, after an agonizing minute of examination, Marie rasped out through a genuine smile, "It's lovely to meet you in person, Nick. Kensie's told me so much about you."

Nick chuckled. "I'm sure she's said some pretty awful things."

Marie's eyes—the same color as Kensie's—sparked. "Oh, yes. For certain." Nick raised his brows at the open admission. Marie continued, "But she also told me this morning about how wrong she was about you and how she was terrified she'd pushed you away for good...yet, here you are."

"Here I am," Nick reiterated, taking a seat next to her bed. "I'm so sorry this happened to you, Ms. Smith."

"Call me Marie, honey." She held her hand up, and Nick awkwardly took it in his, figuring it was what she wanted. "My. What nice hands you have." She patted the backside of his hand. "But can you get my water from the table beside you?"

Heat filled Nick's neck as Marie winked. "Oh, yeah. Of course."

Nonchalantly as possible, he slipped his hand out of hers and got the cup of water for her.

"I can't sit up, honey. You're going to have to help me out here."

With awkward gentleness, Nick held the cup and guided the bendy straw to her lips. She sipped, the crow's feet at her eyes deepening and lips pursing. "Thank you. It's painful, but the water is good for my throat."

Nick offered her a sympathetic smile, unsure of what to say next.

Marie grinned wickedly. "Want to know a secret I'm sure Kensie never told you?"

He leaned closer. "Absolutely, I do."

"After she got the job in Alaska, but before she left, we stalked the school website to see if there were any hot young men. Your picture came up, and Kensie made a joke about you helping her with working out and meal prepping."

Nick rolled his lips into his mouth to keep from laughing at the irony. While he was going through an awful breakup, the woman he now loved was stalking his picture on the school website and already making plans for the two of them. And then she showed up and hated him for two and a half years.

"She threw those plans right out the window," Nick jested. "Instead, she made new plans to loathe me for all of eternity over a stupid email."

"Ah, yes. The email." Marie's eyes went back in time. "I remember when she called me to tell me about that. She was livid, Nick. Livid. But it was because of how she was made fun of in school for her name. Sometimes I wish I had given her a normal name, but let's be honest. Our Kensie isn't a normal girl. She's as lovely and kind as they come. She deserved a name as beautiful as she is."

"Her name is one of my favorite things about her," Nick admitted. "It rolls off the tongue. It's melodic and soft, like her."

A knock sounded at the door, and Nick jumped to his feet.

The doctor from outside opened the door while a nurse wheeled Kensie in on a chair. Her eyes immediately landed on Nick, and if he wasn't seeing things from his lack of sleep, her shoulders relaxed, and a layer of peace blanketed her.

"We ran imaging and blood tests. There are no broken bones or internal bleeding. Her vocal chords will be sore, and she should refrain from talking for at least a day. She's stated she doesn't want to stay for observation, so we are releasing her."

Nick shook the doctor's hand. "Thank you, Doctor."

"Keep an eye on her. If she suddenly spikes a fever, shows signs of intense swelling or mental instability, or loses consciousness, bring her back immediately."

Nick received care instructions from the nurse, and then he was left alone with Kensie and her mom, who was crying.

"Nick, bring her over here."

He obliged, wheeling Kensie, who also had tears running down her cheeks, to her mom's bedside. The women took each other's hands.

"I'm so sorry, baby. I'm so sorry." Marie sniffled, and a slow, haunted smile formed through her tears. "But I'm not sorry, because if it wasn't for that man, I wouldn't have you. I'd go through it all again to have you, Kensington Marie."

Nick watched from the corner, pushing back his own waterworks. He silently thanked God that Kensie was going to be all right. That Marie was alive and surviving. That the man who did this would hopefully be locked away in a more secure facility, never to touch these two strong women again. Nick had so much to learn about Kensie's history here in Mississippi, but if only a fraction of his experience to provide a framework for what she'd gone through, he had empathy for the women.

After a few moments, Kensie spun herself and faced Nick. He couldn't tell if her expression was one of gratitude or fury. But then again, when it came to Kensie, Nick thought both emotions equated to love in her eyes.

Taking him off guard for a second, she slowly signed, "What are you doing here?" Her motions weren't aggressive, but her face still burned. Nick remembered that she knew sign language from the small encounter through the classroom windows. Was that only a few weeks ago? It felt as if lifetimes had passed since that moment.

Nick didn't know if Marie knew sign language, but she was making exactly zero attempts not to act like she wasn't eavesdropping.

He signed back to Kensie, "I'm sorry I went against your wishes, but I couldn't let you go. I love you, Kensington. Don't push me away. Let me in."

"I'm scared."

Nick moved directly in front of her and hit his knees to be on her level, continuing to sign. "I'm scared, too. We both have our demons. But like we vowed earlier, let's fight them together. Don't let them tear us apart. They win when that happens."

Kensie stared at him, a million contemplations in her stark-blue, watery eyes. He could see the battle of options, tumultuous in her mind, and he prayed silently that she would choose to go to war with him. He'd survive if she didn't, but it wouldn't be pretty survival.

Her jaw set and eyes fortified. "I want to win with you. But I'm staying in Mississippi for at least the remainder of the school year. I can't let Mom be alone after this."

A weight rolled off Nick's shoulders, and a brick tumbled off his chest. He could breathe again for the first time in two days. He could do a few months long-long-distance. In fact, it would be good for him not to have access to her touch and her kiss. He signed, "I'm so glad you're alive."

Kensie looked like she wanted to laugh, but the motion hurt her. Nick reached for her, but she put up a hand. After a breath, she signed, "I'm okay. I'm glad I'm alive, too." Then a shyness swept over her, and she averted her gaze. "Are you staying through Christmas?"

Nick reached for her chin and, with the gentleness of a feather, turned her face to him. He spoke aloud. "If it's okay with Marie, I'd love to stay with you both through Christmas break." Nick looked over Kensie's shoulder.

Marie signed languidly with shaky hands, "Who do you think taught her ASL? My mother was deaf. Didn't want to risk Kensie not knowing ASL for genetic reasons." She paused and then spoke aloud. "Of course, you can stay."

Turning to Kensie, her smile broad, Nick could tell the movement caused her discomfort. She motioned for Nick to come closer. He did. Kensie placed her hands on his face and pulled him even closer. He could see the moment her mind pushed back against his nearness, but she closed her eyes and took a breath. When she opened them, all was quiet in their depths. She mouthed, "I love you," then gave Nick the most tender, tear-soaked kiss he'd ever received. One that would stay with him for all time.

"I love you," Nick said through a burning throat as he fought not to cry in this moment of pure joy. A brilliant strike of lightning, illuminating the onyx night.

Kensie lightly pushed him away to sign again. "Oh, and where did you get this? It's beautiful." She pulled the deep ruby ring out of her pocket.

"I found it on the floor at Ted Stevens. I'm going to turn it in at the front desk when I make it back." He took the ring and put it on her finger one last time, though Kensie tried to protest. He grinned at her. "One day, I'll get you one that's all yours."

Her eyes narrowed as she took her hand back and signed, "Appeal to emotion fallacy?"

Taking her hand and pressing his lips to her palm, he whispered, "It's a promise as old as time itself, Kensington. A covenant to last forever."

Chapter Twenty-Six

Kensie

"**I** still can't believe you never told me you were a five-time state spelling bee champion." Nick shook his head, laughing, as he eyed the trophies shoved in a corner of Kensie's childhood room. "So many wasted opportunities to make fun of you."

"I'm sure you will find many opportunities," Kensie said. Her throat was still sore, but she could talk fairly normally as long as she wasn't long-winded. Nick was forcing her to drink plenty of medicinal teas. Though she hated the taste, they were helping.

It was Tuesday, Christmas morning, and they had run to the house to swap out clothes, grab a few things for Marie, and freshen up outside the hospital room. Marie would hopefully be coming home by the end of the week, but her father was already out of the hospital and transferred to a prison in Northern Mississippi so that even if he did manage another escape, he was far away from the women.

Kensie only felt a tad safer. It would take time for her to process everything that happened. The events of the

weekend had only stacked upon the fresh but old memories that had resurfaced a little over a week ago.

She sat on her old twin-sized bed that still had her pink,
floral comforter set covering it. Kensie hadn't changed the
room since she was sixteen, even though she didn't leave
home until a few years ago. There was a mirror across
from her, and Kensie wanted to cry looking at the bruising
finger marks on her neck, but then she thought of her
mother's condition and how Roman had called her Marie.
According to the police, he was trying to kill Kensie's mom
again, and he was apparently doped on prescription drugs
and mistook her for her mother. He had gotten his cuff
loose somehow, and when the officer went inside to check
on him, he had knocked the officer unconscious. Roman
Smith was a brute of a man, but he was still a shadow of
what Kensie remembered from when she was a little girl.

The bed dipped as Nick sat down beside her and took
her hand. "How are you?"

Kensie swallowed and winced at the action. She was
honest with Nick about her thoughts—something they'd
started doing. Short answers such as "I'm fine" or "I'm
okay" weren't allowed. They both promised to be up-front
and truthful, no matter how deep or how dark their
thoughts were.

When she'd finished telling him, Nick held her and
kissed the top of her head, whispering reassurances her
way. "He's far away, Kensie. He's never going to hurt you
or your mom again. You're safe."

"I know." Kensie stood and pulled Nick to his feet; she didn't want to talk about *him* anymore. Not on Christmas. She placed her hands on Nick's shoulders and ran her hands down his arms. She had been touching him a lot over the past couple of days, determined to overcome her fears. He stood still as she explored, her hands running up his spine and through his hair. He sighed, lolling his head back into her hands.

"You have no idea how good it feels when you do that." Nick's Adam's apple bobbed, and Kensie kissed it.

Nick straightened and took control, weaving his hands into her long, curly hair and tilting her lips to his. He kissed her with unwavering control, careful not to hurt her in any way. Kensie whispered against his mouth, "And you have no idea how good that feels."

"Oh, I think I do." Nick chuckled, letting her step backward instead of pulling her closer as he wished to do. Nick stared at her freckled face and wide blue eyes, and she knew he'd move mountains for her. "What are you thinking of?" Kensie asked.

Nick tucked a strand of hair behind her ear as he answered. "Of how much you've changed in me in such a short time. I finally understand what Noah—remember, the guy you met with his wife on their honeymoon?" Kensie nodded, and he continued. "He once told me that he just knew Esme was the woman for him right from the start. While I might not have known from the actual start, there was some point over the past couple of years that I did know but didn't want to admit to myself because I didn't think I ever had a real chance. Plus, I wasn't the man a woman like you deserved."

"Nick, stop saying you don't deserve me." Kensie hated it when he said that, as if she were a perfect little angel. Nick deserved a woman who didn't attempt to push him away because of her trauma.

But Nick shook his head. "It's true. Before you, I would use my good looks and smooth ways to coerce women into...entertaining me." Kensie didn't miss the red tinting his cheeks at the admission. She knew he wasn't a saint, but they'd never openly talked about it. She guessed it was time.

Kensie laughed. "You've definitely tried with me."

"But I knew it would fail every time." Nick scratched the beard coming in on his face. Kensie secretly hoped he'd keep it.

"How so?"

"Because you were you. Good. Wholesome. Kind. You weren't going to cave to my attempts." Nick grinned. "Though I do remember when you flirted with me. Kensie, I about lost my mind. I didn't know what to do when you stomped up to me and batted your lashes and licked your lips. My brain short-circuited."

"You remember that?" Kensie covered her face. "Oh my gosh. I was hoping you'd forget."

Nick grabbed her hands, a lovely smile on his face. "I will forever remember that moment. It was when I really started to think of what it would be like to be yours."

They stood facing one another, holding hands, as Kensie stated, "I don't want you to think that your past sullies you for me. It doesn't. Who you were is not who you are now."

Nick shook his head, as if he was having a difficult time believing her.

So, Kensie dropped his hands and cupped his cheeks. "Listen to me, Nicolas James Lancaster. You are worthy of love as much as I am. Our pasts do not determine who we are today. I'm yours. You're mine. End of the nonfiction-type of story you love so much."

He blinked, and that small dimple made an appearance as he grinned. "I love *you*. So much."

"I love you," she said as she kissed him again. Then she broke free and wrapped a thin scarf around her neck. "Now, let's get back to the hospital. I don't want Mom spending Christmas alone while we make out in my childhood bedroom."

Nick scoffed but took her hand and grabbed the bag she'd packed from the floor. "If you think that's what making out with me is like, you've got another thing coming."

Kensie couldn't help but laugh. "See? You may be a reformed man, but I like that you're still you." She paused, then added with a smirk, "I'm glad I'm the one on the receiving end of your flirty antics, but like, for real this time. I've secretly always liked it despite my protests."

He laughed as if a weight had been lifted from his shoulders, and as they were walking out the door, Nick asked Kensie to get his phone out of his pocket to check the message that had just come through. She saw on the preview that it was his father.

"It's, uh, your dad. He said, 'I choose you, son. Merry Christmas. Be safe. We will talk when you're home.'" Kensie looked up at her frozen man. "What's that mean? What happened?"

Nick dropped the bag on the front porch, took Kensie in his arms, and finally cried a few tears of joy. "I didn't think he would, Kensie." He let her go and beamed through wet liquid. "I'll tell you about it on the way to the hospital."

"Welcome home, Marie!"

Frankie threw confetti in the air as Kensie led Marie into the house while Nick trailed behind carrying bags. It was New Year's Eve, and the doctors finally released her after keeping her a little bit longer due to some internal bleeding.

Marie was slow in her steps, but she was on her feet, and that was great progress.

A banner welcoming her home was strung across the area where the kitchen met the living room. Kensie had made cupcakes, and many cards and gifts had come from her fellow church members and friends. Kensie knew her mom wouldn't want a huge party with lots of people—they were alike in that way—so she only asked Frankie and Gayle to come.

Gayle met Marie inside and hugged her friend. Kensie wrapped her arm around Frankie's waist and rested her head on her shoulder. "I'm so glad we're all together right now."

"Agreed," Frankie said.

Nick set the bags down and motioned for Kensie. "Hey, Liam invited me out to golf. Would you mind if I went for a little while? Give you ladies some time alone and to all catch up?"

"Of course," Kensie said, looking at Frankie. "When did your husband befriend my boyfriend?"

Frankie shrugged. "I don't know. I gave him Nick's number after you gave it to me, and I told him he'd be in town through break and may need some guy time."

"Well, this is a good thing." Kensie kissed Nick's cheek. "Go have fun. Liam's awesome. You'll like him."

After a few rounds of hugs and thank yous, Nick left, and the women settled in the living room, swapping stories, eating cupcakes, and enjoying living.

Hours later, as Kensie was cleaning up while her mom slept, and Frankie and Gayle had gone home, Nick came back carrying a bouquet of roses and a little red gift bag.

"What in the world?" Kensie exclaimed, opening the front door to let Nick inside. She took the flowers from him but eyed the gift bag suspiciously. "What is that?"

"A belated Christmas gift and an early birthday gift. I know things have been wild, but I saw this and wanted to get it for you."

DREW TAYLOR

Kensie closed the door and set the flowers down on the couch before taking the bag, slowly opening it, and seeing a small black box. She glanced up at Nick, who was grinning ear to ear and bouncing with excitement. "This better not be an engagement ring. Despite what you did at the hospital, I'm not ready for that right now."

Nick laughed. "It's not. Just open it."

Kensie pulled it out of the bag. When she popped the box open, it was, in fact, a ring, but not an engagement ring.

She covered her laugh with her hand as she took in the gold-banded ring shaped to look like a castle on the front. Or, as she supposed, a palace. "You shouldn't have gotten me something like this! It's too much."

Nick shook his head and dismissed her. He took the ring and slid it onto her right ring finger. "See? It's a great fit."

She held it up and admired it. It truly was pretty and fit perfectly. "How'd you know my size?"

He grinned as if he were the smartest man in the world, and Kensie soaked in her personal sunshine beaming down upon her. "I had the ring I found sized, and then we determined what your other ring finger would be based on it."

"I love it, Nick. Thank you. It's beautiful." Kensie hugged him. "But I didn't get you anything."

She felt him laugh against her as his voice took on a false seduction. "Don't be crazy. You've already given me a spot next to the Princess of Crescent Cove. You're all I need, Kensington Marie. You're my ride or die. My moonlight in the darkened night. My—"

Kensie pulled back and feigned a gag. "Ew. That was so lame."

"Then gift me with a midnight walk on the beach." Nick pulled her into him and lowered his voice as he ran his fingers down her back. "I want to experience actual sand between my toes while fireworks pop off and I kiss you senseless at midnight."

Kensie couldn't decide if she was flushing or shivering, probably a combination of both. But she agreed. "Meet me at midnight, Mr. Lancaster. Treat me to a senseless kiss on my birthday. Let's make your watch go off again."

Chapter Twenty-Seven

Nick

The post-holiday travel rush was evident as Nick returned his rental car. Kensie wasn't content to tell him goodbye at the house, so she followed behind him until entering the parking garage and meeting him inside the airport.

"I wish I could stay with you until you get on the plane." Kensie sighed into his chest as they stood holding one another while other travelers passed them by. He had visions of never going back and staying here, but he knew losing one teacher over the break was bad enough, though everyone understood.

Nick rubbed circles on her back. "Me too. It's going to be a long five months. I just coerced you into loving me. I'm not ready to give it up yet."

"We aren't giving anything up," Kensie affirmed, toying with his hair. "We are just exploring a new side."

"It's all new. It's crazy how love and loathing are one in the same, don't you think?"

Kensie laughed. "I never believed it could be until I met you."

Checking the time behind Kensie's back, he knew he needed to get through TSA. Squeezing her one last time, he let her go. "I'll call you at every leg of the journey. And be sure to call Braelee. You know she's been worried sick about you. Texting isn't enough for her."

Kensie nodded. "I'll call her on my way back home. Promise."

With one last languid kiss, Nick disappeared to stand in line. Kensie, to his delight, stood there and watched him until they could no longer see each other. His heart ached with every step deeper into the airport.

The journey home was irritatingly slow. When he landed in Seattle, all he could think about was turning right back around. When he landed in Anchorage, he felt the chasm was too wide to ever reach Kensie again. Mississippi was thousands of miles away.

Walking through the point of no return, he made his way to the front desk, winding through all the travelers coming and going. Mostly going, as winters in Alaska were harsh, and people needed at least a few days of warm sunshine to make it through.

"Hey, I was leaving in a rush about two weeks ago, but I found this ring sitting on a stair and figured someone would come by looking for it." Nick held out the ring, smiling sadly at the memories he'd formed with it. This ring was a bright reminder of one of the worst moments of his life and one of the best moments of his life. Thinking the woman he loved was dead, then finding out the woman he loved loved him back.

The customer service agent's face sank with relief. "That's Wilma Grace's ring." He pointed to an elderly woman sitting on a bench across the way. "She's been in here every day looking for it, asking if anyone has found it."

Guilt eased into Nick's bones, but he didn't regret it. Not when it helped him the way that it had.

"I can go give it to her," Nick suggested, seeing a certain sadness in her posture that he hoped he could take away with the ring.

"Yeah, thanks, man."

Nick said goodbye and gingerly made his way to the woman, careful not to spook her since her head was hanging low. "Mrs. Wilma Grace?"

The elderly woman with white curly hair and a wrinkled face met his eyes. *She's so sad*, Nick thought to himself. He cleared his throat and put on his kindest smile. "My name is Nick, and I believe I found something that belongs to you." He held out the ring, and her eyes went from shades of mud brown to light and glowing with tears.

"My ring," she croaked out. With trembling hands, she accepted the ring from Nick and clenched her fist around it. Then she pulled Nick into a rather strong embrace. "Thank you, young man."

Nick laughed, his chest easing at the joy she now seemed to radiate. "I'm happy I could find and return it to you." He took a seat next to her. "I'm sorry it took me so long. I found it as I was leaving in a hurry..." Nick proceeded to tell Wilma Grace what events had transpired, though he couldn't for the life of him figure out why he was opening up to this unknown old lady about his chaotic ride in life.

But she listened, patted his knee, and nodded in sympathy. Then she responded with her own story. "I lost my Rodger a year ago. He was a pilot, and planes were his life. From the moment we met—I was a flight attendant and he was a pilot in training—we knew we were it for each other. He died from sickness last winter. Almost a year ago to this day. I like to come here, to the place he loved to work, and feel a little closer to him as I watch the planes take off. But you know what, boy?" Wilma Grace chuckled as tears rolled down her cheeks.

Nick offered his jacket sleeve, but she just wiped them away with her fingers. "What?" he prompted.

She put her full dentures on display. "We got on each other's nerves like no one else could."

Nick laughed, resting his forearms on his splayed legs and hanging his head. "I guess what they say is true: the one who annoys you the most is the one you'll marry. God's funny like that."

Wilma Grace patted his back. "Nick, I'll tell you one thing about relationships and marriage. If she feels safe enough to put you in your place, and you feel safe enough to call her crap, then that's a love worth clinging to and fighting for."

Nick let her words roll over him. He thought of all the times he'd called out Kensie for her people-pleasing tendencies, and she called him out for roguish, boyish behavior. How true was it that he helped her to stand on her feet while she helped him to ground himself?

"Mrs. Wilma Grace, I think you're a wise woman."

She stood, several inches shorter than Nick, so Nick only had to tilt his head a little to look at her from his seated position. "I don't know why the Good Lord wants me to do this, but He does." Tears shone in her eyes. "I want you to take this ring and make sure it lands permanently on your Kensie's finger. My story's over, but yours has just begun. Let this ring be a reminder that no matter what struggles and troubles you endure together or apart, you always have each other to run home to."

Nick sniffled and pressed his lips together. "I can't tell you how much that means to me, Wilma Grace. But I can't take this ring from you."

The woman grabbed his hand and shoved the ring into it, closing his fingers around it. "I didn't ask your permission, young man. Don't take this blessing God is giving me away from me."

Nick stood and wrapped the woman in a hug, a single drop of liquid pushing free from his eye. "I will cherish this ring forever. And I will get it on my lady's finger as soon as she stops making me have to chase her down to put it on her."

As Nick left the airport, his spirits lifted, he called Kensie to tell her he was on his way home.

"I miss your smile," she whispered on the phone, a tremble in her voice.

"I miss your freckles."

"I miss your dimple."

Nick grinned to himself, his right hand flexing as if to reach for hers, but she was across the country. Not next to him like her voice implied.

When Nick hit the no-service zone, he begrudgingly hung up and listened to his downloaded Spotify playlist. He turned to worship music, and he prayed, asking the Lord to make the months fly by.

His phone buzzing in the cubby took him out of his prayer as his truck announced a text message from his dad.

> Can we meet for lunch tomorrow? I'll be in town.

Nick, already deep in his emotions over the past twenty-four hours, wept with thankfulness. When he was able, he texted his dad back and told him to come over to his place for baked salmon.

Long conversations lingered ahead. Grueling seconds spent missing the woman he loved were going to paint his months. But as he looked at the sprawling mountains steeped in glittering snow, Nick found himself in a state

of contented peace. The stars winked from the sky. A
reminder from God:

   I will never leave you nor forsake you.

Epilogue

Kensie ~ four months later

D ays like today, where walking outside felt like walking into hot soup, Kensie longed for Alaska's "will it snow or will it not?" type of weather during May. Sure, the ground would be soggy and wet, and she'd have to wear her Xtratuf boots everywhere, but that would be a better option than wearing wet clothes.

At least the breeze from the ocean, which was not even a few miles away, was rolling in. She was thankful to live and work near the crushing waters and hot sand.

She'd secured a long-term job subbing for an eleventh-grade English teacher at Willow Bay High School who was on pregnancy leave. She had spent the first nine weeks of the new semester subbing wherever she was needed.

Today was her last day. She had to decide whether to stay with her mom or return to Alaska. That mountainous land called to her like a forgotten home...it had rewired her DNA, and she needed to reconnect.

But Marie...Kensie didn't want to leave her all alone. There was no way Marie would move to Alaska with her. Her mom was tied to Willow Bay the way Kensie found herself stringed to Alaska. Willow Bay didn't feel like home anymore, but Kensie's mom did.

And so did Nick. Kensie missed Nick greatly, and she knew without a doubt she was ready to see him next week after he got back from a hunting trip with his father. The two were still at odds at times, but overall, James was making an effort with Nick, and so she kept encouraging Nick to make an effort with him, hence the hunting trip. Kensie hoped the two came back from it with released inhibitions and not having shot one another. She wanted their future babies to have at least one grandfather in their lives. The other one, she prayed, would stay locked away forever.

Slipping into her car, she noticed the security alert going off on her phone, telling her that someone was on her front porch. Quickly pulling up the app, she had to rub her tired eyes and check again.

Sure enough. He was still standing there with that dimpled smile plastered across his face, a bouquet of roses, and a suitcase. He'd traded his Alaskan spring long-sleeve gear for a Mississippi shorts and T-shirt combo. Kensie wanted to teleport through the screen to hug him and kiss him, a feeling she knew very well thanks to many FaceTime dates.

She pushed the on-screen button that allowed her to speak through the camera. "Mr. Lancaster. What are you doing on my front porch, looking like a fresh spring breeze I want to breathe in forever?"

Nick threw his head back and laughed at her poor flirting. Then he blew her a kiss before attempting a Southern accent. "Windsor, Imma need you to hurry that nice behind of yours home because I'm ready to offer you that forever you're yappin' about."

Placing her phone on her magnetic holder in her car, she watched as Nick dropped his bags and pulled something out of the pocket of his shorts.

Kensie pressed the button. "What's that?"

Nick gave the camera a wide smile before holding up a ring.

The ring.

The deep ruby one he used back in December to pretend to be her husband.

"Nick, why do you still have that?" Kensie felt a little sick over him stealing a ring that gorgeous. He had said he found the sweet little old woman and returned it.

"Get your butt over here and find out."

Kensie had never driven home so fast, going at least fifteen miles over the speed limit.

When she pulled up to the small house tucked between willow trees, she saw Nick standing on the front step with his arms open wide. She threw her car in park, leaving the driver's side door wide open as she ran into Nick's waiting arms. He picked her up and spun her around, peppering her face with sweet kisses. "I've missed you so much, Windsor."

The smell of his forest-rain scent consumed her as she buried her face into his neck. The warmth of him soaking into her bones, despite the muggy May heat. His hands splayed across her back. All of it. It was enough to bring her to tears. "I'm so freaking happy you're here. I've missed the heck out of you."

Nick set her down and wiped a droplet away from her cheek before kissing her. It was chaste but lingered, promises of deeper, languid kisses to come. She adjusted her thin blouse, which had ridden up, and stepped back. That's when she noticed Senator Lancaster, his wife, Stacey, who was clinging to his arm, and Braelee standing beside her mom, Frankie, and Gayle.

"Hi." Kensie waved, embarrassed over her overtly public display of affection in front of their families. Stacey and Braelee waved back, while her mother hid a chuckle behind a cough. Frankie and Gayle just smiled on.

Senator Lancaster, however, was not smiling or waving. He looked entirely uncomfortable and looked everywhere else except at Kensie and Nick.

"Did you kidnap him and force him to come down here?" Kensie whispered.

"Actually, it was his idea for everyone to come down. Our hunting trip was just a ruse to throw you off. He's just not a touchy-feely type, as you might have presumed."

"Where do you get it from then?"

Nick took Kensie's hand and led her to the porch, whispering, "My mother. Duh. Look at the way she's clinging to Dad's arm."

Kensie laughed, embraced everyone except Senator Lancaster, who simply shook her hand, and was about to step inside the house when Nick stopped her.

"What?"

He cleared his throat. "I told you I had something for you. Have you forgotten that already?"

She had. The moment she saw Nick, everything else left her brain. But now, as Nick held out the ring and it glittered under the bright sunlight, she felt an entirely new reason to be excited.

"Wilma Grace wouldn't let me give her the ring back. She said to give it to you, and so I promised her I would when the time was right." Nick slid down to one knee as cameras flashed around them, squeals erupting from their family and friends. Kensie tuned them out as Nick took her hand. The adoration in his eyes spoke volumes. She wanted to shout her answer, but she waited, biting her lip.

"Kensington, I'm not asking you to save me a dance at homecoming, but I'm asking for all your dances. I'm not looking for a one-and-done situation. I'm requesting all of your nights. Bicker with me every day, as long as we end sitting in our pajamas, munching on popcorn, watching *Jane Eyre*. Call me out on my fallacies, and be prepared for me to call you on yours. Then kiss the crap out of me to punish me for arguing with you. Force me to read fiction because it's good for me. Share your demons with me, and let's take them to the Lord together. We can do it here or back in Alaska, I don't care. I'm wherever you are." Nick paused, blowing out a puff of air as he laughed nervously. "I don't know how this goes down in your fiction books you love so much, but Windsor, this is real. Will you do this messy life with me? Forever? As my wife?"

"And you say I overexplain my reasonings," Kensie exclaimed, heart beating out of her chest, before nodding profusely and pulling her brand-new fiancé to his feet, squeezing the life out of him. "Yes, Nick. I want all of that with you forever. And I want it where we get snow on the beach in winter. Take me back to Alaska, Nick. I miss our home." Claps echoed off the trees around them, the light wind offered its congratulations, and after a moment secluded in the bubble they'd created, they turned to their family, hand in hand.

The onslaught of hugs marched forward, with James Lancaster lingering behind. Exchanging glances, Nick didn't even have to open his mouth, and Kensie knew exactly what he was thinking. She stood on her toes and whispered the profound yet basic advice Tarin had once told her. The advice that opened her heart to Nick in the first place.

"Love him like Jesus."

Bonus Content

Loved what you read? Please consider leaving a review on Amazon and Goodreads!

Sign up for my newsletter where you will receive access to playlists, bonus scenes, additional chapters, extended epilogues, and much more! New content added at random!

Scan the QR code or click on the link to learn more about Drew Taylor's books!

www.drewtaylorwrites.com

Book Club Questions

1. Kensie shows up in Alaska ready to reinvent everything about herself—even her name. How does that desire to "start fresh" influence the way she interacts with people (especially Nick), and what does this tell us about what she's really struggling with internally?

2. Let's talk first impressions, because these two did not start off strong. Nick and Kensie immediately misunderstand each other from the very first interaction. How much of their early tension is miscommunication versus personal baggage they brought with them? How do we as humans tend to jump to conclusions?

3. Faith comes up early, especially through Tarin's advice to 'love Nick like Jesus.' Do you think Kensie actually tries to apply that? Where do you see her wrestling with

what she believes versus how she feels toward Nick? How is this reflective in your own life?

4. The banter. The arguing. The tension. Why do you think their enemies-to-lovers works so well? What moments make you think their verbal sparring is hiding something deeper? In life, do you find yourself saying everything but what you genuinely mean?

5. Kensie is sweet and helpful to literally everyone... except Nick. Meanwhile, Nick defends her behind her back even when she's driving him crazy. What do you think this says about who they each are at their core?

6. Community plays a huge role in Kensie's story. She moved thousands of miles to start over, so how do her friendships with Braelee, Tarin, and the other staff shape the way she grows? Where do you see her longing for belonging? Have you ever been in a situation where you'd do anything to fit in?

7. Nick is dealing with way more than just a grumpy attitude; He's navigating past heartbreak, family expectations, and his shaky relationship with his faith. How do those things influence the way he treats Kensie? Does knowing his backstory make him more sympathetic?

8. Arguing is basically their shared love language. Do you feel like their teasing brings them closer together, or

is it just a shield so they don't have to be vulnerable? What moments show the shift from playful annoyance to actual connection? What do you tend to hide behind?

Acknowledgments

To my Savior and Lord, Jesus. Thank you for Your perfect, providential timing. I'm thankful this book was published a year later than I wanted it to be.

To my *Chasing Kensie* team—Ally, Leah, Melody, Tawni, Heather, Amanda, Latisha, and Charity—you all are lovely, God-fearing ladies. Thank you for feeding into this story in a myriad of ways.

To the Taylorverse—thank you all for your constant, unwavering support. I couldn't do what I love every single day without you all.

To my readers—whether you're new or have been with me for a while, thank you for choosing my stories amidst the thousands of other books you could pick up.

To my family and best friends—thanks for being a bedrock, a solid place to land.

To Taryn and Misty, thanks for being two women I could run to at any given moment during my time in Alaska. I will forever cherish our friendship and the countless nuggets of wisdom you both spoke to me. This book is a result of Y'ALL.

To Alaska—you will forever hold a piece of me that I could never get back even if I wanted it back, which I don't. Thanks for refining, stretching, and growing me.

About the Author

Drew Taylor writes modern closed-door chick-lit romance stories from a Christian worldview. She believes faith-based romance can be full of heart, humor, healing, and hope while showcasing the reality of our fallen human condition. Her redemptive and engaging stories point to the One who embodies true love–Jesus Christ. Drew lives in the great state of Mississippi where she teaches high school English. When not teaching or writing, she enjoys reading, baking, researching conspiracy theories, and spending quality time with the people who mean the most to her.

Follow Drew:
Instagram: @authordrewtaylor
Facebook: Drew Taylor, Author
TikTok: @drewtaylorwrites
Pinterest: @authordrewtaylor
YouTube: @authordrewtaylor